what is not yours
is not yours

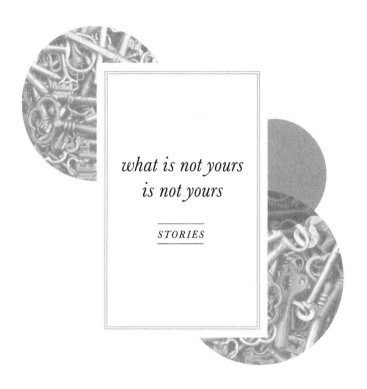

*what is not yours
is not yours*

STORIES

Helen Oyeyemi

HAMISH HAMILTON
an imprint of Penguin Canada, a division of Penguin Random House Canada Limited

Penguin Canada, 320 Front Street West, Suite 1400, Toronto, Ontario M5V 3B6, Canada
Penguin Group (USA) LLC, 375 Hudson Street, New York, New York 10014, U.S.A.
Penguin Books Ltd, 80 Strand, London WC2R 0RL, England
Penguin Ireland, 25 St Stephen's Green, Dublin 2, Ireland
(a division of Penguin Books Ltd)
Penguin Books Australia, 707 Collins Street, Melbourne, Victoria 3008, Australia
Penguin Books India, 11 Community Centre, Panchsheel Park, New Delhi – 110 017, India
Penguin Books New Zealand, 67 Apollo Drive, Rosedale, Auckland 0632, New Zealand
Penguin Books South Africa, 24 Sturdee Avenue, Rosebank,
Johannesburg 2196, South Africa
Penguin Books Ltd, Registered Offices: 80 Strand, London WC2R 0RL, England

Published in Hamish Hamilton paperback by Penguin Canada, 2016
Simultaneously published in the United States by Riverhead Books,
an imprint of Penguin Random House LLC

1 2 3 4 5 6 7 8 9 10 (RRD)

The following stories have been previously published: "Books and Roses" (excerpt,
Granta 129: Fate); "Drownings" (*The White Review*); " 'Sorry' Doesn't Sweeten
Her Tea" (*Ploughshares*); "Dornička and the St. Martin's Day Goose"
(Hayward Gallery anthology *Carsten Höller: Decision*).

The lines on page 53 are from "Rice," originally published in the poetry collection
No Place to Go Back for Longing by Jak-ga-jeong-shin, Seoul, South Korea, 1998.
Reproduced by permission of Chun Yang Hee.

The lines on page 259 are from Karel Jaromír Erben, *Kytice*, translated from the Czech
by Susan Reynolds (London: Jantar Publishing, 2013).

*Publisher's note: This book is a work of fiction. Names, characters, places and incidents either are the
product of the author's imagination or are used fictitiously, and any resemblance to actual
persons living or dead, events, or locales is entirely coincidental.*

Manufactured in the U.S.A.

Book design by Lauren Kolm

LIBRARY AND ARCHIVES CANADA CATALOGUING IN PUBLICATION

Oyeyemi, Helen, author
What is not yours is not yours / Helen Oyeyemi.

ISBN 978-0-14-319783-6 (paperback)

I. Title.

PR6115.Y49W43 2016   823'.92   C2015-906638-7

eBook ISBN 978-0-14-319784-3

www.penguinrandomhouse.ca

contents

open me carefully

—written on an envelope containing a letter from
Emily Dickinson to Susan Huntington Gilbert,
June 11, 1852

books and roses

FOR JAUME VALLCORBA

Once upon a time in Catalonia a baby was found in a chapel. This was over at Santa Maria de Montserrat. It was an April morning. And the baby was so wriggly and minuscule that the basket she was found in looked empty at first glance. The child had got lost in a corner of it, but courageously wriggled her way back up to the top fold of the blanket in order to peep out. The monk who found this basket searched desperately for an explanation. His eyes met the wooden eyes of the Virgin of Montserrat, a mother who has held her child on her lap for centuries, a gilded child that doesn't breathe or grow. In looking upon that great lady the monk received a measure of her unquestioning love and fell to his knees to pray for further guidance, only to find that he'd knelt on a slip of paper that the baby had dislodged with her wriggling. The note read:

1. *You have a Black Madonna here, so you will know how to love this child almost as much as I do. Please call her Montserrat.*

2. *Wait for me.*

A golden chain was fastened around her neck, and on that chain was a key. As she grew up, the lock of every door and cupboard in the monastery was tested, to no avail. She had to wait. It was both a comfort and a great frustration to Montse, this . . . what could she call it, a notion, a suggestion, a promise? This promise that somebody was coming back for her. If she'd been a white child the monks of Santa Maria de Montserrat might have given her into the care of a local family, but she was as black as the face and hands of the Virgin they adored. She was given the surname "Fosc," not just because she was black, but also because her origin was obscure. And the monks set themselves the task of learning all they could about the needs of a child. More often than not they erred on the side of indulgence, and held debates on the matter of whether this extreme degree of fondness was a mortal sin or a venial one. At any rate it was the Benedictine friars who fed and clothed and carried Montse, and went through the horrors of the teething process with her, and rang the chapel bells for hours the day she spoke her first words. Neither as a girl nor as a woman did Montse ever doubt the devotion of her many fathers, and in part it was the certainty of this devotion that saw her through times at school and times down in the city when people looked at her strangely or said insulting things; the words and looks sometimes made her lower her head for a few steps along the street, but never for long. She was a daughter of the Virgin of Montserrat, and she felt instinctively and of course heretically that the Virgin herself was only a symbol of a yet greater sister-mother who was carefree and sorrowful all at once, a goddess who didn't guide you or shield you but only went with you from place to place and added her tangible presence to your own when required.

When Montse was old enough she took a job at a haberdashery in Les Corts de Sarrià, and worked there until Señora Cabella found her relatives unwilling to take over the family business and the shop closed down. "You're a hardworking girl, Montse," Señora Cabella told her, "and I know you'll make something of yourself if given a chance. You've seen that eyesore at the Passeig de Gràcia. The Casa Milà. People call it La Pedrera because it looks like a quarry, just a lot of stones all thrown on top of each other.

An honest, reliable girl can find work as a laundress there. Is that work you can do? Very well—go to Señora Molina, the *conserje*'s wife. Tell her Emma Cabella sent you. Give her this." And the woman wrote out a recommendation that made Montse blush to read it.

She reported to Señora Molina at La Pedrera the next morning, and the *conserje*'s wife sent her upstairs to Señora Gaeta, who pronounced Montse satisfactory and tied an apron on her. After that it was work, work, work, and weeks turned into months. Montse had to work extra fast to keep Señora Gaeta from noticing that she was washing the Cabella family's clothes along with those of the residents she'd been assigned. The staff turnover at La Pedrera was rapid; every week there were new girls who joined the ranks without warning, and girls who vanished without giving notice. Señora Gaeta knew every name and face, even when the identical uniforms made it difficult for the girls themselves to remember each other. It was Señora Gaeta who employed the girls and also relieved them of their duties if their efforts weren't up to scratch. She darted around the attic, flicking the air with her red lacquered fan as she inspected various activities. The residents of Casa Milà called Señora Gaeta a treasure, and the laundry maids liked her because she sometimes joined in when they sang work songs; it seemed that once she had been just like them, for all the damask and cameo rings she wore now. Señora Gaeta was also well liked because it was exciting to hear her talk: She swore the most powerful and unusual oaths they'd ever heard, really unrepeatable stuff, and all in a sweetly quivering voice, like the song of a harp. Her policy was to employ healthy-looking women who seemed unlikely to develop bad backs too quickly. But you can't guess right all the time. There were girls who aged overnight. Others were unexpectedly lazy. Women who worried about their reputation didn't last long in the attic laundry either—they sought and found work in more ordinary buildings.

It was generally agreed that this mansion the Milà family had had built in their name was a complete failure. This was mostly the fault of the architect. He had the right materials but clearly he hadn't known how to make the best use of them. A house of stone and glass and iron should be stark and sober, a watchtower from which a benevolent guard is kept on society. But the white stone of this particular house rippled as if reacting to a hand that had found its most pleasurable point of contact. A notable newspaper critic had described this effect as being that of "a pernicious sensuality." And as if that wasn't enough, the entire construction blushed a truly disgraceful peachy-pink at sunset and dawn. Respectable citizens couldn't help but feel that the house expressed the dispositions of its inhabitants, who must surely be either mad or unceasingly engaged in indecent activities. But Montse thought the house she worked in was beautiful. She stood on a corner of the pavement and looked up, and what she saw clouded her senses. To Montse's mind La Pedrera was a magnificent place. But then her taste lacked refinement. Her greatest material treasure was an egregiously shiny bit of tin she'd won at a fairground coconut shy; this fact can't be overlooked.

THERE WERE A FEW more cultured types who shared Montse's admiration of La Pedrera, though—one of them was Señora Lucy, who lived on the second floor and frequently argued with people about whether or not her home was an aesthetic offense. Journalists came to interview the Señora from time to time, and would make some comment about the house as a parting shot on their way out, but Señora Lucy refused to let them have the last word and stood there arguing at the top of her voice. The question of right angles was always being raised: How could Señora Lucy bear to live in a house without a single right angle . . . not even in the furniture . . . ?

"But really who needs right angles? Who?" Señora Lucy

would demand, and she'd slam the courtyard door and run up the stairs laughing.

SEÑORA LUCY was a painter with eyes like daybreak. Like Montse, she wore a key on a chain around her neck, but unlike Montse she told people that she was fifty years old and gave them looks that dared them to say she was in good condition for her age. (Señora Lucy was actually thirty-five, only five years older than Montse. One of the housemaids had overheard a gallery curator begging her to stop telling people she was fifty. The Señora had replied that she'd recently attended the exhibitions of some of her colleagues and now wished to discover whether fifty-year-old men in her field were treated with reverence because they were fifty or for some other reason.) Aside from this the housemaids were somewhat disappointed with Señora Lucy. They expected their resident artist to lounge about in scarlet pajamas, drink cocktails for breakfast, and entertain dashing rascals and fragrant sirens. But Señora Lucy kept office hours. Merce, her maid of all work, tried to defend her by alleging that the Señora drank her morning coffee out of a vase, but nobody found this credible.

———

MONTSE FOUND WAYS to be the one to return Señora Lucy's laundry to her; this sometimes meant undertaking several other deliveries so that her boss Señora Gaeta didn't become suspicious. There was a workroom in Señora Lucy's apartment; she often began work there and then had the canvases transported to her real studio. Thirty seconds in Señora Lucy's apartment was long enough for Montse to get a good stare at all those beginnings of paintings. The Señora soon saw that Montse was curious about her work, and she took to leaving her studio door open while she etched on canvas. She'd call Montse to come and judge how well the picture was progressing. "Look here," she'd say, indicating a faint shape in the corner of the frame. "Look here—" Her fingertips glided over a darkening of color in the distance. She sketched with an effort that strained every limb. Montse saw that the Señora sometimes grew short of breath though she'd hardly stirred. A consequence of snatching images out of the air—the air took something back.

MONTSE ASKED SEÑORA about the key around her neck. It wasn't a real question, she was just talking so that she could

stay a moment longer. But the Señora said she wore it because she was waiting for someone; at this Montse forgot
herself and blurted: "You too?"

The Señora was amused. "Yes, me too. I suppose we're
all waiting for someone." And she told Montse all about it
as she poured coffee into vases for them both. (It was true!
It was true!)

"TWO MOSTLY PENNILESS WOMEN met at a self-congrat-
ulation ritual in Seville," that was how Señora Lucy began.
The event was the five-year reunion of a graduating class
of the University of Seville—neither woman had attended
this university, but they blended in, and every other person
they met claimed to remember them, and there was much
exclamation on the theme of it being wonderful to see
former classmates looking so well. The imposters had done
their research and knew what to say, and what questions to
ask. Their names were Safiye and Lucy, and you wouldn't
have guessed that either one was a pauper, since they'd
spent most of the preceding afternoon liberating various
items of priceless finery from their keepers.

These two penniless girls knew every trick in the book,
and their not being able to identify each other was one of
the downsides of being an efficient fraud. Both women

moved from town to town under an assortment of aliases, and both believed that collaboration was for weaklings. Lucy and Safiye hadn't come to that gathering looking for friendship or love; they were there to make contacts. Back when they had toiled at honest work—Lucy at a bakery and Safiye at an abattoir—they'd wondered if it could be true that there were people who were given money simply because they looked as if they were used to having lots of it. Being blessed with forgettable faces and the gift of brazen fabrication, they'd each gone forth to test this theory and had found it functional. Safiye loved to look at paintings and needed money to build her collection. Lucy was an artist in constant need of paint, brushes, turpentine, peaceful light, and enough canvas to make compelling errors on. For a time Lucy had been married to a rare sort of clown, the sort that children aren't afraid of: *After all, he is one of us, you can see it in his eyes,* they reasoned. *How funny that he's so strangely tall.* Lucy and her husband had not much liked being married to each other, the bond proving much heavier than their lighthearted courtship had led them to expect, but they agreed that it had been worth a try, and while waiting for their divorce to come through Lucy's husband had taught her the sleight of hand she eventually used to pick her neighbor's pocket down to the very last thread. The night she met Safiye she stole her earrings right out of her earlobes and, having retired to a quiet corner of the mansion to inspect them, found that the gems were paste. Then she discovered that her base metal bangle was missing and quickly realized that she could only have lost it to the person she was stealing from; she'd been distracted by the baubles and the appeal of those delicate earlobes. Cornered by a banker whose false memory of having been in love with her since matriculation day might prove profitable, Lucy wavered between a sensible decision and a foolhardy one. Ever did foolhardiness hold the upper hand with Lucy; she found Safiye leaning against an oil lantern out in the garden and saw for herself that she wasn't the only foolish woman in the world, or even at that party, for Safiye had Lucy's highly polished bangle in her hand and was turning it this way and that in order to catch fireflies in the billowing, transparent left sleeve of her gown. All this at the risk of being set alight, but then from where Lucy stood Safiye looked as if she was formed of fire herself, particles of flame dancing the flesh of her arm into existence. That or she was returning to fire.

They left the reunion early and in a hurry, along with a small group of attendees who'd found themselves unable to sustain the pretense of total success. Having fallen into Lucy's bed, they didn't get out again for days. How could they, when Lucy held all Safiye's satisfactions in her very fingertips, and each teasing stroke of Safiye's tongue summoned Lucy to the brink of delirium? They fell asleep, each making secret plans to slip away in the middle of the night. After all, their passion placed them entirely at each other's command, and they were bound to find that fearsome. So they planned escape but woke up intertwined. It was at Lucy's bidding that Safiye would stay or go. And who knew what Safiye might suddenly and successfully demand of Lucy? *Stop breathing. Give up tea.* The situation improved once it occurred to them that they should also talk; as they came to understand each other they learned that what they'd been afraid of was running out of self. On the contrary the more they loved the more there was to love. At times it was necessary to spend months apart, coaxing valuable goods out of people using methods they avoided discussing in detail. Lucy sent Safiye paintings and orange blossoms, and Safiye directed a steady flow of potential portrait subjects Lucy's way. The lovers fought about this; it seemed to Lucy that Safiye was trying to trick her into making a "respectable" living. Lucy had promised herself that she'd only paint faces she found compelling and it was a bother to have to keep inventing excuses for not taking on portraits.

"It's all right, you're just not good at gifts," Lucy said, with a smile intended to pacify. Gifts didn't matter when they were together, and gifts didn't have to matter when they were apart either. But Safiye was outraged.

"What are you talking about? Don't you ever say that I'm bad at gifts!"

If there are any words that Lucy could now unsay, it would be those words about Safiye being bad at gifts; if Lucy hadn't said them Safiye wouldn't have set out to steal the gift that would prove her wrong, and she wouldn't have got caught.

The lovers spent Christmas together, then parted— Lucy for Grenoble, and Safiye for Barcelona. They wrote to each other care of their cities' central post offices, and at the beginning of April Safiye wrote of the romance of St. Jordi's Day. *Lucy, it is the custom here to exchange books and roses each year on April 23rd. Shall we?*

LUCY HAPPILY settled down to work. First she sent for papyrus and handmade a book leaf by leaf, binding the leaves together between board covers. Then she filled each page from memory, drew English roses budding and Chinese roses in full bloom, peppercorn-pink Bourbon roses climbing walls and silvery musk roses drowsing in flowerbeds. She took every rose she'd ever seen, made them as lifelike as she could (where she shaded each petal the rough paper turned silken), and in these lasting forms she offered them to Safiye. The making of this rose book coincided with a period in Lucy's life when she was making money without having to lie to anyone. She'd fallen in with an inveterate gambler who'd noticed that she steadied his nerves to a miraculous degree. He always won at blackjack whenever she was sitting beside him, so they agreed he'd give her 10 percent of each evening's winnings. This man only played when the stakes were high, so he won big and they were both happy. Lucy had no idea what was going to happen when their luck ran out; she could only hope her gambler wouldn't try to get violent with her, because then she'd have to get violent herself. That would be a shame, because she liked the man. He never pawed at her, he always asked her how Safiye was getting on, and he was very much in love with his wife, who loved him too and thought he was a night watchman. The gambler's wife would've gone mad with terror if she'd known how close she came to losing her life savings each night, but she didn't suspect a thing, so she packed her husband light suppers to eat at work, suppers the man couldn't even bear to look at (his stomach always played up when he was challenging Lady Luck), so Lucy ate the suppers and enjoyed them very much, the flavor of herbed olives lingering in her mouth so that when she drank her wine she tasted all the greenness of the grapes.

FROM WHERE LUCY sat beside her gambler she had a view through a casement window, a view of a long street that led to the foot of a mountain. And what Lucy liked best about her casement window view was that as nighttime turned into dawn, the mountain seemed to travel down the street. It advanced on tiptoe, fully prepared to be shooed away. Insofar as a purely transient construction of flesh and blood can remember (or foretell) what it is to be stone, Lucy understood the mountain's wish to listen at the window of a den of gamblers and be warmed by all that free-floating hope and desolation. Her wish for the mountain was that it would one day shrink to a pebble, crash in through the glass, and roll into a corner to happily absorb tavern life for as long as the place stayed standing. Lucy tried to write something to Safiye about the view through the casement window, but found that her description of the mountain expressed a degree of pining so extreme that it made for distasteful reading. She didn't post that letter.

Safiye had begun working as a lady's maid—an appropriate post for her, as she had the requisite patience. It can take months before you even learn the location of a household safe, let alone discover the code that makes its contents available to you. But was that really Safiye's plan? Lucy had a feeling she was being tricked into the conventional again. Safiye instigated bothersome conversations about "the future," the eventual need for security, and its being possible to play one trick too many. From time to time Lucy paused her work on the rose book to write and send brief notes:

Safiye—I've been so busy I haven't had time to think; I'm afraid I'll only be able to send you a small token for this St. Jordi's Day you wrote about. I'll beg my forgiveness when I see you.

Safiye replied: *Whatever the size of your token, I'm certain mine is smaller. You'll laugh when you see it, Lucy.*

Lucy wrote back: *Competitive as ever! Whatever it is you're doing, don't get caught. I love you, I love you.*

On April 23rd, an envelope addressed in Safiye's hand arrived at the post office for Lucy. It contained a key on a necklace chain and a map of Barcelona with a black rose drawn over a small section of it. Lucy turned the envelope inside out but there was no accompanying note. *She couldn't even send a book,* Lucy thought, tutting in spite of herself. She hadn't yet sent the book she'd made, and as she stood in the queue to post it she began to consider keeping it.

The woman in line ahead of her was reading a newspaper and Lucy saw Safiye's face—more an imperfectly sketched reproduction of it—and read the word "Barcelone" in the headline. Some vital passage narrowed in her heart, or her blood got too thick to flow through it. She read enough to understand that the police were looking for a lady's maid in connection to a murder and a series of other crimes they suspected her of having committed under other names.

MURDER? IMPOSSIBLE. Not Safiye. Lucy walked backward until she found a wall to stand behind her. She rested until she was able to walk to the train station, where she bought train tickets and a newspaper of which she read a single page as she waited for the train to come. She would go where the map in her purse told her to go, she would find Safiye, Safiye would explain and they would laugh. They'd have to leave the continent, of course. They might even have to earn their livings honestly like Safiye wanted, but please, please please please. This pleading went on inside her for the entire journey, through three train changes and the better part of a day. A mountain seemed to follow along behind each train she took—whenever she looked over her shoulder there it was, keeping pace. She liked to think it was her mountain she was seeing, the one she'd first seen in Grenoble, now trying its best to keep faith with her until she found Safiye.

Safiye's map led Lucy to a crudely hewn door in a wall. This didn't look like a door that could open, but a covering for a mistake in the brickwork. The key fit the lock and Lucy walked into a walled garden overrun with roses. She waded through waves of scent, lifting rope-like vines of sweetbriar and eglantine out of her path, her steps scattering pale blue butterflies in every direction. Safiye had said that Lucy would laugh at the size of her gift, and perhaps if Lucy had found her there she would have. After all she'd never been given a secret garden before. But the newspapers were saying that this woman who looked like Safiye had killed her employer, and Lucy was very much afraid that it was true and this gift was the reason. At nightfall she considered sleeping among the roses, all those frilled puffs of air carrying her toward some answer, but it was better to find Safiye than to dream. She spent two weeks flitting around the city listening to talk of the killer lady's maid. She didn't dare return to the rose garden, but she wore the key around her neck in the hope and fear that it would be recognized. It wasn't, and she opted to return to Grenoble before she ran out of money. Her gambler was in hospital. There'd been heavy losses at the blackjack table, his wife had discovered what he'd been up to, developed a wholly unexpected strength ("inhuman strength," he called it), broken both of his arms, and then moved in with a carpenter who'd clearly been keeping her company while he'd been out working on their finances. Still he was happy to see Lucy: "Fortuna smiles upon me again!" What could Lucy do? She made him soup, and when she wasn't at his bedside she was picking pockets to help cover the hospital bills. They remain friends to this day: He was impressed by her assumption of responsibility for him and she was struck by the novelty of its never occurring to him to blame anybody else for his problems.

A FEW WEEKS after her return to Grenoble there was a spring storm that splashed the streets with moss from the mountaintops. The stormy night turned the window of Lucy's room into a door; through sleep Lucy became aware that it was more than just rain that rattled the glass . . . someone was knocking. Half-awake, she staggered across the room to turn the latch. When Safiye finally crawled in, shivering and drenched to the bone, they kissed for a long time, kissed until Lucy was fully woken by the chattering of Safiye's teeth against hers. She fetched a towel, Safiye performed a heart-wrenchingly weak little striptease for her, and Lucy wrapped her love up warm and held her and didn't ask what she needed to ask.

After a little while Safiye spoke, her voice so perfectly unchanged it was closer to memory than it was to real time.

"Today I asked people about you, and I even walked behind you in the street for a little while. You bought some hat ribbon and a sack of onions, and you got a good deal on the hat ribbon. Sometimes I almost thought you'd caught me watching, but now I'm sure you didn't know. You're doing well. I'm proud of you. And all I've managed to do is take a key and make a mess of things. I wanted to give you . . . I wanted to give you . . ."

"Sleep," Lucy said. "Just sleep." Those were the only words she had the breath to say. But Safiye had come to make her understand about the key, the key, the key, it was like a mania, and she wouldn't sleep until Lucy heard her explanations.

From the first Safiye had felt a mild distaste for the way her employer Señora Del Olmo talked: "There was such an interesting exchange rate in this woman's mind . . . whenever she remembered anyone giving her anything, they only gave a very little and kept the lion's share to themselves. But whenever she remembered giving anyone anything she gave a lot, so much it almost ruined her." Apart from that Safiye had neither liked nor disliked Señora Del Olmo, preferring to concentrate on building her mental inventory of the household treasures, of which there were many. In addition to these there was a key the woman wore around her neck. She toyed with it as she interviewed gardener after gardener; Safiye sat through the interviews too, taking notes and reading the character references. None of the gardeners seemed able to fulfill Señora Del Olmo's requirement of absolute discretion: the garden must be brought to order, but it must also be kept secret. Eventually Safiye had offered the services of her own green thumb. By that time she'd earned enough trust for Señora Del Olmo to take her across town to the door of the garden, open it, and allow Safiye to look in. Safiye saw at once that this wasn't a place where any gardener could have influence, and she saw in the roses a perpetual gift, a tangled shock of a studio where Lucy could work and play and study color. Señora Del Olmo instructed Safiye to wait outside, entered the garden, and closed the door behind her. After half an hour the Señora emerged, short of breath, with flushed cheeks—

"As if she'd just been kissed?" Lucy asked.

"Not at all like that. It was more as if she'd been seized

and shaken like a faulty thermometer. I asked her if there was anybody else in the garden, and she almost screamed at me. *No! No. Why do you ask that?* The Señora had picked a magnificent bunch of yellow roses, with lavender tiger stripes, such vivid flowers that they made her hand look like a wretched cardboard prop for them. Señora Del Olmo kept the roses in her lap throughout the carriage ride and by the time we'd reached home she was calm. But I thought there must be someone else in that garden—the question wouldn't have upset her as much otherwise, you know?"

"No one else was there when I was," Lucy said.

Safiye blinked. "So you've been there."

"Yes, and there were only roses."

"Only roses . . ."

"So how did you get the key?" They were watching each other closely now; Safiye watching for disbelief, Lucy watching for a lie.

"In the evening I went up to the Señora's sitting room, to see if there was anything she wanted before I went to bed myself. The only other people the Señora employed were a cook and a maid of all work, and they didn't live with us, so they'd gone home for the night. I knocked at the door and the Señora didn't answer, but I heard—a sound."

"A sound? Like a voice?"

"Yes—no. Creaking. A rusty handle turning, or a wooden door forced open until its hinges buckle, or to me, to me it was the sound of something growing. I sometimes imagine that if we could hear trees growing we'd hear them . . . creak . . . like that. I knocked again, and the creaking stopped, but a silence began. A silence I didn't feel good about at all. But I felt obliged to do whatever I could do . . . if I left a door closed and it transpired that somebody might have lived if I had only opened it in time . . . I couldn't bear that . . . so I had to try the door no matter what. I prayed that it was locked, but it opened and I saw the Señora standing by the window in the moonlight, with her back to me. She was holding a rose cupped in her hands, as if about to drink from it. She was standing very straight, nobody stands as straight as she was standing, not even the dancers at the opera house . . ."

"Dead?"

"No, she was just having a nap. Of course she was fucking dead, Lucy. I lit the lantern on the table and went up close. Her eyes were open and there was some form of *comprehension* in them—I almost thought she was about to hush me; she looked as if she understood what had happened to her, and was about to say: *Shhh, I know. I know. And there's no need for you to know.* It was the most terrible look. The most terrible. I looked at the rest of her to try to forget it, and I saw three things in quick succession: one, that the color of the rose she was holding was different from the color of the roses in the vase on the windowsill. The ones in the vase were yellow streaked with lavender, as I told you, and the one in the Señora's hand was orange streaked with brown."

Lucy mixed paints at the back of her mind. What turned yellow to orange and blue, purple to brown? Red.

"I also saw that there was a hole in the Señora's chest."

"A hole?"

"A small precise puncture"—Safiye tapped the center of Lucy's chest and pushed, gently—"It went through to the other side. And yet, no blood."

(It was all in the rose.)

"What else?"

"The stem of the orange rose." Safiye was shivering again. "How could I tell these things to a policeman? How could I tell him that this was how I found her? The rose had grown a kind of tail. Long, curved, thorny. I ran away."

"You took the key first," Lucy reminded her.

"I took the key and then I ran."

The lovers closed their eyes on their thoughts and passed from thought into sleep. When Lucy woke, Safiye had gone. She'd left a note: *Wait for me*, and that was the only proof that the nighttime visit hadn't been a dream.

A DECADE LATER, Lucy was still waiting. The waiting had changed her life. For one thing she'd left France for Spain. And the only name she now used was her real one, the name that Safiye knew, so that Safiye would be able to find her. And using her real name meant keeping the reputation associated with that name clean. She showed the book of roses she'd made for Safiye to the owner of a gallery; the man asked her to name her price, so she asked for a sum that she herself thought outrageous. He found it reasonable and paid on the spot, then asked her for more. And so Safiye drew Lucy into respectability after all.

Señora Lucy's separation from Safiye meant that she often painted landscapes in which she looked for her. Señora Lucy was rarely visible in these paintings but Safiye always was, and looking at the paintings engaged you in her search for a lost woman, an uneasy search because somehow in these pictures seeing her never meant the same thing as having found her. Señora Lucy had other subjects; she was working on her own vision of the Judgment of Paris, and Montse had been spending her lunch breaks posing for Señora Lucy's study of Aphrodite. Montse was a fidgeter; again and again she was told, "No no no no as you were!" Then Señora Lucy would come and tilt Montse's chin upward, or trail her fingers through Montse's hair so that it fell over her shoulder just so. And the proximity of that delightful frown clouded Montse's senses to a degree that made her very happy to stay exactly where she was as long as Señora Lucy stayed too.

BUT THESE WEREN'T the paintings that sold. It was Señora Lucy's lost woman paintings that had made her famous. The lost woman was thought to be a representation of the Señora herself, but if anybody had asked Montse about that she would have disagreed. She knew some of these paintings quite well, having found out where a number of them were being exhibited. Sunday morning had become her morning for walking speechlessly among them. Safiye crossed a snowy valley with her back to the onlooker, and she left no footprints. In another painting Safiye climbed down a ladder of clouds; you turned to the next picture frame and she had become a gray-haired woman who closed her eyes and turned to dust at the same time as sweeping herself up with a little brush she held in her left hand.

"And the garden?" Montserrat asked.

Lucy smiled. "Still mine. I go there once a year. The

lock never changes; I think the place has been completely forgotten. Except maybe one day she'll meet me there."

"I hope she does," Montse lied. "But isn't there some danger there?"

"So you believe what she said?"

"Well—yes."

"Thank you. For saying that. Even if you don't mean it. The papers said this Señora Fausta Del Olmo was stabbed . . . what Safiye described was close enough . . ."

MONTSE THOUGHT that even now it wouldn't be difficult to turn half-fledged doubt into something more substantial. She could say, quite simply, I'm touched by your constancy, Señora, but I think you're waiting for a murderer. Running from the strangeness of such a death was understandable; having the presence of mind to take the key was less so. Or, Montse considered, you had to be Safiye to understand it. And even as herself Montse couldn't say for sure what she would have done or chosen not to do in such a situation. If that's how you find out who you really are then she didn't want to know. So yes, Montse could help Señora Lucy's doubts along, but there was no honor in pressing such an advantage.

"And what about your own key, Montserrat?"

Lucy's key gleamed and Montse's looked a little sad and dusty; perhaps it was only gold plated. She rubbed at it with her apron.

"Just junk, I think."

ALL THE SHOPS would be closed by the time Montse finished work, and the next day would be St. Jordi's Day, so Montse ran into the bookshop across the street and chose something with a nice cover to give to Señora Lucy. This errand combined with the Señora's long story meant that Montserrat was an hour late returning to the laundry room. She worked long past dinnertime, wringing linen under Señora Gaeta's watchful eye, silently cursing the illusions of space that had been created within the attic. All those soaring lines from ceiling to wall disguised the fact that the room was as narrow as a coffin. Finally Señora Gaeta inspected her work and let her go. Only one remark was made about Montse's shamefully late return from lunch: "You only get to do that once, my dear."

MONTSE WENT HOME to the room and bed she shared with three other laundry maids more or less the same size as her.

She and her bedfellows usually talked until they fell asleep. They were good friends, the four of them; they had to be. That night Montse somehow made it into bed first and the other three climbed in one by one until Montse lay squashed up against the bedroom wall, too tired to add to the conversation.

WHILE MONTSE had been making up her hours the other laundry maids had attended a concert and glimpsed a few of La Pedrera's most gossiped about couples there. For example, there were the Artigas from the third floor and the Valdeses from the fourth floor, lavishing sepulchral smiles upon each other. Señor Artiga and Señora Valdes were lovers with the tacit consent of his wife and her husband. Señora Valdes's husband was a gentle man many years older than her, a man much saddened by what he saw as a fatal flaw in the building's design. The lift only stopped at every other floor; this forced you to meet your neighbors as you walked the extra flight of stairs up or down, this was how Señora Valdes and Señor Artiga had first found themselves alone together in the first place. It was Señor Valdes's hope that his wife's attachment to "that popinjay" Artiga was a passing fancy. Artiga's wife couldn't wait that long, and had made several not so discreet inquiries regarding the engagement of assassins until her husband had stayed her hand by vowing to do away with himself if she harmed so much as a hair on Señora Valdes's head. Why didn't Artiga divorce his wife and ask Señora Valdes to leave her husband and marry him? She'd have done it in a heartbeat, if only he'd ask (so the gossips said). Señor Artiga was unlikely to ask any such thing. His mistress was the most delightful companion he'd ever known, but his wife was an heiress. No man in his right mind leaves an heiress unless he's leaving her for another heiress. "Maybe in another life, my love," Artiga told Señora Valdes, causing her to weep in a most gratifying manner. And so in between their not so secret assignations Artiga and Señora Valdes devoured each other with their eyes, and Señora Artiga raged like one possessed, and Señor Valdes patiently awaited the vindication of an ever-dwindling hope, and their fellow residents got up a petition addressed to the owners of the building, asking that both the Artigas and the Valdeses be evicted. The *conserje* and his wife liked poor old Señor Valdes, but even they'd signed the petition, because La Pedrera's reputation was bad enough, and it was doubtful that this scandalous peace could hold. Laura, Montse's outermost bedmate, was taking bets.

—————

ON THE MORNING of St. Jordi's Day, before work began, Montse climbed the staircase to the third floor. *To Lucy from her Aphrodite.* The white walls and window frames wound their patterns around her with the adamant geometry of a seashell. A book and a rose, that was all she was bringing. The Señora wasn't at home. She must be in her garden with all her other roses. Montse set her offering down before Señora Lucy's apartment door, the rose atop the book. And then she went to work.

"MONTSERRAT, have you seen the newspaper?" Assunta called out across the washtubs.

"I never see the newspaper," Montserrat answered through a mouthful of thread.

"Montserrat, Montserrat of the key," Marta crooned beside her. The other maids took up the chant until Montse held her needle still and said: "All right, what's the joke, girls?"

"They're talking about the advertisement that's in *La Vanguardia* this morning," said Señora Gaeta, placing the newspaper on the lid of Montse's workbasket. Montse laid lengths of thread beneath the lines of newsprint as she read:

ENZO GOMEZ OF GOMEZ, CRUZ AND MOLINA AWAITS
CONTACT WITH A WOMAN WHO BEARS THE NAME
MONTSERRAT AND IS IN POSSESSION OF A GOLD KEY
ONE AND ONE HALF INCHES IN LENGTH.

Without saying another word, the eagle-eyed Señora Gaeta picked up a scarlet thread an inch and a half long and held it up against Montse's key. The lengths matched. Señora Gaeta rested a hand on Montse's shoulder, then walked back up to the front of the room to inspect a heap of newly done laundry before it returned to its owner. The babble around Montse grew deafening.

"Montse don't go—it's a trap! This is just like that episode in *Lightning and Undetectable Poisons*—"

"That's our Cecilia, confusing life with one of her beloved radio novellas again . . . so sordid an imagination . . ."

"Let's face it, eh, Montse—you're no good at laundry, you must have been born to be rich!"

"Montserrat, never forget that I, Laura Morales, have always loved you . . . remember I shared my lunch with you on the very first day?"

"When she moves into her new mansion she can have us all to stay for a weekend—come on, Montse! Just one weekend a year."

"Ladies, ladies," Señora Gaeta intervened at last. "I have a headache today. Quiet, or every last one of you will be looking for jobs in hell."

Montse kept her eyes on her work. It was the only way to keep her mind quiet.

THE SOLICITOR ENZO GOMEZ looked at her hands and uniform before he looked into her eyes. Her hands had been roughened by harsh soap and hard water; she fought the impulse to hide them behind her back. Instead she undid the clasp of her necklace and held the key out to him. She told him her name and he jingled a bunch of keys in his own pocket and said: "The only way we can find out is by trying the lock. So let's go."

THE ROUTE they took was familiar. "Sometimes I go to an art gallery just down that street," Montse said, pointing. He had already been looking at her but when she said that he began to stare.

"You sometimes go to the Salazar Gallery?"

"Yes . . . they exhibit paintings by—"

"I don't know much about the artists of today; you can only really rely on the old masters . . . but that's where we're going, to the Salazar Gallery."

Gomez stopped, pulled a folder out of his briefcase, and read aloud from a piece of paper in it: *Against my better judgment but in accordance with the promise I made to my brother Isidoro Salazar, I, Zacarias Salazar, leave the library of my house at 17 Carrer Alhambra to one Montserrat who will come with the key to the library as proof of her claim. If the claimant has not come forth within fifty years of my death, let the lock of the library door be changed in order to put an end to this nonsense. For if the mother cannot be found, then how can the daughter?*

Enzo put the folder back. "I hope you're the one," he said. "I've met a lot of Montserrats in this capacity today, most of them chancers. But you—I hope it's you. Are you . . . what do you know of the Salazar family?"

"I know that old Zacarias Salazar was a billionaire, left no biological children but still fathers many artworks through his patronage . . ."

"You read the gallery catalog thoroughly, I see."

A gallery attendant opened the main gate for them and showed them around a few gilt-wallpapered passages until they came to the library, which was on its own at the end of a corridor. Montse was dimly aware of Enzo Gomez mopping his forehead with a handkerchief as she placed the key in the lock and turned it. The door opened onto a room with high shelves and higher windows that followed the curve of a cupola ceiling. The laundry maid and the solicitor stood in front of the shelf closest to the door. Sunset lit the chandeliers above them and they found themselves holding hands until Gomez remembered his professionalism and strode over to the nearest desk to remove papers from his briefcase once again.

"I'm glad it's you, Montserrat," he said, placing the papers on the desk and patting them. "You must let me know if I can be of service to you in future." He bowed, shook hands, and left her in her library without looking back, the quivering of his trouser cuffs the only visible sign of his emotions.

Montse wandered among the shelves until it was too dark to see. She thought that if the place was really hers she should open it up to the public; there were more books here than could possibly be read in one lifetime. Books on sword-swallowing and life forms found in the ocean, clidomancy and the aurora borealis and other topics that reminded Montse how very much there was to wonder about in this world: There were things she'd seen in dreams that she wanted to see again and one of these books, any of them, might lead her back to those visions, and then further on so that she saw marvels while still awake. For now there was the smell of leather-bound books and another faint but definite scent: roses. She cried into her hands because she was lost: She'd carried the key to this place for so long and now that she was there she didn't know where she was. The scent of roses grew stronger and she wiped her hands on her apron, switched on a light, and opened the folder Enzo Gomez had handed her.

This is what she read:

Montserrat, I'm very fond of your mother. I was fond of everyone who shared my home. I am a fool, but not the kind who surrounds himself with people he doesn't trust. I didn't know what was really happening below stairs; we upstairs are always the last to know. Things could have been very different. You would have had a home here, and I would have spoiled you, and doubtless you would have grown up with the most maddening airs and graces. That would have been wonderful.

As I say, I was fond of everyone who lived with me, but I was particularly fond of Aurelie. I am an old man now—an old libertine, even—and my memory commits all manner of betrayals; only a few things stay with me. Some words that made me happy because they were said by exactly the right person at exactly the right time, and some pictures because they formed their own moment. One such picture is your mother's brilliant smile, always slightly anxious, as if even in the moment of delighting you she wonders how she dares to be so very delightful. I hope that smile is before you right now. I hope she came back to you.

Please allow me to say another useless thing: Nobody could have made me believe that Aurelie ever stole from me. The only person who could possibly have held your mother in higher esteem than I did was my brother, Isidoro. He told me I should give my library to her. Then he told me she'd be happier if I gave it to her daughter. Do it or I'll haunt you to death, he wrote. The rest of this house is dedicated to art now; it's been a long time since I lived here, or visited. But the library is yours. So enjoy it, my dear.

Zacarias Salazar

PS: I found Aurelie's letter to you enclosed among my brother's papers. I am unsure how it got there.

Aurelie's letter made Montse stand and walk the paths between the shelves as she read, stopping to sit in the cushioned chairs scattered across the library's alcoves. She kept looking up from the page, along the shelves, into the past.

Dear Montserrat,

I should make this quick because I'm coming back for you, so really there's no need for it. I suppose really I'm writing this to try to get my brain working properly again. It will be hard to let you go even for a little while, but Isidoro thought that even if worse comes to worst (which it won't) the library key will bring you back here somehow.

I'll tell you about your key: A wish brought it to me. It was my birthday, my thirtieth birthday, and Fausta Del Olmo was the only one who knew. There are people who are drawn to secrets as ants are to jam. Fausta's one of them. She searches out all things unspoken and unseen—not to make them known, but to destroy them so that nobody knows they ever existed. That's what makes her heart beat faster, the destruction of invisible foundations. Why? Because she finds it funny. The master once told us about a cousin of his, a lovely, cheerful girl, but touched in the head, he said. This cousin committed suicide one day, quite out of the blue. She did it after talking to her friend on the telephone. That friend now spends her days searching her brain for those disastrous words she must have said, and has become ill herself. As our master was telling us this I watched Fausta Del Olmo out of the corner of my eye. She was laughing silently, but the master didn't notice until Fausta's laughter grew so great that she began to choke. She explained that she was overcome by the sadness and the mystery of it all, and she made the sign of the cross. By then I was already so frightened of her that I didn't dare contradict her. There's no stopping Fausta because she believes in hell. The master thinks this belief in hell keeps her on the straight and narrow, but the truth is she's so sure she's going there that she doesn't even care anymore. When Fausta brought me a little cake with a candle in it and told me to make a wish I wanted to say no. It's stupid but I didn't want Fausta to know my birthday, in case she somehow had the power to take it away. If she made it so I was never born I'd never have had a chance to be me and to hear your father's honey-wine voice and to fall in love with him. He ran off, your father, and if I ever find him I won't be able to stop myself from kicking him in the face for that, the cowardly way he left me here. I didn't yet know I was pregnant, but I bet he knew. He must have developed some sort of instinct for those things. He once said, "Babies are so . . ." and I thought he was going to say something poetic but he finished: "expensive."

I should be making you understand about the key! When I blew out my birthday candle I wished for a million books. I think I wished this because at that time I was having to force my smiles, and I wanted to stop that and to really be happier.

The master has a husband, Pasqual Grec. Not that they were married in church, but that's the way they are with each other. Some of the other servants pretend they've no eyes in their heads and say that Pasqual is just the master's dear friend, but Fausta Del Olmo says that they definitely share a bed and that since they are rich they can just do everything they want to do without having to take an interest in anybody's opinion. Your key doesn't seem to want me to talk about it, but I will. I will. The master is not an angry man, but he's argumentative in a way that makes other people angry. And Pasqual is an outdoorsman and doesn't like to wait too long between hunts; when he gets restless there are fights—maybe three a week. The master retires to the library for some time and takes his meals in there, and Pasqual goes out with the horses. But when the master comes out of the library he's much more peaceful. I thought it must be all the books that calmed the master down. Millions of books—at least that's how it looks when you just take a quick glance while pretending not to be at all interested. And the day after I made my wish the key to the library fell into my hands. The master had left it in the pocket of a housecoat he'd sent down to me in the laundry. Of course it could have been any key, but it wasn't. The key and the opportunity to use it came together, for the master and Pasqual had decided to winter in Buenos Aires. I was about four months pregnant by then, and had to bind my stomach to keep you secret and keep my place in the household. I went into the library at night and found peace and fortitude there.

I didn't know where to begin, so I just looked for a name that I knew until I came to a life of Joan of Arc, which I sat down and read really desperately. I read without stopping until the end, as if somebody were chasing me through the pages with a butcher's knife. The next night I read more slowly, a life of Galileo Galilei that took me four nights to finish because his fate was hard to take. I kept saying, "Those bastards," and once after saying that I heard a sound in another part of the library. A library at night is full of sounds: The unread books can't stand it any longer and announce their contents, some boasting, some shy, some devious. But the sound I heard wasn't the sound of a book. It was more like a suppressed cough or a sneeze, or a clearing of the throat, or some convulsive, impulsive mix of the three. Everything became very still. Even the books shut up. I looked at the shelf directly in front of me; I read each title on it, spine after spine. There was a gap between the spines, and two eyes looked out of it. Not the master's, or Pasqual's, not the eyes of anybody I could remember having met.

I found the courage to ask: "What are you doing here?"

"What are YOU doing here?" asked the man. I could hear in his voice that he wasn't well, and then fear left me; I felt we both had our reasons.

"Can't you see I'm reading?" I said. "Maybe you should read too, instead of SPYING on people."

"Maybe I should," he said. "It's just that I thought you might be like the other one."

"The other one?"

"Yes. But don't tell her you've seen me."

"Why not?"

"Because then she'd know that I've seen her . . . and I don't want her to know that until I've spoken to my brother."

"Your brother?"

"Too much talking, pretty thief. I have to rest now. But promise you won't tell her."

He didn't need to describe her; it had to be Fausta he was talking about. I didn't even want to know what she'd been up to.

"I'm not a thief," I said. "And I won't say anything to her. I haven't seen you, anyway. Only your eyes."

"Well? What do you think of my eyes, pretty thief?"

"They are an old man's eyes," I answered, and I held the Life of Galileo up in front of my face until I heard him walking away. He walked all the way to the back of the library, and up some stairs— I hadn't known there was a staircase in the library until I heard him going up it—look, Montserrat, and you'll see that there is one, built between two shelves, leading up to a door halfway up the wall. Through that door is a wing of the main house that only a few of the servants were familiar with, though we all knew that Isidoro Salazar, the master's younger brother, lived in that part of the house. Lived—well, we

knew the man was dying there, and did not wish to be talked to
or talked about. A special cook prepared his meals according to
certain nutritional principles of immortality that a Swiss doctor
had told the master about, and Fausta had told us how she laid
the table and served the meals in Isidoro's rooms. He waited in
the next room while she did it, and no matter what he ate or
didn't eat he was still dying. When I thought about that I
worried that my words might have added to Isidoro's troubles.

The next day, after Fausta had brought him his lunch, I
wrote: "I should not have been like that to you—Rude and
thoughtless maid from the library" on a piece of paper, ran up to
his rooms and pushed the note under his door. And I stayed
away from the library for a while, only returning when the
chatter of the books reached me where I slept in the maids'
dormitory on the other side of the house. He wasn't there that
night, but when I went to my shelf of choice to take down
Galileo, I saw a slip of paper sticking out of the neighboring
book. The slip read: "To the pretty thief—read this book, and
then look for more."

I loved some of the books he chose, others sent me to sleep. I
turned his slips of paper over and wrote down my thoughts. One
of the books he chose was a slim pamphlet of poetry that didn't
make much sense to me: I dismissed it with a line borrowed
from other poems he'd introduced me to: It may wele ryme
but it accordith nought. He responded with a really long

and angry letter—I think he must have been the author of those poems I didn't think were good.

Isidoro wouldn't come near me, even when I began to want him to. We'd spend nights reading together, on separate sides of a shelf, not speaking, listening to the books around us. According to Stendhal it takes about a year and a month to fall in love, all being well. Maybe we fell faster because all was not well with us: every day it got harder for me to keep you to myself, and he could not forget that he was dying; he fought sleep until the nightmares came to take him by force. He fell asleep in the library one night—he had done this twice before, but out of respect for him I had left using a route that meant I could pass him without looking at him. But when I heard him saying: "No, no . . ." I went to him without thinking and leaned over him to try to see whether I should wake him. He was younger than the look in his eyes suggested. I don't know what his sickness was—it had some wasting effect—even as I saw his face I saw that its beauty was diminished. You can read character in a sleeping face, and his was quite a face. The face of a proud man, vengeful and not a little naive, a man with questions he hadn't finished asking and answers to some questions I had myself. He opened his old man eyes and took a long, deep breath, as if breathing me in. It must have looked as if I was about to kiss him. Our faces were very close and curtains of my hair surrounded us; if we kissed it would be our secret to keep. I kissed him. Then I asked if it had hurt. He said he wasn't sure and that we'd better try it again. And he kissed me back. I didn't want to leave him after that, but I had to be back in bed by the time the other maids began to wake up.

Montserrat, I wrote that being in love with your father was nice, but being in love with Isidoro Salazar was like a dream. Not because of money or anything like that—! The man loved foolishly and without regard for the time limit his learned doctors had told him he had; he made me feel that in some way we had always known about each other and that he would be at my side forever. When Fausta Del Olmo took me aside and asked: "Is there anything you want to tell me?" my blood should have run cold, but it didn't. After all she could have been asking about the pregnancy.

Beyond Isidoro's staircase is a door that connects to a walled garden. The garden is Isidoro's too: he planted all the roses there himself and took care of them until he got too sick to do anything but just be there with them of an evening. We were often there together. It's a long walk from the top of the garden to the bottom, and I'd carry him some of the way. Yes, on my back, if you can imagine that. He was drowsy because of his medication—he had to take more and more—but even through the haze of his remedies he remembered you. "The baby!" I told him you didn't mind (you don't, do you?) and that his weight was balancing me out. He grew more lucid when we lay down on the grass. He was so fond of the roses; one night I told him that he wouldn't die, but that he would become roses.

"I wouldn't mind this dying so much if that were true," he said, slowly. "But wait a minute . . . roses die too."

"Well, after that you'd become something else. Maybe a wasp, because then you could go around stinging people who don't like your poems."

It was around that time that I kept finding gifts on my bed. Little gifts, but they got bigger and bigger. A mother of pearl comb, a calfskin purse, a green cashmere shawl. I told Isidoro to stop giving me gifts. The other servants were asking about them. Isidoro simply smiled at first, but when he asked me to show him the gifts I saw that he was perplexed and that they hadn't come from him.

"Are you sure there's nothing you want to tell me?" Fausta Del Olmo asked, and maybe it was just a beam of sunlight that struck her eye, but I thought she squinted at my stomach. She added that the master would return in two weeks' time. I didn't even answer her. Suddenly she pushed me—if I hadn't clutched the stair rail I would have fallen—and as she passed me she hissed: "Why should it be you who sees him?"

That afternoon I found the last gift under my pillow. It was a diamond ring. I put the box in the pocket of my apron and kept it there until nighttime, when I went to the library. I showed the ring to Isidoro and asked him what I should do. He said I should marry him. He had instructed Fausta Del Olmo to put the ring beneath my pillow; he was sure that she had been responsible for the other gifts, even though they were nothing to do with him. She was planning something, but it didn't matter, or wouldn't if I married him.

"Time is of the essence," Isidoro said. All I could do was look at him with my mouth wide open. And then I said yes. He said I must fetch a priest at once, and I didn't know where to find a priest, so I went and woke Fausta Del Olmo up and asked her to help me. She gave me the oddest look and said: "What do you want a priest for?"

"I'm marrying Isidoro Salazar tonight," I said.

"Oh, really? And I suppose he's the father of your child too?" she whispered, her eyes glinting the way they do when she gets hold of a secret at last.

"Please just hurry."

Fausta Del Olmo put on her coat and slippers and ran out to fetch a priest, and the man of God arrived quickly; he was calm and had a kind face and took my hand and asked me what the trouble was. "But didn't you tell him, Fausta, that this is a wedding?"

Fausta shrugged and looked embarrassed and I began to be frightened of her all over again. Something was wrong. I took the priest to the library, and Fausta Del Olmo followed us.

Isidoro wasn't there, but when I opened the library door, a door at the far, far end of the room slammed shut. Isidoro had seen Fausta and escaped into the rose garden. I went after him, but Fausta and the priest didn't follow me—they were talking, and Fausta was pointing at something . . . I now realize it was the door to Isidoro's rooms that she was pointing at.

Isidoro wasn't in the garden; after searching for him I went back into the library, which was also empty. I could hear a lot of noise and commotion in the rest of the house, footsteps hurrying up and down the wing where Isidoro's rooms were. I saw his rooms, the inside of them, I mean, for the first time that night. The priest Isidoro and I had sent for was praying over a waxen body that lay in the bed. When the priest finished his prayers he said that I must not be afraid to tell him the truth, that no one would punish me, that I'd done well to send for him.

"What do you mean?" I said.

"This man has been dead for at least a day. No, don't shake your head at me, young lady. See how stiff he is. He'd been very ill, poor soul, so this is a release for him. You came here this morning and found him like this, isn't that what happened? And your master is away, so you worried all day about who to tell and what you would say until the worry made you cook up this story in your head about a wedding. Isn't that so?"

All the servants were listening, but I still said no, that he was wrong. I put my hand in my pocket to take out my ring and show it to him, but the ring was gone too.

"My ring," I said, turning to Fausta Del Olmo, who replied in the deadliest, most gentle voice: "What ring, Aurelie? Be careful what you say."

After that I stopped talking. I looked at the body in the bed and told myself it was Isidoro and no one else. This was a truth that I had to learn, things would go very badly for me if I refused to learn it, but the lesson was very hard indeed.

The priest left, promising to write to the master as soon as he got home, and all we servants went to bed. Fausta was the last to leave Isidoro's room, closing the door behind her as quietly as if he was just sleeping. Then she took my arm and dragged me downstairs to the maids' dormitory, where judge and jury were waiting. Was I mad or was I simply a liar? They'd already taken out the little gifts I'd received and were talking about them: Now Fausta told them where the gifts had come from. I'd taken the key to the library from the master's laundry, she announced, and I'd been selling off a number of his valuable books. I inferred from this that this is what Fausta herself had been doing before I'd interrupted her with my library visits.

"But how stupid, to spend the money on things like this," the cook said, flapping the green shawl in my face.

"Some people just don't think of the future," Fausta Del Olmo said. A couple of the other maids hadn't joined in and looked as if they didn't entirely believe Fausta Del Olmo. Perhaps they'd had their own problems with her. But then Fausta announced that even Isidoro Salazar had known I was a thief. She showed them some of the slips of paper Isidoro had left for me in the library, slips he must have left that time I stayed away. The words "pretty thief" persuaded them. The master is a generous man and stealing from him causes all sorts of unnecessary difficulties. Now that some of his books are gone he may well become much less generous. The servants drove me out of the dormitory. They went to the kitchen and took pots and pans and banged them together and cried: "Shame! Shame! Shame!" I stayed in my bed for as long as I could with my covers pulled over my head, but they were so loud. They surrounded my bed, shame, shame, shame, so loud I can still hear it, shame, shame, shame. I fled, and Fausta and the servants chased me through the corridors with their pots and pans and screeching—someone hit me with a spatula and then they all threw spoons, which sounds droll now that it's over, but having silver spoons thrown at you in a dark house is a terrifying thing, you see them flashing against the walls like little swords before they hit you. It would've been worse if those people had actually had knives: they'd completely lost their minds.

I made it into the library by the skin of my teeth and locked the door behind me. I wrote, am writing, this letter to you, my Montserrat. The servants have given up their rough music and have gone to bed. You will be born soon, maybe later today, maybe tomorrow. I feel you close. I know where I will have to leave you. As for this letter, I will give it to the roses, and then I must get out of here for a while. How long? Until I am sure of what happened, or at least the true order of it all. Did I somehow give him more time than he would have had on his own? The entire time I have been writing this letter I have felt Isidoro's eyes on me. He seems to be telling me that we could still have been married, that if I'd only brought the priest and not Fausta we could still have been married. Of course he cannot really be telling me anything: I have seen him as a dead man. Why am I not afraid?

Montse found that she'd walked the length of the library as she read her mother's letter. Now she stood at the door to Isidoro's garden, which opened with the same key. Outside, someone in the shadows took a couple of startled steps backward. Señora Lucy.

"I saw all this light coming out from under that door," Lucy said. "That was new." She peered over Montse's shoulder. "Swap you a rose for a book," she said.

"sorry" doesn't sweeten her tea

천양희 / 밥

외로워서 밥을 많이 먹는다던 너에게
권태로워 잠을 많이 잔다던 너에게
슬퍼서 많이 운다던 너에게
나는 쓴다

궁지에 몰린 마음을 밥처럼 씹어라
어차피 삶은 너가 소화해야 할 것이니까

To you who eat a lot of rice because you are lonely

To you who sleep a lot because you are bored

To you who cry a lot because you are sad

I write this down.

Chew on your feelings that are cornered

Like you would chew on rice.

Anyway life is something that you need to digest.

—*CHUN YANG HEE*

B e good to Boudicca and Boudicca will be good to you," Chedorlaomer said. Boudicca and I eyed each other through the blue-tinted glass of Ched's fish tank, and I said: "Tell me what she is again?"

To the naked eye Boudicca is a haze of noxious green that lurks among fronds of seaweed looking exactly like the aftermath of a chemical spill. But Ched's got this certificate that states Boudicca's species is *Betta splendens*, colloquially known as Siamese fighting fish because fish of this kind have a way of instigating all-out brawls with their tank mates. It's almost admirable. Boudicca doesn't care how big or pretty her fellow fish are; if they come to her manor she will obliterate them, whether that means waiting until the other fish is asleep before she launches her attack or, in the case of a fish that simply refused to engage with her, eating the eggs that the other fish had spawned and then dancing around in the water while the bereaved mother was slain by grief.

So now Boudicca lives alone, which is exactly what she wanted all along.

I get this vibe that Ched the eternal bachelor sees Boudicca as a fish version of himself, but he's never said that out loud, at least not to me. We don't have those kinds of talks. Even if Ched and Boudicca are on some level the same person, the fact remains that the man is able to feed himself and the fish needs someone to see to her nutrition a couple of times a week.

Ched called me over to tell me he was going away for two years and he expected me to take care of Boudicca. Twice a week for two years! Plus Ched's house is spooky. The House of Locks, it's called. That's the actual address: House of Locks, Ipswich, Suffolk. He travels a lot and I have his spare set of keys for use while on best friend duty, watering his house plants when he used to have house plants, collecting post, etc., but when I'm in there I don't linger. Nothing has actually happened to me in there. Not yet, anyway. But every time I go into that bloody house there's the risk of coming out crazy. Because of the doors. They don't stay closed unless they're locked. Once you've done that you hear sounds behind them; sounds that convince you you've locked someone in. But when you leave these doors unlocked they swing halfway out of the doorframe so that you can't see all the way into the next room and it's just as if somebody's standing behind the door and holding it like that on purpose. The windows behave similarly—they won't fully open unless you push them up slowly, with more firm intent than actual pressure. Only Ched really has the knack of it. Apparently the house's first owner took a particular pleasure in fastening and releasing locks—the feel and the sound of the key turning until it finds the point at which the lock must yield. So for her the house was a lifetime's worth of erotic titillation.

IT'S A NICE HOUSE for Ched too, in that it's big and he got it on the cheap, and anyway he's not really comfortable in overly normal situations. As it is he hears voices. Nobody else hears these voices but they're not just in Ched's head, you know? In this world there are voices without form; they sing and sing, as they have from the beginning and will continue until the end. Ched borrows their melodies: That's the music part of the songs he writes. For words Ched uses rhymes from our village, the kind that nobody pays attention to anymore because they advocate living by a code that will surely make you one of life's losers. A lot of stuff about living honestly and trying your best. Even if you only have one tiny job to do, do it well, do it well, do it well . . .

These songs of Ched's turned out to be a hit with a lot of people outside our country. Ched got Internet famous and then magazine famous and all the other kinds of famous after that. It was fun to see. His mother still says to me: "But don't you think people overreact to our Chedorlaomer? These girls screaming and fainting just because he looked at them or whatever. He's just some boy from Bezin."

That's the power of those true voices, man.

And now that you know that Ched and I are from a small village that might make you say Oh OK, so that's why this guy believes in voices he's never heard. But trust, living in a small village in a country that's not even sure it's really a country you see a lot of shit that's stranger than a shaman (which is what Ched is, or was, before he started making money from the voices). Every day there was news that made you say "Oh really." Some new tax that only people with no money had to pay. Or yet another member of the county police force was found to have been an undercover gangster. If not that then a gang member was found to have been an undercover police officer. An Ottoman-style restaurant opened in a town nearby; it served no food but had a mineral water menu tens of pages long, and fashion models came to drink their way through it while we played football with their bodyguards. Speaking even more locally there was this one boy at our school who had quite a common first name and decided to fight every other boy in our postal code area for the right to be the sole bearer of that name—can you imagine? I was one of the boys on his hit list, and I was already getting picked on because I didn't have a father. But what a ridiculous place we were born into, that fatherlessness was a reason why people would flick a boy's forehead and say insulting things to him, then pile on four against one when he took offense . . . it's not our fault we're ridiculous people, Ched and me. How could we be anything else?

Ched was the absurd-looking boy who suddenly grew into his features and became really good-looking overnight. That didn't seem right, so he got picked on too. But Ched had been thinking, and the result of that was his going around offering assistance to the other boys who had the same name as me, arguing that if our little problem fought us individually he would easily beat us but if we stood up to him together none of us would have to change our name. The others feared duplicity more than anything else (this was wise, since duplicity was all we knew) and decided it was better to take their chances as individuals.

I BELIEVED Ched though. With the solemnity of a couple exchanging vows we slipped knuckle-dusters onto each other's fingers, four for each hand. Then I walked over to the boy who didn't think he should have to share his name with anybody and without saying a word I smacked the pot of chocolate pudding he was eating right out of his hand. He was so astounded he just stood there pointing at me as his friends came loping over like bloodthirsty gazelles. I didn't even check whether this Chedorlaomer boy really had my back, but I trusted that he did, and he did. What a great day, a day that a modest plan worked. That guy changed his own name in the end. And it's been like that ever since with Ched and me. He was lucky enough to be a year older than me and when he graduated from our school it was like I was the only sane one left in an asylum. There was more and more bullshit every day. But Ched waited for me at the school gates, and he had a lot of good pep talks.

That's why it's pretty odd that Chedorlaomer went back for mandatory military service. Only passport holders have to do that, and I thought he'd given up his passport, like I had.

"No, I never told you that," Ched said.

"But why would you keep it? Haven't you seen the stuff they write about you over there? You've sold out, you're scum, blah blah blah. So what, now you're trying to change people's minds? Why those minds in particular? I thought we—"

"Yeah, I know what you thought," Ched said. He laughed and ruffled my hair. All of his was gone; he'd just come back from the barber's. Baldness made him look younger than I'd ever seen him, and toothier too. Like a stray, but a dangerous stray; you could take him home if you wanted to but he'd tear the walls down. "It's time for me to be part of something impersonal," he said. "Duty is as big as it gets. Do these people like me? Do I like them?

Am I one of them? All irrelevant. I'll be directing all of each day's effort toward one priority: Defend the perimeter."

Other things my best friend said to me: That two years was but a short span. And in the meantime he hoped his house of locks would become a kind of sanctuary for me. It would've been a really nice speech if Boudicca hadn't been blinking balefully at me the whole time. *You there . . . forget to feed me once, just one time, and you're dead.* I mumbled that I had a lot on at work but I'd see what I could do.

I DON'T TELL Ched how often the things he says come true. That's for his own good of course, so that he stays humble. But here's an example: This past couple of weeks alone I've come to the House of Locks seven times. Four times to feed Boudicca and walk the length of her tank—the first time she raced me to the farthest corner, and all the other times she's turned her back. The rest of my visits have been for sanctuary, I suppose. Just like Ched said. All I've seen or heard of him since his departure are blurry photographs of his arrival at barracks, these posted on various fan sites. He hasn't called or replied to e-mails, so I walk through the wing of the house that he favors, passing the windows with various views of his fountain. A girl of pewter stands knee-deep in the water, her hands cupped, collecting streams and letting them pour away. Her eyes are blissfully closed. In the room I'm watching her from the curtains hang so still that breathing isn't quite enough to make me believe there's air in here. The front door is the only one I lock behind me, so as I go through the house all the doors behind me are ajar. It's still hair-raising, but it's reassuring too. The house is wonderfully, blessedly empty—nobody else will appear in the gap between the doors—that gap is a safe passage across all those thresholds I crossed without thinking.

ABOUT WORK: I run a clinic for my Aunt Thomasina's company. A "Swiss-Style Weight-Loss Clinic," to quote the promotional materials. This basically means that people come here for three days of drug-induced and -maintained deep sleep, during which they're fed vitamins through a drip. This is a job I jumped at when it was my non-Ched-dependent ticket out of Bezin. It's not as peaceful as I expected; most of the sleeping done here is the troubled kind. A lot of sleep talking and plaintive bleating. None of the sleepers are OK, not really. On the bright side the results are visually impressive: Most clients drop a clothing size over those seventy-two hours. Aunt Thomasina experienced this herself before she ever tried it out on anybody else. Something awful happened to her when she was young— she's never even hinted at what that might be—and she took what she thought was a lethal dose of valerian and went to bed, only to wake up gorgeously slender three days later. "This will be popular," she said to herself. And she was right. Most days the waiting room is full of clients happily shopping on their tablet devices; the whole new wardrobe they just ordered will be waiting for them at home after their beauty sleep. Of course weight loss that drastic is unsustainable, which makes the clinic a great business model. We send our monthly customers Christmas and birthday cards; they're part of the family.

We have doctors who make sure that we're not admitting anyone likely to suffer serious complications from our treatment, so my job is mainly monitoring and addressing complaints and unrealistic expectations. I can fake sympathy for days: Aunt Thomasina says I am a psychopath and that it's a good thing I came under the right influences at a young age. I also do night shifts, since we can't lock anybody into their rooms and I'm good with sleepwalkers. Last week we had two. One guy rose up pulling tubes out of his skin because he's not used to sleeping indoors in summer. He grew up in an earthquake-prone region and his family hit upon the strategy of sleeping in a nearby field so as to avoid having their house fall down on them. My shift partner got him back into bed with warm assurances of safety, but when it was my turn I merely whispered: "You are interrupting the process, my friend. Do you want her to regret or not?" He sleep-ran back down the corridor and had to be restrained from re-attaching himself to the vitamin machine. That was what he'd written in his questionnaire beside "objective": TO BE SEXY SO THAT SHE REGRETS.

Our other sleepwalker was just extremely hungry. You can't coax someone out of that. This client got up and searched for food with such determination that she had to have her drug dose significantly elevated. For a couple of hours it seemed her hunger was stronger than the drugs. I sat out the third intervention and stayed in the monitor room watching the camera feed: It was fascinating to watch her returning to the surface of sleep crying, "Chips . . . chips . . . ," but eventually she went down hard and stayed under. Ultimately she was happy with her results but apart from the usual disorientation she also looked really thoughtful, as if asking herself: *Worth it?* She probably won't be back.

The sleepwalkers upset my shift partner Tyche. Her being upset helps her get through to them, I think. They can tell that she cares about them and isn't judging them like I am. Tyche is someone that I think Ched should meet.

She's only a part-timer at the clinic; her business card states that the rest of the time she does ODD JOBS—INVOCATIONS. Invocations. Something she learned while trying to do something else, she says. So she can relate to Aunt Thomasina's weight-loss discovery. Tyche's beauty is interestingly kinetic; it comes and goes and comes back again. Or maybe it's more that you observe it in the first second of seeing her and then she makes you shelve that exquisite first impression for a while so she can get on with things. Then in some moment when she's not talking or when she suddenly turns her head it hits you all over again. There's a four-star constellation on her wrist that isn't always there either. When it is, its appearance goes through various degrees of permanence, from drawn on with kohl to full tattoo. I mentioned this to her, but she laughed it off: "But don't you stare at me too much? Everything OK with your boyfriend?" In my matchmaking capacity I've paid closer attention to her visuals than I would pay to anybody on my own behalf. On to inner qualities: She's powerful. Not just in doing whatever she does to make people listen to her instead of watch her, but . . . I think she heals herself. She wears a wedding ring, so I made reference to her partner, but she held her hand up and said: "Oh, this? I found it." Then she told me about it. A while ago she'd been in a relationship with someone who was adamant about keeping her a secret, to the extent that they didn't acknowledge each other if there was even one other person in sight. Her superpower was picking emotionally unavailable partners and she doubted she'd get a better offer. She also assumed that the relationship would gradually get less secret. Nothing changed, and while she continued to profess her commitment to her secret boyfriend, her body disagreed and tried to get her out of it. She got sick. Her hair started falling out and her skin went scaly; she was cold all the time, and could only fall asleep by reciting words of summoning.

NOBODY CAME, but one evening at the pub down the road from her house she found a ring at the bottom of a pint of lager she was drinking. The ring was heavier than it looked, and she recognized it without remembering exactly where she'd seen it before. Since no one at the pub seemed to know anything about the ring, she took it to the police station, only to return there to collect it at the end of the month: There had been no inquiries related to the item, so it was hers. And when she wore it she felt that a love existed. For her . . . her, of all people. And it was on all the time. Of this love there would be no photographs, no handwritten declarations, no token at all save the ring. If this was the only way that what she'd called could come to her then it sufficed; she was content. The hand that wore the ring grew smooth, and she recouped her losses.

"Didn't some nuns used to wear wedding rings?" I asked her.

She nodded and said that that was something she thought about a lot.

I'd best introduce her to Ched before the nuns get her. Ched's voices are bullies: They won't let him play unless it's for keeps. Tyche might have an answer for them.

BUT WHY AM I treating Ched's celibacy as something to be fixed? Maybe because I am so much in his debt for so many things and I can't think of any other way to settle up. Maybe I've become evangelical ever since I got a little family of my own. The scene at the homestead is different every day. My boyfriend has joint custody of his two daughters with his ex-wife, whose schedule is ever-changing, so the girls might be at home or they might not.

DAYANG IS THE ELDER at sixteen; Aisha's eighteen months behind her. Day is studious and earnest, a worrier like her father—she carries a full first aid kit around in her school bag and tells me off for calling her boyfriend by a different name every time I see him. In my defense the boy genuinely looks different every time he comes over, but Day's concerned that he'll think she has other boyfriends. This would be catastrophic because Mr. Face-Shifting Boyfriend is The One. And how can she tell he's the one, I ask. Well how did I know that her dad is my One, she asks. Some things are just completely obvious, GOSH.

DAY IS GREAT, but Aisha is my darling and my meddlesome girl. She's the one who gets the question "But why are you like this?" at least once a day from her father. If she isn't growing something (she is the reason Noor finds toadstools in his shoes) or brewing something (she's the reason it's best not to leave any cup or drinking glass unattended when she's at home) she'll pass by singing and swishing her tail around (she put her sewing machine to work making a set of tails that she attaches to her dresses. A fox's tail, a dragon's tail, a tiger's tail, a peacock's. On a special occasion she'll wear all of them at once). Last month Matyas Füst released a new album and Aisha hosted a listening party for five bosom friends. The bosom friends wore all their tails too . . .

———

THOSE WERE THE GOOD old days, when Aisha's love for Matyas Füst was straightforward idol worship. Her wall was covered with posters of him; she sometimes got angry with him for being more attractive than she thought anyone was allowed to be and would punch a poster right in the face before whispering frantic apologies and covering it with kisses. She had Noor or me buy certain items because she'd read an interview in which he mentioned he loved this or that particular scent or color on a woman. All of Aisha's online IDs were some variation of her official motto: "Matyas Füst Is Love, Matyas Füst Is Life."

CHED HAD MET Füst a few times and said he wouldn't want any daughter of his going anywhere near "that dickhead," but the first time he said that I took it with more than a pinch of salt. For starters Aisha's polite refusal to have a crush on her friendly neighborhood pop star was something of an ego bruiser. There were a few other small but influential factors: Füst's being ten years younger than Ched, and its being well-known that Füst composes, arranges, and writes the lyrics for all his (mostly successful) songs himself . . . no voices. It just wasn't really possible for Ched to like him. Füst was forever being photographed wearing dark gray turtlenecks, was engaged to be married to a soloist at the Bolshoi Ballet, didn't seem to go to nightclubs, and reportedly enjoyed art-house film, the occasional dinner party, and the company of his cat Kleinzach. A clean-shaven man with a vocal tone reminiscent of post-coital whispers, that was Matyas Füst. The way he sings "Twinkle Twinkle Little Star" is no joke.

CHED HAD been away for about a month when I got home to find "love to hatred turn'd." Noor was making dinner, checking his recipe board after each step even though he knew it just as well as if he'd written it himself. The not-so-hidden charms of a man who takes his time over every detail . . . especially once you distract him for just long enough to turn all his attention onto you. It didn't occur to me to ask about the kids until halfway through our very late dinner. Bad stepfather.

"Er . . . have the kids already eaten?"

Noor shook his head. "They promised they'd have something later."

"Hmmm. Why?"

"Not sure. Heartbreak, I think."

"Ah, so the face shifter isn't The One after all?"

"No, it's not Day—well, it is Day, but only because she can't let Aisha go through it all on her own."

The sisters were huddled together on Aisha's bed with a laptop between them. They closed the laptop when I came into the room, leaving me to look around at the bare walls and wonder what had happened. Both girls were red-eyed and strenuously denied being upset. When I left the room I clearly heard Day say: "You've got to stop watching it," and Aisha answered: "I know, but I can't." Then she said, "Maybe it isn't true, Day? It probably isn't true," and Day said, "Oh, Aisha."

NOOR AND I WATCHED the video ourselves downstairs. It was called "A Question About Matyas Füst." Noor found it hard to watch in one go; he kept pausing it. This cowardly pacing would normally have been grounds for a dispute; I agreed with him just that once, though. The video opened with a woman sitting on the floor in her underwear, showing us marks all over her body. A lot of the marks were needle track marks, but they were outnumbered by marks I hadn't wanted Day and Aisha to ever become acquainted with: bruises left by fists and boots. I dreaded the end of the camera's journey up to the woman's face and didn't know what to think when I saw that it was untouched, even a subdued kind of pretty. No makeup, clean, mousy-looking hair, age absolutely anywhere between twenty-five and forty-five. I'd seen girls who resembled her waitressing in seedy bars across the Continent, removing customers' hands from their backsides without turning to see who the hand belonged to, their gestures as automatic and unemotional as swatting midges.

She pulled a T-shirt on and looked at the camera for a little while before she started talking. You could tell from her eyes that she was out of her head on something and probably couldn't have told you her own name if you'd asked her. Her English was far below fluency, but since she was in her happy place she didn't bother struggling with pronunciation, just said what she had to say and left us to figure it out. She wanted us to know that "the entertainer" Matyas Füst had picked her up on a street corner a few hours after he'd played a sold-out concert in Greenwich. She'd spent the rest of the night with him and he hadn't proved very entertaining at all. *Tell us a bit more about yourself,* the person holding the camera said—a woman, I think, trying to sound gentle, but her voice was thick with anger. The woman on camera obediently stated that she was often on street corners trying to get money, and that she didn't often get lucky: The men she signaled to could usually tell just by looking at the backs of her hands that she'd gone too far into whatever she was doing. But Matyas Füst didn't care about that: He'd had a fight with his controlling bitch of a girlfriend and it had taken all he had not to hit the girlfriend. Taking your fists to a prima ballerina with an adoring host of family and friends would be a very messy and expensive blunder. So he went looking for some-one nobody cared about. *And he found . . . me . . .* the woman on-screen said, and giggled. Noor pressed pause again and left the room, went upstairs, and knocked on Aisha's bed-room door. "Come and eat," he said, and Aisha and Day said they'd come in a minute.

HOURS LATER they still hadn't come downstairs. We'd watched the rest of the clip by then. The whole thing was only three minutes and thirty seconds long, but we kept try-ing to watch it through Aisha's and Day's eyes, this woman telling us that after they'd had sex Füst had insulted her so that she slapped him, and once he'd received the slap he'd smiled (her fingers plucked at the corners of her mouth until we could see just how he'd smiled), told her she'd "started it," and proceeded to beat her until she couldn't stand up. She'd hit back, she said, even from her place at his feet she'd hit back, but every time he hit harder. Then he stood over her in all his wealth and fame and arrogance and shrugged when she said she wasn't going to keep quiet about this. Matyas Füst had shrugged and asked her if she thought anybody was going to give a shit that someone like her had got hurt. A nameless junkie with seriously crazy English. *Look at you,* he said. *And look at me.* He threw a handful of money at her and told her it was better for her to keep her mouth shut and spend that, or save it for a rainy day. Then he went back to his girlfriend. They must have made up, because she'd seen photos of them having a romantic dinner in a restaurant, and hints had been dropped about their wedding plans. *I look him on Google.* The woman on-camera seemed proud of her diligence. Then she asked us her question about Matyas Füst: *Did* anybody care that he'd hurt her, someone like her? She was just wondering. She laughed and gave us a perky little wave at the end. *Thank you. Nice day to you.*

Aisha came in cradling her laptop in her arms. Day followed, hands helplessly rising and falling. "It's not just the clip, it's the *comments*," she said, when she saw us.

Ah yes, the comments.

Noor couldn't make himself look, so Aisha and I read some of them aloud. There was a lot of *LOL cool allegations junkie, maybe it was all a dream?* and *LMAO people will say anything to ruin a good man's reputation stay strong Matyas!*

If only that was the worst of it. Aisha's haggard face as

she read: *Oh boohoo. What's this one complaining about? He paid her, didn't he? She hit him, didn't she? Admitted all this herself. Does she think you can hit someone and just walk away?* I read: *She should count herself lucky: men probably treat broken down old whores worse than that in her country. And she got to bang Matyas! Matyas Füst can beat me up any time baby LOL*

Then the apologists came out to play: *Even if this is true is it the full story? We know that Matyas wouldn't just lash out like that so we need to be asking what she did . . .*

Day showed us a screenshot she'd saved. She'd posted a comment of her own: *Guys are you being serious? I'm appalled and really scared by this and all the reactions I'm seeing . . . this isn't the world I want to live in.* She'd received so many replies telling her to kill herself that she'd decided to delete her account.

"I still don't think it's true," Aisha said. "He couldn't have done something like this." When Noor put on his solicitor voice to point out that the video had been up for half a day, had a view count of half a million, and would have had Matyas Füst's team of lawyers swinging left and right if the content hadn't had any basis in fact, Aisha said through gritted teeth: "But he hasn't said anything at all."

"He'll probably make a statement in the morning," Noor said. We were failing as the men in Day and Aisha's life. We weren't doing what we were supposed to do. This came through very clearly in the way that Day and Aisha were looking at us, or more not looking at us, really.

THE MORNING brought no statement from Füst, and Noor sounded relieved (and ashamed of his relief) when he said: "Looks like she hasn't got any proof and he's going to ignore or deny it." In the afternoon there were reports of an eyewitness to the beating coming forward, and about an hour after that Füst's legal team announced that he'd voluntarily made himself available to the police for questioning.

AT THE CLINIC my concentration was poor and I mixed up checkout forms so that departing clients got to read details of each other's low self-esteem and experience the outrage of not being unique. Tyche Shaw and I were on the same shift again, and got authorization to offer free secondary sleep sessions all round so we wouldn't be sued. But like Aisha, Tyche was addicted to the YouTube clip. She spent her break time watching it over and over on her phone and ran the battery right down.

"I found that one tough to watch," I told her.

"Really?" she said. "But it's just someone talking about this time she got beaten up. No bullets or gore or bombs or anything. This is nothing compared to other things you can see on this site."

"I don't know what to say. I can't explain it."

"Well, I hope she sees the view count and accepts that as an answer to her question about whether people care. These numbers are up there with the numbers for footage of the world's most brilliant strikers scoring the decade's most brilliant goals. So it's not that we're indifferent . . . we care . . . just in a really really really fucked-up way . . ."

Matyas Füst's fiancée released a statement as we were leaving work: She was shocked and upset to hear of "the events described in the video" and would be paying the victim a visit to see if there was anything she could do for her. She had never seen a violent side to Matyas's character but it was now undeniable that he'd been struggling with some issues and they'd be spending some time apart while he completed a course of anger management therapy.

"No jail time for Füst . . . just a fine and some therapy," Tyche predicted, even as she admired the photo of the prima ballerina, who was elfin and ethereal and all the rest of it.

"Yeah, well, I beg to differ," I said.

Tyche stuck her hand out. "Bet you a hundred pounds."

"I suppose this is all just a joke to you, but I know a girl who's pretty badly shaken up by all this."

Tyche sighed. "She was a fan?"

"She's still trying to be one, I think. Clinging to every possible delusion."

Tyche's sigh deepened. "Let me know if intervention's required."

"OK, thanks . . ." I had it in my mind to ask Tyche what she thought she might be able to do for a girl she'd never met—in a spirit of curiosity, not hostility—but had to hurry over to the House of Locks. Terry, the man who maintained Boudicca's fish tank, was waiting for me to let him in. After Terry left I stayed a few more hours, reading Matyas Füst updates aloud to Boudicca, who looked suitably incredulous. YouTube woman was glad she'd had the chance to meet the woman she'd found herself taking a beating for and wouldn't be pressing charges. She'd hit Füst first—that was an excessive response to some words he'd said, and his response in turn had been excessive; all she asked was acknowledgment of that. A sincere apology. So Matyas Füst was preparing a sincere apology.

HAS SHE READ ANY OF THE COMMENTS? That's what I wondered. Did the woman from the YouTube video understand that the public wasn't on her side? She made her requests with such placid mirth, as if talking into a seashell or a shattered telephone, as if Matyas Füst fans weren't actively looking for her, probably in order to finish her off. Even those who'd begun to condemn Füst believed his apologies should be directed elsewhere ("It's his fiancée I feel sorry for in all this . . ."). Those who claimed they *wanted* to feel concern for YouTube woman didn't like that she'd filmed her allegations while high. And yet she might not have been able to talk about it sober.

NOOR TEXTED that he was considering taking Aisha's laptop away until the Füst case died down. She seemed to have spent the entire evening engaged in a long and rambling argument with her friends via six-way video call. She attacked Füst's reputation, defended it, then attacked again, berated the friends who'd gone off him for their faithlessness, cursed the infinite stupidity of his unchanged fans and threatened to put on a Füst mask and beat them up to see how they liked it. She'd skipped dinner again and was running a temperature. When was I coming home?

Two firsts: being reluctant to leave Ched's house and being reluctant to enter my own. I said I'd been at the gym. Ched does have a home gymnasium; he works out a lot, his body being his back-up plan in case he gets ugly again. But I don't know why I lied.

AISHA WILL GET over this. But what of her tails and her plant-growing projects and the remarkably potent gin she was perfecting? "That gin was going to make us richer than an entire network of 1920s bootleggers," I said, to see if that wouldn't rouse her. She likes money. Now it seems she liked it because she could exchange it for Matyas Füst–related items. What worries Noor is that three of Aisha's graven images fell off their pedestals at once: him, me, and Matyas Füst. The girls seemed to pity our weakness. Noor's brusque talk of judicial process and media treatment. My awkward, awkward silence. Is it really bad that the girls have found us out, though? I never projected strength. Not on purpose, anyway.

"What are you really worrying about, Noor?"

He shuffled papers into his briefcase, rearranged his pens, straightened his tie. "It just . . . I think I've lost them. Just like that, overnight. Their mother says they're fine with her . . ."

I loosened the knot of his tie a little, just a little. It still looked neat, so he couldn't complain.

"Nah. I don't even know them as well as you do and I

can tell they're just thinking." A casual overview of all their main emotional attachments reveals that Noor and his ex have been better parents than they realize; while Day and Aisha appreciate strength, lack of it isn't a deal breaker in the matter of whether they respect a person or not.

ALL WAS QUIET on the Matyas Füst front for a few months; I kept an eye on that situation (among others) and read that the reporters who managed to get a sound bite out of Füst all got the same one. He was completing his anger management therapy and was still preparing his apology. This sound bite was paired with another obtained from YouTube woman: *Looking forward to it.*

It was around that time Ched and I started talking again—not often, but enough. I'd be entering or leaving the House of Locks, the phone would ring, and it would be Ched. He described his current existence as a cycle of drills and chores, and was so tired he'd fall asleep mid-sentence. It was good to speak to him, not just because it was him but because he didn't know the first thing about the incident that had rocked my household. When I gave him a brief outline he said: "Oh, you know the apology Füst's preparing is going to be a song, right? And that song is going to become an anthem of repentance. It's probably going to be called 'Dress Made of Needles.'"

"Nice—I'll go down to the betting shop tomorrow."

There was something else I wanted to talk about while I had him on the line. When I answered his phone calls he needed half a second to adjust his greeting, and it sounded as if he was disappointed that I was the one who'd answered. Well, disappointed is too strong a word. It was more as if I wasn't his first preference. Which was fine, except that I'm the only other person who has keys to his house. His mum's been trying to get a set for years without success.

"So what's going on? You met someone?"

"Not sure," he said. "I . . . think so."

"And this person has keys?"

After a lot more questioning he eventually confessed that he hadn't given a set of keys to anybody else and had never actually met this woman in person, but was fairly sure that she had keys because she sometimes answered the phone when he called. When he said that I adjusted my position so that I was able to watch all the open doors and I said: "That's wonderful, Ched. I'm really happy for you."

"Don't overreact," he said. "She's a nice voice at the moment, nothing more. Like one of the ones that sing. Except that she just talks."

"Did you ask her how she got in?"

"Of course."

"Well, what did she say?"

"She encouraged me to think of a better question."

I glared at Boudicca; no wonder she'd been filling out lately. "Maybe she feeds your fish too."

"Haha, maybe. But while we're talking about this, could you do me a favor? I don't think she wants to be seen, so if you let yourself in and happen to notice that she's around just leave immediately, OK?"

"OK, Ched. No problem."

Just another day in the lives of two boys from Bezin. Still, I checked every room in Ched's wing of the house before I left. His alarm system's in working order and none of his valuables have moved. For now.

CHED'S PHONE GIRLFRIEND earned me the first direct smile I'd got from Aisha in weeks. "You stupid boys," she said, lovingly. A string of text messages appeared on her phone and her smile vanished as if it had never been.

"Brace yourself," Noor shouted from the next room. "It's Matyas Füst's apology."

Day wasn't ready to leave her bubble bath—"Oh no, no apology for me, thank you," so Aisha grabbed a couple of foam stress balls, jumped onto Noor's lap, and said: "Go." We watched and listened to Matyas Füst singing a song about a girl who walked the earth in a dress made of needles that she couldn't remove without maiming herself. People with good intentions kept trying to pull the needles out and give her something soft and warm to wear instead, but the needles pricked their fingers so much that they gave up. Then the girl met a bad man who drove the needles in deeper. Not with a hammer, but with his hands, for the thrill of joining his own torture to hers. Luckily, luckily the bad man managed to bleed out before he could kill her—it turned out his bones were magnetic(?). I might have misunderstood that part of the song, but whatever it was about his bones, they drew the needles from her and into him, he died in the utmost agony, the end. I kept waiting for Füst to wink, but he didn't.

"My favorite thing about this song is the way it starts out all about her and ends up all about him," Noor said, as we refreshed the page and fat red love hearts accumulated in the comments beneath the video.

Matyas understands

This is exactly how I'm feeling today

Thank you Matyas

Think we can all agree he shouldn't have done it in the first place but now he's done the decent thing

We forgive u

All I could say was: "Amazing."

How did it go from "Füst should apologize to the woman he beat up" to "Füst should apologize to his fiancée" to "Füst should apologize to us"?

Aisha spoke through the stress ball she'd stuffed into her mouth, removed it, and started again: "Maybe this is a piece of conceptual art? Like something out of one of Matyas's favorite films. Couldn't YouTube woman be an artist who's worked out a concept that uses the media to show us something about fame and its . . . its magic touch? So what if that touch is a punch? She's famous now. Maybe she's trying to get us thinking about the different ways people get famous. By excelling at something, or by suffering publicly. Maybe what that eyewitness saw was a performance? What if she already had an agreement with Matyas that he would beat her up for the concept? Doesn't it seem like there's no way to avoid getting punched by someone or other? Doesn't matter who you are, it's just a fact of life. So isn't it a little better if you get to choose who punches you? You know, I think if I could pick I would have chosen him too."

She was doing well until Noor, who'd stopped me from countering every single one of her speculations, said: "Ah, darling. Would you?" Then she buried her head in her dad's jumper and howled. We couldn't tell if it was heartbreak, rage, mirth, or simply the difficulty she was having unimagining Mr. Matyas Füst.

THE REHABILITATION of Matyas Füst was in full swing. His compulsory course of therapy was over, but he was continuing of his own accord. His fiancée quietly moved back into his house and he was doing a fuckload of charity work. The charity work was the last straw for me. Before I explain the part I may or may not have played in another man's complete mental and physical breakdown I just have to quickly praise myself here. Yes, I have to be the one to do it; nobody else even understood how patient I was with Aisha's mourning process in the midst of every other grief-worthy event going on in the world. Aisha herself was in a hurry to attain indifference to "the Füst matter" but you can't rush these things. The cackling with which Aisha greeted YouTube woman's simple and dignified acceptance of Matyas Füst's apology, that cackling was not ideal. Words were better, a little less opaque, so I was patient with her outbursts. More patient than Jesus himself!

The first I knew of my contribution to the charity of Matyas Füst's choice was an e-mail that arrived while I was pursuing quotes from satisfied customers. The e-mail thanked me for my ten-thousand-pound auction bid—the winning bid!—and expressed hope that my daughter Aisha would enjoy the private concert that Matyas Füst would accordingly perform for her. Ten thousand of my strong and painstakingly saved pounds, Matyas Füst, that was all I was able to compute. Oh, and I saw red arrows between the two. Ten thousand pounds to Matyas Füst. I had some sort of interlude after that, running between my keyboard and the nearest wall, flapping my hands and choking. Tyche came into my office, glanced at my computer screen, threw a glass of water in my face, and left. That got me to sit back down, at least. Five minutes later Aisha Skyped me from her school computer lab. I accepted the call, put my face right up to the camera, and bellowed her name until she resorted to typing:

> OMG PLS CALM DOWN
>
> YOU'VE GOT TO CALM DOWN
>
> I'M CASHING THE VOUCHER
>
> I SAID I'M CASHING THE VOUCHER!

"What voucher?" I asked the camera.

Aisha held up a finger, rummaged in her schoolbag and

held up a voucher I'd given her on her last birthday, the last of a booklet of six. There in my own handwriting were the words: *This voucher entitles you to one completely fair and wrath-free hearing.*

"Ahhhhhh," I said, banging my chest, trying to open up some space in there. "OK, OK, I'm ready."

"I used your emergency debit card," Aisha said. "You know Dad always wants to know why I'm like this and all I can say is I'm sorry I am. But I think—no, I'm sure, I'm sure, that if I just look him in the eye . . . I know it's a lot of money. I didn't really think the bid would go through. I didn't know you had that much on there! But please understand. I will pay you back. I'm going to get a job, and I'm going to make some stuff and sell a lot of it."

"It's OK," I said. "It's OK." My heartbeat was returning to normal. Aisha had been operating on the principle that I wouldn't want to be that guy who embarrasses himself by withdrawing a ten-thousand-pound donation he made to an enormously deserving cause. But I am that guy, so it's fine for me to do that.

NOOR'S EX-WIFE came over for coffee and spoke of seeking psychiatric assistance for Aisha, particularly in the light of Day's discovery that Aisha had made a purchase from her laptop: a liter of almost pure sulfuric acid—96 percent. The three of us sat silently with our coffee cups, picturing Aisha and Füst alone in some garland-bedecked bower, Füst singing his heart out, maybe even singing his latest hit, "Dress Made of Needles" . . . then as the last notes of the song died out, Aisha uncapped the bottle of acid hidden beneath her dress and let fly. For about a week Noor couldn't look at Aisha without shouting: "What are you?"

All we'd hear from Aisha was the bitter laugh, and I tried to soothe her by saying, "He's been forgiven, Aish. Everyone else has forgiven him," but I stopped that because there was a look that replaced her laughter, and that look haunted me.

It was Ched's opinion that it might have been all right if the apology had been something that Aisha could consider real, but now this thing wouldn't end unless she was able to take or witness vengeance upon Matyas Füst. Tyche agreed, but with a slight modification: Aisha would be able to move on if Matyas Füst was able to deliver a sincere apology for what he'd done. "At least . . . that's how it would be for me," Tyche added, twirling her wedding ring around her finger. "I mean, the galling thing about 'Dress Made of Needles' is that as a piece of music it's fine, but as an apology it takes the piss. But you know what, at least we got a meaningful song out of it, at least he wrote this good song because of her . . ."

The constellation on Tyche's wrist was definitely a tattoo that day and her breeziness was macabre. I thought for a long time, or what felt like a long time, anyway, before I asked her if there was anything she could do for Aisha.

"Let me talk to her," Tyche said.

I wasn't allowed to listen to their conversation, but I know that it concerned the invocation of a goddess and Tyche was very well prepared for it, arrived at our house wearing an elegant black suit and carrying a portfolio full of images and diagrams that she and Aisha pored over at length.

"Just FYI, we decided on Hecate," Tyche said on her way out.

"Yeah? Who she?"

"Oh, nobody you need to worry about . . ."

"Come on, let me have the basics."

"Well . . . she keeps an eye on big journeys from the interior to the exterior, or vice versa. She's there for the step that takes you from one state to another. She's someone you see at crossroads, for instance. Well, you sort of see her but don't register what you've seen until it's too late to go back. She holds three keys . . . some say they're keys to the underworld, others that they're access to the past, present, and future. And—ah, you're zoning out on me . . ."

Tyche struck and held a warlike pose in the doorway.

"Picture the image of me fixed in this doorway, and

also in every other doorway you pass, sometimes three-dimensional and sometimes vaporous, whatever I feel like being at the moment you try to get past me," she said. "Imagine not being able to stop me from coming in, imagine not being able to cast me out because I own all thresholds. As an additional bonus, imagine me with three faces. That's who we're sending to have a little chat with Matyas Füst."

"Oh! Why didn't you just lead with that instead of the benevolent stuff? But listen, hang on, Tyche, is that not a bit much—"

She was already gone.

SUMMER HAS COME BACK around, and with only a week until Ched returns from military service, I write this from a bench beside Ched's water fountain at the House of Locks. The woman with the voice he likes came in while I was feeding Boudicca, so I left.

Anyway, events of recent months, presented without comment, for who am I to comment after all?

- The day after Tyche and Aisha had their meeting, a black-bordered notice appeared in one of the national newspapers:

R.I.P. MATYAS FÜST,

HAPPY BIRTHDAY MATYAS FÜST

AND GOOD LUCK.

YOUR REBIRTH WILL BE A DIFFICULT ONE.

- Naturally a lot of questions were asked, since Matyas Füst was alive and, at that time, well. It proved impossible to discover who was responsible for the notice.

- The day after the notice appeared Matyas Füst phoned into a five p.m. radio show that was popular with commuters all over the country and announced that he'd like to apologize for his apology, which had come more from his head than his heart. He also asked that his fans cease their verbal abuse of the victim of his attack, since she had "been through a lot" and hadn't asked for a penny in compensation beyond their original transaction. The hosts of the radio show had to ask him to repeat his declarations of remorse several times because his weeping made them unintelligible.

- About a week after that, Füst interrupted his performance on the live taping of a variety show to state that he was being "hounded" and that he feared for his life, that "they" pricked him with needles and slammed his hands in doors. When members of the audience pointed out that he was uninjured he appeared confused and said that it had only happened "inside where no one could see." Before the broadcast was halted he also managed to say that he believed that in attacking the woman he'd met on the street he'd been following a bad example set by his father, who had frequently beaten his mother in front of him. His parents issued a joint denial that basically boiled down to: *We have no idea why he's saying these things but it's making us sad.* Füst's fiancée moved out of his house again with talk of plans to "focus on her career" . . . that was funny, and rather sweet . . . if there was ever anybody born focused on her career it was this prima ballerina, but her statement suggested she thought it didn't show. As for her ex-fiancé, a few close members of his family moved into his home, "to look after him." The close family members were unable to prevent him from phoning into radio shows and appearing on breakfast TV to apologize for his previous apologies and make further apologies. He ended his most recent TV appearance with the reflection that quality was probably better than quantity and that he'd take his time to find a genuine expression of his thoughts. He'd been told that the key to a real apology was the identification of one's real mistake. He hoped to be able to do that soon.

• Health-care professionals were reported to have joined the close family members surrounding Füst at his home, but he escaped them all and was reported missing for six months.

• Füst was found to have been sleeping rough all winter—a very hard winter, so much surprise was expressed that he'd lived through it. He gave one interview, to a reputable chronicle of paranormal phenomena. I think he intended for the interview to dispel the rumors of his insanity but it had the opposite effect. Especially when he spoke about "them." "They" demanded that he apologize and then called his apologies glib. He said that "they" were three women and yet "they" were one, and that one of them took his pain away so that the others could return it to him and so it went on. He said he should have died during the winter but it pleased "them" to keep him alive in order for him to learn what he could say or do to keep them off. If there was anybody who knew how to convince this woman that he was sorry, Matyas Füst begged to know that secret at any price.

- Aisha may have abandoned tails for good, but all-heal plants are flowering in her window box, she's working on reducing the aphrodisiac effect of an otherwise very convenient headache cure, and she's looking forward to Matyas Füst's forthcoming book, *An Outcast's Apology.* She reckons Füst is getting closer to identifying his mistake, and says he should keep trying.

is your blood as red as this?

I.

(NO)

YOU ALWAYS SAID, Myrna Semyonova, that we weren't right for each other. And it always made my heart sink when you said that, but my answer was always: *You're wrong. I'll show you. I'll show you.* I've got something that other lovers would give a great deal to possess: a perfect memory of the very first time I saw you. I was fifteen, and my handsome, laconic eighteen-year-old brother burned brightest among my heroes. I followed him everywhere—well, he sometimes managed to escape me, but most of the time he didn't make too much of an effort. That's Arjun's gift; never trying too hard, always doing just enough. Somehow he knew how to be with people, when to make eye contact and when to gaze thoughtfully into the distance, how to prove that you're paying attention to what you're being told. It was Jyoti's breaking up with him that improved his people skills. For three years Jyoti had been warning him and warning him about his tendency not to listen to her, or to anyone. *Don't you ever think that one day you might miss something really important, Arjun,* she'd say. *Something that someone can only say one time?* He tried to focus. Well, he claimed that he was trying, but he still tuned out. If Jyoti was talking, then he'd gaze adoringly at her but not hear a word, and with everyone else he'd just fall silent and then insert a generic comment into the space left for him to speak in. God knows where his mind used to go.

One day Jyoti met up with him at the café down the road for a make-or-break conversation. She had a favor to ask him, she said, and if he didn't at least consider doing it then there was no point in their being together. *Jyoti, you have my full attention,* he said immediately. *Tell me—I'm listening.* Fifteen minutes later, she checked her watch, kissed him on the cheek, and left the café beaming. She was late to meet a friend, but he'd agreed to do her the big favor she'd asked for. Only he had no idea what the favor was supposed to be. She'd lost him about four words in.

He asked a woman sitting nearby if she'd overheard the conversation, and if she could by any chance tell him what had been asked of him, but the woman was elderly and said: "Sorry love, I'm a bit hard of hearing nowadays."

A couple on the other side of him categorically denied having heard anything, even after he told them the future of his relationship depended on it—this was England after all, where minding one's own business is a form of civil religion. So all he could do was wait for Jyoti's furious I CAN'T BELIEVE YOU phone call, and vow to win her love again one day, when he'd become a better man. I was learning a lot from Arjun. And I had lots more to learn. In those days when anyone spoke to me I became a flustered echo, scrambling up the words they'd said to me and then returning them as fast as I could. Blame it on growing pains, or on the ghost I shared my bedroom with.

MYRNA, BEFORE YOU I could only really talk to my brother and the ghost. There was something disorganized about the way she spoke that rubbed off on me. Plus she (the ghost) had warned me that the minute I grew up I wouldn't be able to see her anymore. "How will I know when I've grown up?" When I started using words I didn't really know the meaning of, she said. I said I did that already, and she said yes but I worried about it and grown-ups didn't. (Of course I'm paraphrasing her; when I think back on her syntax it's like hearing a song played backward.) So then there's this trepidation that you're going to suddenly find yourself having a conversation that turns you into a grown-up, a conversation that stops you being able to see things and people that are actually there. My brother knew about the ghost, but described her as an alarmist, said I needed to get out more and invited me to his friend Tim's nineteenth birthday party. The party where I met you, Myrna.

"You can be my date tonight if you like," Arjun said.

"Won't people think it's creepy?" I asked.

"Nah . . . if anything females are into males who are nice to their verbally challenged little sisters," he said. "Gives the impression of having a caring side and stuff like that."

"What a relief! I'd hate to come between you and the females."

"Don't even worry about that, Radha. That's never going to happen." (And so on.)

I know what it is to have a brother that people like

talking to, so I brought a book just in case the evening took Arjun away from me. But he stuck with me, introduced me to the birthday boy, called upon his friends to observe the way I calmly matched him beer for beer, generally behaved in a way that made me feel as if I was something more than a stammering fly on the wall. Then a boy approached us—well, Arjun, really—a nondescript sort of boy, I'm surprised to say, since his hair was green. He had a look of rehearsal on his face, he was silently practicing sentences he'd prepared, and Arjun said to me quietly: "Wonder what this one's after."

The boy, Joe, was Tim's cousin.

"Joe who goes to the puppet school?" Arjun asked.

"Yeah . . ."

"Seen, seen," Arjun said. "What you saying?"

"Girls like you, don't they?" Joe asked.

Arjun lowered his eyelids and shrugged; if I'd been wearing sleeves I'd have laughed into one of them. Joe had a twenty-pound note, which he was willing to hand over to my brother right now if Arjun would go over to a certain girl, dance with her, talk to her, and appear to enjoy her company for a couple of hours. Once I realized what he was asking, I thought: *Even Arjun will be lost for words this time.* But my brother must've had similar requests before (can teenage boys really be so inhuman?) because he asked: "Is she really that butters? I haven't seen any girl I'd rate below a seven tonight. A good night, I was thinking."

The boy had the good grace to blush. "No, she's not that ugly. Just . . . not my type."

"Why did you even bring her then, if she's not your type?" Arjun asked.

"It was a dare," Joe said, miserably. "I don't usually do things like this—you can ask Tim—just believe me when I say I didn't have much of a choice. I didn't think she'd say yes. But she did."

"Mate . . . don't pay people to hang out with her."

"I don't know what else to do. She's got to have a good time. She's my headmaster's daughter. I don't think she'd get me expelled or anything—maybe she won't even say anything to him. But she's his daughter."

"Better safe than sorry," my brother agreed. Myrna, by that point I was already looking around to see if I could spot you (what level of unattractiveness forces people to pay cash so as to be able to avoid having to look at it or speak to it?) and when Joe said that he'd been trying to talk to you but you just sat there reading your book, I searched all the harder.

"What kind of person brings a book to a party," Arjun said expressionlessly, without looking at me, but he gave a little nod that I interpreted as a suggestion that I seek this girl out.

"What's her name?" I asked. Joe told me. I found you half buried in a beanbag, pretending to read that dense textbook that takes all the fun out of puppeteering, the one your father swears by—Brambani's *War Between the Fingers and the Thumb*. Curse stuffy old Brambani. Maybe his lessons are easier to digest when filtered through stubbornly unshed tears. You had a string of fairy lights wrapped around your neck. I sort of understood how that would be comforting, the lights around your neck. Sometimes I dream I'm falling, and it's not so much frightening as it is tedious, just falling and falling until I'm sick of it, but then a noose stops me short and I think, well, at least I'm not falling anymore. Clearly I hadn't arrived in your life a moment too soon. You looked at me, and this is how I saw you, when first I saw you: I saw your eyes like flint arrows, and your chin set against the world, and I saw the curve of your lips, which is so beautiful that it's almost illusory— your eyes freeze a person, but then the flickering flame of your mouth beckons.

Thank God Joe was so uncharacteristically panicky and stupid that evening. I discovered that I could talk to you in natural, complete sentences. It was simple: If I talked to you, perhaps you would kiss me. And I had to have a kiss from you: To have seen your lips and not ever kissed them would have been the ruin of me . . .

AS FOR WHAT you saw of me—I think you saw a kid in a gray dress gawping at you like you were the meaning of life. You immediately began talking to me as if I were a child at your knee. You told me about how stories come to our aid in times of need. You'd recently been on a flight from Prague, you told me, and the plane had gone through a terrifyingly long tunnel of turbulence up there in the clouds. "Everyone on the plane was freaking out, except the girl beside me," you said. "She was just reading her book—maybe a little bit faster than usual, but otherwise untroubled. I said to her: 'Have you noticed that we might be about to crash?' And she said: 'Yes I did notice that actually, which makes it even more important for me to know how this ends.'"

I got you to dance, and I got you to show me a few of the exercises you did for hand flexibility, and I got you to talk about your school and its classrooms full of students obsessed with attaining mastery of puppets. I liked the sound of it. Your eyes narrowed intently as you spoke of your final year there: The best two students were permitted to choose two new students and help them through their first year. It was in your mind to play a part in another puppeteer's future, that much was clear. You believed in the work that puppet play can do—you'd seen it with your own eyes. Before your father began teaching, back in the days when he performed, you had seen a rod puppet of his go down on its knees before a girl who sat a little aside from his audience of schoolchildren. This girl had been looking on with her hair hanging over her face, only partly hiding a cruel-looking scar; her eyes shone with hatred. Not necessarily hatred of your father or of puppets or the other children, but a hatred of make-believe, which did not heal, but was only useful to the people who didn't need it. Man and long-bearded puppet left the stage, walked over to the girl, and knelt—the puppet's kneeling was of course guided by your father's hand, and every eye in the audience was on your father's face, but his uncertain expression convinced everyone that the puppet had suddenly expressed a will of its own. "Princess, I am Merlin, your Merlin," the puppet man said to the girl. "At your service forever."

"Me?" the girl said, suspicious, on the edge of wrath—*you just try and make me the butt of your joke*—"Me, a princess? You, at my service?"

"It's no mistake." The puppet's hand moved slowly, reverently; it held its breath despite having no breath to hold, the girl allowed that wooden hand to fondly brush her cheek—watching, you were absolutely sure that no hand of flesh and bone would have been allowed to come that close. "This is the sign by which we recognize you," the puppet said, "but if you wish you may continue as you are in disguise."

And your father and his puppet returned to the stage, never turning their backs on the girl, as is the protocol regarding walking away from royalty. The girl's teacher cried, but the girl herself just looked as if she was thinking. She continued to think through the second act of the puppet play, but by the third act she was clapping and laughing as loudly as the rest of them. I really don't know why I thought your reaching the end of that story would be a good moment to kiss you; I wasn't entirely surprised that it didn't work.

"YOUNG LADY, I'm flattered—and tempted—but—how old are you, anyway?" you asked. Then you said I was too young. Too young, not right for you, blah blah blah. Always something.

Joe and Arjun appeared with our coats, and you slid my book out of my coat pocket. "What's this?"

Fate is what it was. Yes, fate that the book I had with me was a novel written by my great-grandfather, a text you couldn't read because my great-grandfather had put a permanent ban on any of his works being translated into English, Russian, or French. He was adamant that these three are languages that break all the bones of any work translated into them. Since people like getting around rules, there are various unofficial translations of my great-grandfather's books floating around online, but all of them just seem to prove his point.

"JUST TELL ME the beginning of it, then," you said, and I opened the book to translate for you. You liked the beginning—a woman opens her front door to find a corpse on her doorstep, but before the body can topple across the threshold of her home she says, "Oh no you don't," pushes it back out with a broom, and legs it out of the back door.

"Wait," you were saying, as I walked away arm in arm with my brother—"Hang on, Radha, I need to know—"

"I'd say she's at least an eight," my brother said, surprised. (You have my permission to make him regret marking girls' physical appearance out of ten.) When I got home the ghost immediately knew something was up. She said she'd been wondering when I'd meet someone.

"If I—I don't know, if some sort of miracle happens and I have sex with someone, will I stop being able to see you?"

The ghost looked crafty for a moment, then relented and said no, I was stuck with her. And she was pleased for me when you phoned me the next day to ask me to translate the next paragraph of my great-grandfather's book. You hung up as soon as I gave you the paragraph, but the ghost said you'd come back for more, and you did. You began to talk to me a little after each day's translation, asking me questions about myself and my day and whatever music happened to be playing in my bedroom whenever you called. "Glad you like it—I don't know what this song is called, but it's probably quite a bit older than we are. The truth is we've got a nostalgic ghost for a DJ around here," I'd say, and you'd laugh, thinking I'd made a joke.

The ghost observed that I was going to come to the end of my translation one day.

"Yeah, but come on. We're only halfway through the second chapter. And after this book there are fifteen others by the same author."

The ghost asked if I thought my great-grandfather would be impressed by this use of his hard work.

"Oh, ghost—what have you got against love?"

Nothing, said the ghost, sounding injured. She had nothing whatsoever against love. She was just saying.

The ghost showed that she was on my side when she heard you mention the news that you were one of the two final-year students who got to select a newcomer to mentor. "It's going to be fun. We get to watch the applicants through hidden panels in a soundproofed room so they don't hear us booing or cheering them."

This terrified me, but the ghost breathed on the windowpane and wrote FOR GO IT on the misted glass.

"Who's the other student?" I asked. "Not green-haired Joe?"

"Haha, no. Though he does put on interesting Punch and Judy shows. Dad says he's going to be very good one day. The other student's a boy called Gustav Grimaldi. I don't like the way he performs; it's scruffy. And I'd say his puppets have a nihilistic spirit, if you'd understand what I meant by that."

"Nihilistic, eh . . . sounds bad," I said, pinning the phone to my ear with my shoulder as I googled "nileistic."

"Sometimes his puppets won't perform at all. He just lets them sit there, watching us. Then he has them look at each other and then back at us until it feels as if they have information, some kind of dreadful information about each and every one of us, and you begin to wish they'd decide to keep their mouths shut forever. There's no entertainment in it at all, and I don't understand why he chooses this way to put on a show when he knows so many other ways. He shouldn't be allowed to choose any new students.

If there's anyone bound to introduce unsavory elements into our group, it's Grimaldi."

"Good thing I'm extra wholesome then. Do applicants have to have experience with puppets and all that?" I asked, and when you said that in fact your father liked people to come to the field fresh, I asked if fifteen was too old to start.

"Not if you're serious. Are you?"

"As serious as I can be. I don't feel one hundred percent sure that I'm not a puppet myself," I said.

"No wonder I like you," you said. The ghost gave me a high five.

"You need a puppet," you went on. "Competition for places is quite fierce—people do what they can to stand out. Some people make their own puppets. I did, out of paper and pins. The thing fell apart mid-performance, but I built that into the story."

MUM AND DAD wouldn't be thrilled by my new career ambitions. *Don't forget your Uncle Majhi . . . Majhi the mime . . . and ask yourself, do we really want more people like that in our family?* My parents worked a lot—no need to bother them with something that might not work out. The thing to do was gain admission first and talk them round later. I bought a brown-skinned glove puppet. He came with a little black briefcase and his hair was parted exactly down the middle. The precision of his parting made me uneasy; somehow it was too human at the exact same time as exposing his status as a nonhuman. I got him a top hat so I wouldn't have to think about the cloth hair falling away from the center of his cloth scalp. You gave me a hand with some basics of ventriloquism, even though you definitely weren't supposed to help—it was then that I began to hope that you'd stop saying I wasn't right for you—and I taught my puppet to tell jokes with a pained and forlorn air, fully aware of how bad the jokes were. Sometimes you laughed, and then my glove puppet would weep piteously. When you took the glove puppet he alternated between flirtatious and suicidal, hell-bent on flinging himself from great heights and out of windows. I noticed that you didn't make a voice or a history for the puppet, but you became its voice and history. I'd have liked to admire that but felt I was watching a distressing form of theft, since the puppet could do nothing but suffer being forced open like an oyster.

WE DECIDED it would be better for my puppet to continue the daily translations—my great-grandfather's book, line by line, first in Hindi, next in English, as you listened, rapt, and then repeated the line in Russian and French. Thus the book's bones were broken. I didn't realize it until about a week before my audition, when I reread the book's last chapter, which I was yet to translate for you, and the bright words flew through my mind like comets. That feeling was gone from the other chapters; somehow it had seeped out. And I told my glove puppet that it was not to say the final words of the book.

The ghost approved, but she was also quite sure that you wouldn't choose me if my glove puppet didn't say the words we'd planned it would say, you and I. The ghost even advised me not to bother turning up. Naturally I disregarded her advice. A couple of days later, the waiting room of your grand old school encased me in marbled fog as I watched other hopefuls practicing with their puppets. Some were more actors than puppeteers, but others handled their marottes and tickle puppets and Bunraku puppets with an ease and affection that didn't exist between my glove puppet and me. I think the soul must be heavy and smooth, Myrna: I deduce this from the buoyant, jerky movements of puppets, which lack souls. The girl beside me was very pretty—tousled dreadlocks, dimples, and night-sky skin—you know, with this radiance blended into the darkness. But I considered myself taken, and so I merely asked where her puppet was. "It's this." She took a small box out of her jacket pocket, and out of that box she took a porcelain chess piece. A plum-colored queen, her only features her crown and a slight wave that conceded the existence of hips and a bosom.

"Did you make her yourself?"

"No, I found her. I know she doesn't look like a puppet, but she is one. I know it because when I first picked her up I said something I'd never said before. I put her down and then when I picked her up I said the thing again without meaning to, and again it was something I hadn't said before, even though the words were the same."

"What's her routine?"

"At the moment she only asks this one question, but I'm hoping to learn how to get her to ask another."

"What's her question?"

The girl looked uncomfortable. She pointed at her nametag: "This is me, by the way." Tyche Shaw. My own nametag was lost in my hair, so I shook hands with her and said: "Radha Chaudhry. What's your puppet's question?"

Tyche mumbled something, too low for me to hear. I'd just decided not to ask again—maybe she was saving it up for the audition—when she repeated herself: "Is your blood as red as this."

A chess piece asking a personal question, possibly one of the most personal questions that could be asked. I didn't know how to answer. At my instruction my glove puppet shook its head, *No, surely your blood is redder.* Tyche turned the purple queen around on her palm and asked the question again; this time the note of challenge left her voice and the question became droll; the next time the chess piece asked her question she sounded worried, seeking comparison for the sake of measuring normality. Frustration came next (after all, the chess piece wasn't even red . . . therefore as red as what, compared to what). From what you'd said about Gustav Grimaldi's puppets I knew you would strongly disapprove of the question Tyche Shaw's puppet asked; in fact you would hate it. But this tiny queen's question was large; she spoke and you couldn't think of anything else but her question, and how to answer it. The sharpest thing I had on me was a brooch—I could prick my finger with my brooch pin, and then we would see.

"You're good, Tyche," I said, and I wasn't the only one who walked out for fresh air. Several other demoralized applicants followed me out and had last-minute conversations with their puppets.

"I'm not going to be able to get this job done for you," my own glove puppet said to me.

"Shhh, I won't let you pretend this is your fault," I told it. "I'm just going to have to find another way to show Myrna."

———————

THERE WAS A FRAMED photograph hung on the wall in front of me, and when I said your name I saw you in the picture. Well, I saw your back, and your long, bright pony-tail fluttering. The image is black and white, and you're running, and you cast a number of shadows that cluster about you like a bouquet. There's a figure running a little ahead of you and at first that figure seems to be a shadow too, except that it casts a backward glance that establishes an entirely separate personality. The figure's features are wooden, but mobile—some sort of sprite moves within, not gently, but convulsively. A beauty that rattles you until you're in tears, that was my introduction to Rowan Wayland. You and the puppet—I decided it was a puppet—were leaping through one upright rectangle into another. An open door seen through an open door, and in the corner of that distant room was a cupboard, fallen onto its side. There was a sign on the cupboard door. (I tilted my head: The sign read TOYS.)

It's a photo in which lines abruptly draw back from each other and ceilings and floors spin off in different directions, but for all that the world that's pictured doesn't seem to be ending. You were both running in place, you blurred around the edges, the puppet hardly blurred at all, and the puppet was looking back, not at you, but at me. It felt like the two of you were running for your lives, for fear I'd take them. Or you could've been racing each other to that cupboard door, racing each other home. TOYS, the sign reads, but signs aren't guarantees. Either way I wanted to go too, and wished the puppet would hold out its hand to me, or beckon me, or do something more than return my gaze with that strange tolerance.

WHEN MY NAME was called I entered the audition room and my glove puppet made an irresolute attempt to eat a sugar cube from a bowlful that had been left on a table, then gave in to despair and decided to sleep. After a minute there was a crackling sound in the corner of the room and I heard your voice through the speaker, Myrna, trying to give me a chance. "Miss Chaudhry, don't you have anything prepared? You've only got ten more minutes and as you may have seen in the waiting room, we're observing quite a few applicants today."

This reminder had no effect on me; I continued as I was until someone knocked on the audition room door and then came in, glancing first at the clock and then through the mirrored wall to the spot where I presumed you were sitting. It was a boy who came in—he had a hand behind his back, and I think I would've found that threatening if it weren't for his deep-set, elephantine eyes, the patience in them.

"I'm Gustav," he said. "Give me your puppet and you shall have a different one."

"What will you do with mine?"

"It's up to him. He can sleep all he wants and have as much sugar as he likes, make new friends, maybe change the position of the parting in his hair if he's feeling daring. Quickly, take her."

I handed over my glove puppet and received a brass marionette in exchange. "I got this one out of the store cupboard. She hasn't been out in a while . . . a lot of people find they can't work with her; she's haunted," Gustav said over his shoulder, as he left the room. Smashing.

ORCHESTRATING this new puppet's movements seemed hopeless; I was holding the wooden bar that controlled all her strings correctly, and none of the strings were tangled, but that had been Gustav's quick, deft work, not mine. Though we both stood still I felt the marionette advance upon me, and without moving I shrank away.

"Five minutes," you said through the speaker, not hiding the note of incredulity in your voice. I spoke to the puppet in the looking-glass English that my ghost friend speaks. I asked her if she was haunted or something worse. She answered eagerly, as you do in a foreign country when you need assistance and come upon someone who speaks your language: "Worse thingsome," was her answer. "Worse thingsome." *And if I help you now, you must help me later.*

You won't ask me to harm anyone? I asked.

Never.

Then I accept.

Good. Simply translate what I say. I will speak; don't worry about the controls, I will match your posture, it'll look better.

She spoke the way that my ghost friend spoke—it cannot be that all ghosts speak the same way, I knew that even then—and I translated. It didn't take long:

I am not a haunted puppet, we said, *I am living. My name is Gepetta and a long time ago I was an apprentice to two puppeteers whose names are honored in this place. I took care of the puppets in the workshop—I was a kind of nurse to them, tending to their damage, and making sure that they lasted. Their masters grew old and died, and I stayed with the puppets. They were not living, but one step away from living, always one step away. They know when human life is near them, and they need human life to be near them; it keeps them from going . . . wrong.*

I began to train others in the care of puppets. In my time it seemed such knowledge was dying out . . . I trained a few boys and girls who wanted to learn, but a plague came. Not a plague that revealed itself in the skin, this one crept through the air. My apprentices died, and I would have too, but my puppet charges forbade it.

Each puppet sacrificed something—a leg, an arm, torso, head, and so on . . . you will replace these things when you are ready, they said.

They assembled a body, but didn't join up the parts.

Look at your new body. You will go in, they said.

I said I would not, but it happened hour by hour; I would drowse a little and when I woke another part of me had been replaced. It began with my left hand and ended with my right foot. Think of it: looking down at your human foot out of a pair of brass eyes. And then I grew smaller, and all of a piece, as I am today. My name is Gepetta; long have I wanted to say this, but nobody would help me to say it . . .

SO THAT WAS how I met my friend Gepetta. And as you know, Myrna Semyonova, three days later I was called back to your school, our school, and I found Tyche Shaw waiting for me. And you were there, and so was Gustav Grimaldi. Then I knew I'd been chosen, and I went to you. You smiled and said, "Well done," but it was Gustav who took my hand and said: "Welcome, Radha. We'll do such things together!"

My ghost friend was right: I disobeyed you and so you didn't choose me. But what were your reasons for choosing Tyche? I saw even then that you would try your best to break what she carries.

Why are you telling me all this again, you say impatiently, but a person doesn't easily recover from the sadness of finding that it's not always affinity that draws us together (not always, not only), that you can be called to undo the deeds of another. You make a lot of work for me— my blood runs cold to think of it all—but you see I take strength from remembering that you began with intentions that were pure.

II.

(YES)

RADHA AND GUSTAV had a shaky start. She brought me along to their first meeting and the three of us walked around Berkeley Square. "Hi, Gepetta," Gustav said to me. He always says hello to me, even though I never reply. His good manners are his own affair. Radha threw bread-crumbs to pigeons. Gustav kept his sunglasses on the entire time and talked at length about the work of several mid-twentieth-century filmmakers Radha had never heard of. I could see Radha making up her mind that if she was going to learn anything from Gustav it would be by accident, and I saw her changing her mind when he introduced her to his puppets—"You've brought yours," he said to Radha, nod-ding in my direction, "and I've brought mine." Four of them had accompanied him to this meeting; two peeping out from each of his coat pockets. They were good-natured fatalists one and all, never in a rush, preferring to put off action until matters had resolved themselves without any-one in the troupe having had to lift a finger. The leader of the pack was a disheveled sophisticate named Hamlet. It was Hamlet who became Radha's chief extracurricular guide, her lecturer, heckler, cheerleader, and coconspira-tor. At those times we all forgot whose voice and hands Hamlet and company were making use of, and the next day Radha would report mastery of some minor voice con-trol trick to Gustav as if he hadn't been there in the room with us. Initially it seemed that this type of forgetfulness seriously displeased Gustav, but as we grew more comfort-able with him I began to see that when Radha told him something odd or amusing that Hamlet or one of his other puppets had said or done, what Gustav actually expressed was restrained interest. He was observing a process we were not yet privy to.

I CAUGHT ON LONG before Radha did. She spoke to Gustav's troupe in a way that she would never have spoken to him directly. As this confidence flourished, so did a sympathy between Radha and Gustav's puppets, who devoted themselves to making her laugh and would materialize en masse outside her classroom door and walk her to the bus stop at the end of the day, crying: "Make way for boss lady!" Gustav surrounded her with her especial favorites: Hamlet with his pudding bowl haircut, Chagatai, who was both assassin and merman (he kills sailors with his sexy falsetto!), Brunhild the shipbuilder, and an astronaut named Petrushka, who answered any question put to him in exhaustive detail. Also present was a toddler-sized jumping bean known as Loco Dempsey. Their master walked behind Radha, arms raised as he worked the controls high above her head. Under Gustav's command all the strings stayed separate; Radha marveled at that and leaned into him so as not to be the body that tangled those clean lines.

He nudged a few of the controls into her hands, lowered his arms so that he was holding her—not tightly, since there's only so much you can do with your elbows. He whistled a brisk polonaise and her gestures led his as she set Brunhild and Loco to marching. Radha looked so happy that I thought some kind of admission was forthcoming later, but instead she turned to me and said: "That can't be the same gang Myrna told me about."

THE NIGHT a fortuneteller outside KFC seized Radha by both hands and told her that little by little she was falling for an invisible man, she was confounded and kept me awake until dawn asking who on earth it could possibly be . . .

I couldn't decide whether the Grimaldi boy was to be pitied, congratulated, or scolded. Granted, this was one way to have a secret love affair, but there was no telling what his own feelings were, or whether this was just a routine seduction for him. Put yourself in his place: You're descended from generations of people who speak and have spoken primarily through puppets . . . as such you're a kind of champion at psychological limbo. And you happen to like girls with brilliant eyes that see hidden things and dark hair from which they occasionally retrieve forgotten notes to themselves. Then you meet a new one. Wouldn't you try and see how close you could get without her noticing?

RADHA TOOK to checking her phone constantly but with no clear objective—most of her messages were from Tyche Shaw, who she felt both jealous and protective of and would have preferred not to have to deal with at all. Tyche was in the Orkney Isles with Myrna and her father, and in addition to relying on Radha to keep her updated on puppet school assignments, the girl insisted on being friendly and requesting personal news. Unaware that she had any, Radha settled for sending pictures of herself sitting on the curbstone outside her house drinking homemade smoothies with her brother. I was in the photo too, sat on Arjun's shoulders. I never spoke to him and so he viewed me as a kind of fashion accessory of Radha's. At that time I was getting some of my best fun from being alone with him and sporadically opening and closing my mouth whenever he blinked.

Me, Gepetta, and A.J. on the corner drinking heavy juice all day long. What about you and my wife?

That was all the invitation Tyche needed to flood Radha's in-box with angst that Radha unintentionally increased by responding only with emoticons.

Where do I begin . . . well, everything I do pisses "your wife"
off

I keep answering her rhetorical questions & then not daring
to answer her non-rhetorical questions

Oh and her specialty seems to be saying insanely awful stuff
out of nowhere

The kind of things you have to forget in order to be able to go
on living, you know?

This one comment about my hands made me want to cut
them off & just throw them away. Has anyone ever spoken to
you like that

Never mind, I just avoid looking at my hands now, hahaha
sob

Never been good at comebacks, so I just pick up rocks and
pretend to clobber her when her back is turned.

How's it going with Gustav anyway

Radha, what exactly do you like about this WENCH?

Her dad genuinely thinks she's human . . .

———————

FOR EVERY TEN MESSAGES from Tyche there were perhaps three or four from Myrna (all in praise of Tyche) and one from Gustav. One night, just as Radha had lain down on her bed, he sent a photo of his glove puppet Cheon Song Yi wielding a tube of lipstick like a sword. Accompanying text: *Somebody stop her.* As for Gustav, all that could be seen of him was a full, shapely lower lip stained orchid pink from Song Yi's lipstick attack. He was positioned behind the puppet, but it was one of those photos where the background very gradually becomes the foreground. At first glance Radha snorted and rolled her eyes. Then she tilted her head, took another look, and slowly crossed and uncrossed her legs. Still studying the photo, she absentmindedly traced the shape of her own mouth and sucked the tip of her index finger. The bedroom ghost and I looked at each other and silently agreed to vacate the room.

I MISSED DESIRE. And I was glad my friend's heart had been given a puzzle to work on while it ached over Myrna Semyonova. Even if it became necessary to drop Gustav, Radha had other tutoring options. Her classmates were a friendly bunch, lacking in the competitive spirit their teachers would have liked to see. They worked on one another's ideas. Their puppets swapped costumes, props, catchphrases, and sometimes even characters. This kind of camaraderie made the ostracization of Rowan Wayland all the more marked.

HISTORY OF PUPPETRY was the hour of the week in which Radha and others played with paper, making puppets with pinned joints and hands and feet that spun like weather vanes. They were learning histories of Punchinello, a beak-nosed figure who stands for nothing. The place and century of his birth is the sort of thing learned people in tweed jackets argue about, but for a couple of centuries he's been present in Austria, where he is Kasperle, setting his cunning aside to concentrate on brutality without pause, until every other puppet in his world is dead and then his master must see to it that he doesn't go after his audience too. In Hungary he's the terse and sardonic Vitéz László, in France the twinkle returns to his eyes and he becomes Polichinelle, a demon from the merriest of hells. In England Punch is a sensitive chap; any passerby who so much as looks at him the wrong way is promptly strangled with a string of sausages. When he takes up his Turkish residence Karagöz is too lazy to attempt very much murder, though he has a reservoir of verbal abuse to shower upon anyone who comes between him and his meals. Wherever you find him, he is careful not to discuss the past. Whatever it is you're asking about, he didn't do it and hasn't the faintest idea who might be responsible, in fact he doesn't know anything at all, he wasn't "there," see, he's been "here" the whole time . . . which begs the question, where were you?

WHEN RADHA and I walked into the History of Puppetry classroom the first thing we noticed was the ocean of space that surrounded Rowan Wayland, and for caution's sake we chose seats that maintained his solitude. We watched him but had difficulty finding out whether keeping our distance was weak or wise; nobody would talk about him. Wayland himself behaved as if his pariah status was perfectly natural, walking around the building looking straight ahead with his collar popped up around his ears. Radha remarked that he gave her the strange feeling of being an extra on a film set. It took two weeks for curiosity to change our seating vote. "Maybe he's just misunderstood," I said. Radha agreed to risk it.

He had a pair of red needles and a heap of wool on top of his books and was knitting while he waited for the teacher to arrive. There's a gentle assurance many knitters have as they fix their patterns in place. Rowan's knitting wasn't like that. He stared at his sock-in-progress with an insistence that brooked no compromise, as if he'd learned that this was the only way to ensure that each stitch stayed where he'd put it. We took the seats alongside him, Radha said hello, and kept saying it until he acknowledged her with a sidelong glance.

"I'm Radha," Radha said, before he could look away again.

"OK," he said. "Why—I mean, what do you want?"

"Nothing," Radha answered, with the guileless good cheer that makes her so dear to me. "Just saying hello. This is Gepetta."

He smiled at me, and kept knitting. At first, second, or even third glance it was difficult to pin down what made him so much avoided. Rowan's physical effect—godlike jawline, long-lashed eyes, umber skin, rakish quiff of hair— is that of a lightning strike. In full sunlight the true color of his hair is revealed to be navy blue, and when he scratches his head, as he sometimes does when he's thinking, his hair parts so that the two tiny corkscrews of bone at the front of his skull are visible. Yes, horns. Not scary ones—I think these were intended as a playful touch. The problem with Wayland is that he's a puppet built to human scale.

Masterless and entirely alive. No matter how soft his skin appears to be he is entirely wooden, and it is not known exactly what animates him—no clock ticks in his chest. Rowan is male to me, since he moves and speaks with a grace that reminds me of the boys and men of my Venetian youth. He's female to Myrna. For Radha and Gustav Rowan is both male and female. Perhaps we read him along the lines of our attractions; perhaps it really is as arbitrary as that. He just shrugs and says: "Take your pick. I'm mostly tree, though." His fellow students already had all those confusing hormone surges to deal with. So most of them stayed away, though I'm sure they all dreamed of him, her, hir, zir, a body with a tantalizing abundance of contours, this Rowan who is everything but mostly tree. I'm sure Rowan Wayland was dreamed of nonstop.

AND HE'S AS EVASIVE as any Punchinello I've met. You ask him a question and he somehow makes you answer it for him. Rowan and Radha never really moved past what she called their "eye candy and eye candy appreciator" relationship. I was the one the eye candy befriended. That surprised me. I remember Radha introducing me to the ghost in her bedroom in anticipation of our knowing each other, at least wanting to know each other because we spoke the same language. But that ghost is a little too aloof for her own good.

Rowan Wayland, on the other hand, calls me "Gepetta, Empress of the Moon." Since neither of us needs sleep we take night buses, sharing earphones and listening to knitting podcasts. If anyone else on the bus notices anything about us they assume it's because they're drunk. I've been trying to find a way to make him reveal how he came to be. In my own mind I've already compared my condition with his and have decided that his condition is preferable. He breathes; I do not. It's not that I believe that I could ever have my body back again—the one I used to have, I mean. Those who drove me into this form did what they did and that's all. I was on my way out and they thought they were helping me; instead they turned motion and intelligible speech into a currency with which personhood is earned.

This craving for consideration is the only real difference between my youthful self and the old, old Gepetta of today. The puppets who made me were shocked when I sold them. Shocked because puppets don't need money, but also because of the care I took to separate them—they couldn't understand that at all. No two to the same home, or even to neighboring cities. I consulted maps and made sure each of those puppets would be held apart by forests and deserts and the spans of rivers. The likelihood of any kind of reunion is almost impossible for them, us. I wonder if that broke their bond, but being able to find an answer to that question would mean my project failed. A shattering so absolute that no word can be picked up again—that's my success.

AT THE END of the second week of Tyche and Myrna's absence a personal essay was due. The title was something along the lines of "What Can a Puppet Do?" The students were required to state their current ambitions, and though the statement would receive a grade it would remain private. In an environment that relied so heavily on public demonstration of progress this was a rare opportunity to be earnest without simultaneously putting yourself at a severe disadvantage; for this reason the teachers imposed a word limit so things didn't get out of hand. Rowan claimed that the title made his mind go blank, so I dictated his essay to him word for word. What can a puppet do? We didn't have an uncynical answer between us, so I simply reassembled a few lines I remembered from lectures I'd heard Brambani give back when he was still in the process of writing *War Between the Fingers and the Thumb*. The role of the puppeteer is to preserve childlike wonder throughout our life spans, etc. Radha's essay was so brief that it only met half the required number of words; she copy-pasted the paragraph she'd already written and added a line at the beginning explaining that she was making use of the technique of repetition for the sake of emphasis. Hard copies were required, so Tyche e-mailed her essay to Radha, who handed it in without reading it and ran off hand in hand with the Grimaldi boy. Rowan Wayland intercepted Tyche's essay before it reached Ms. Alfarsi's desk, putting a finger to his lips when I began to ask him what he was doing. He read it twice, and then I read it, to see what he was looking for.

Last night was moonless, and we took a boat out onto Scapa Flow. There was broken light all across the sky, and columns of cloud twisting and turning through the pieces. Dust and dragon fire. Professor Semyonova said: "That's the Milky Way. As much of it as we can see, anyway."

It was so beautiful I kept my eyes on it in case it suddenly disappeared, or turned out to be some gigantic illusion. Maybe it was the rocking of the deck, or maybe I stared for too long, but after a while I felt it all moving against me, the light and the clouds and the darkness, countless stars and planets flying like arrows from a bow hidden farther back. Not that we three on the boat were the target; that was an accident of scale. We crush ants all the time just walking through a park. I thought the best plan was to leave before the sky arrived, just jump into the sea and drown directly. The second best plan was to close my eyes, but Myrna made me keep looking up. She said her own fear had been that those pinpricks of light were growing and that as they did, she shrank. She made me keep looking up until the panic was singed away. All I knew how to do with puppets, all I used to want to do, was play unsettling tricks. That's not enough anymore. I want to put on stubborn little shows, find places here and there where we get to see what we'd be like if we were actually in control of anything. Cruel fantasies, maybe, but they can't hurt any more than glimpsing a galaxy does.

Tyche Shaw

"Good grief, the puppeteers of today," I said, at the same time as Rowan asked me how much I thought Tyche disliked Myrna on a scale of one to ten.

"Eight," I said. "Maybe eight and a half. Though judging from the essay, she's come round."

"Judging from the essay, Gepetta, the dislike currently exceeds ten. Myrna knows how to make people do what she wants, but she doesn't know how to alter their actual thoughts. Yet here's Tyche suddenly claiming Myrna's aims as her own. Can't you just smell burning in the distance? In a way it would be entertaining to just sit back and watch Myrna get out-manipulated for once. But I can't do that."

"Why not? I would."

ROWAN TOLD me about a girl who responded to all external stimuli except human touch. That, she did not feel at all, which was the reason why from an early age other people scared her and kept getting scarier and scarier until they became almost impossible to cope with. She could see and hear her fellow human beings but making physical contact was identical to grabbing at thin air. It was like living with hallucinations that would neither disappear nor become tangible. The worst part was having to pretend that this pack of ghouls was nothing to be concerned about. She quickly learned that getting upset was counterproductive because then there were attempts to comfort her with hugs and the like. She said whatever she had to say and did whatever she had to do to circumvent unnecessary physical contact, but her situation was further complicated by the effect that her touch had on others. She was walking pain relief. She didn't cure or absorb the source of pain—it was more that she dismantled the sensation itself for a few hours, or up to half a day depending on the duration of skin contact. It didn't matter what kind of affliction the other person suffered, if the girl held his or her hand pain departed and all other impressions expanded to fill the space it left.

THIS, MORE THAN her numbness, twisted her relationships beyond imagining. People in her immediate vicinity some-how sensed what she could do for them and reached for her without really thinking about it, then clung to her, friends, family, and strangers, making use of her without perceiving that they were doing so, clinging so tightly that her ribs all but cracked. It seemed everybody was in all kinds of pain all the time. Shaggy-haired young men camped on her doorstep with their guitar cases and the girl's father re-sorted to spending a part of each evening standing backlit in the sitting room window with his arms folded so that the doorstep campers got a good view of his lumberjack biceps. The incongruous combination of white hair, beard, and powerful arms usually caused the boys to scatter with the muddled impression that Father Christmas was angry with them.

AS A FORM of escape from involuntary giving, the girl tried to identify those who were in the most pain and spent eve-nings at her local hospital just sitting with people, holding hands for as long as she could. She tried to do the same on the psychiatric ward but the security was tighter there. When she came home she stayed near her mother, whose addiction to painkillers had already caused her to injure herself for the sake of high-strength prescriptions. The woman's nerves tormented her so that only medication prevented her howling becoming a source of public or even domestic disturbance. From the little that the woman had been able to explain to her, the girl knew that her mother thought strange thoughts she could never tell anyone. Graphic structures appeared on the insides of her eyelids, a minute exhibition of X-ray photographs. There was affection between mother and daughter, but they'd given up trying to express it; rather than force a display they simply asked for each other's good faith. And no matter how many times the girl offered her hand, her mother refused it. It was the usual struggle between one who loves by accepting burdens and one who loves by refusing to be one. Really the mother's pursuit of pills wasn't motivated by the necessity of avoiding pain, but a determination to avoid any feeling at all. That's why the pills were better than holding the child's hand.

THE GIRL's father was a puppeteer, and there came a day when he was called to perform in Prague; an honor it would've been difficult to disregard. He'd never dreamed of being noticed by the puppeteers at work in that city, let alone considered a colleague. The professor's wife read this as a sign that she must either break or bend. She told her husband it would be good for him to take their daughter traveling, and checked into a clinic as an answer to her family's anxieties about her being alone. So the girl found herself living in Prague. Rowan himself has no particular view of Prague, but I know it a little, and it was fitting that the likes of Myrna Semyonova was let loose in a city whose streets combined sepia-filtered rainbows and shapes of nightmarish precision. If I truly remember the street Rowan mentioned, then Myrna and her father lived in a building that looked like an avenue of concrete gallows welded together with steel. Apart from enforcing her school attendance, her father left her to her own devices; she was free to watch his rehearsals and performances or to improve her graffiti skills, aggravate swans on the banks of the Vltava, or anything else that seemed like a good idea. Myrna loved to watch her father with his puppets—he showed her the influence it was possible to have from a slight distance—so she spent a lot of time at the theater that became his second home. But she also began a correspondence with her mother that pleased them and led to the discovery that both strudel and currant buns remain on the edible side after delivery by forty-eight-hour courier service. From time to time they briefly discussed recovery, and Myrna began to hear a change in the language her mother used to describe her pain—they were words that spoke more of bending than breaking.

MYRNA HAD ASSUMED command over two boys who lived in the flat above her own: Jindrich and Kirill, the Topol brothers. Myrna was both boys' grand passion . . . they called her "London" and longed for a chance to rescue her from some danger or other. Sometimes one brother would menace her so that the other could defend her, even though she'd emphasized from the beginning that all she required of them was that they both die for her if and when such endeavor became necessary. The Topols were in the process of teaching Myrna some Czech, so her instructions were mostly mimed, but the brothers understood her at once. Death frequently crossed their minds, and why shouldn't it, when Myrna had become a participant in their Sunday afternoon wrestling matches in Olšany cemetery? Kirill was ferocious and Jindrich was fleet of foot, but Myrna was nimbler still, and her brutality was fed by her desire not to cheat. Instead of laying hands on her opponent she wove figures of eight until he was exhausted and some obliging tree branch gave her the height to safely grab Jindrich or Kirill with both feet and slam him to the ground, with the additional offense of forcing him to break her own fall.

WITH ITS TENS OF THOUSANDS of graves, Prague's Olšany cemetery is a large village, a small town, in itself. I, Gepetta, have been there, and I know that something travels in that place, something passes among the trees. I cannot say what this traveler is, since we've never crossed paths, but what I've been able to see for myself is that in some of Olšany clearings leaves lock together and form shadowy bridges from branch to branch, and the barks of these bridged trees peel back to show a color that glistens with rawness and decay, sap and old bone. The Topols and Myrna followed this trail, switching wrestling arenas for about a month, scrambling through swathes of undergrowth, administering the occasional surprise fly-kick (no matter how many times it's happened before, it's always startling to be assaulted by a bush) before they discovered the little wooden devil. The wooden devil had been aware of them for weeks. She was carved of rowan wood, and she retained the opinions of trees: one of them being that it was best not to have anything to do with human folk. "Firstly, they cut us down," Rowan said. "Secondly they're all insane, though I suppose they can't help that, being rooted in water instead of earth."

THE WOODEN devil got a good laugh out of the ones who passed by, though. They were so funny she couldn't even feel sorry for them. They tried so hard to keep track of time. Whenever they were together they couldn't let sixty of their minutes pass without asking each other what time it was; as if time was a volatile currency that they either possessed or did not possess, when in fact time was more of a fog that rose inexorably over all their words and deeds so that they were either forgotten or misremembered. The wooden devil's official duty was to guard the grave of an alchemist named Rowan Wayland. The grave was empty; in fact it was one of seven scattered across the continent, and the other six were empty too. As an alchemist, Wayland had liked the idea of implying that he'd excelled at his profession—this could only work if he left absolutely no evidence of having died. His plan had worked. Six centuries had passed and the residents of the streets surrounding the cemetery still didn't feel they could rule out the possibility of his being around somewhere. Every fourteenth of July without fail the town council received a bag of antique gold from an anonymous benefactor; symbolic payment for Wayland's burial plot. It was actually somewhat unlikely that this payment came from Wayland himself, since the main reason King Rudolf had ordered the alchemist's execution was his failure to produce gold from base metal as promised. Wayland had good friends. They arranged for a wooden puppet to be buried in place of his body. The man himself had fled the Czech lands and lived to advance his career in other royal courts.

The wooden devil had been through a lot since she'd been discovered to be the grave's sole inhabitant—she'd been waxed and lacquered and pegged to the earth, frozen, drenched, and dried out again. She'd even seen the traveler in the trees: "Spinning, as a wheel does." The life in the wooden devil was slight and vague, only a little more than that possessed by inanimate puppets, but it was maintained by the fact that the first impression she gave was one of humanity. Graveyard visitors approaching the wooden devil from behind tended to mistake her for someone about the same age as Myrna Semyonova was at that time, and would confidently strike up conversation, though they were either sheepish or oddly repulsed when they discovered their mistake. At any rate this persistence of address cultivated a silent response. The wooden devil had a good vantage point, and served as secret audience to a few Topol-Semyonova wrestling matches. The devil was slightly worried that Myrna and the boys would make a nuisance of themselves once they found her. But there was one tree that the wooden devil thought of as her mother, because this tree had murmured soothingly to her when she'd still been coming up as sapling. That tree watched over her still, and murmured what the elder trees at Olšany always murmured:

"To pominulo; stejně může i tohle." That went by; so can this.

The tree was right. This situation wasn't unique. The children were most likely to run for their lives as soon as they saw her.

MYRNA SAW THE DEVIL before the Topol brothers did, and she approached without calling out. She read the name on the headstone and brushed a little lichen out of the devil's hair. Her gentleness left the devil nonplussed. It was highly irregular for anyone to be curious enough about the feel of her to voluntarily touch her. And nobody had ever seemed quite so pleased by their findings.

The boys overdid their nonchalance, treating the devil's shoulders as coat pegs. The girl's front door keys were always falling out of her pockets, so she left them on the devil's lap before chucking her under the chin and saying:

"Thanks, Rowan." A sequence of elaborate stretches followed, and then Jindrich and Kirill were ready to fight, with Myrna playing referee. It was a highly unusual afternoon for the wooden devil, who was intensely aware of the arm that Myrna had casually flung around her shoulders, as if they were friends who had come to that place together.

AROUND DINNERTIME the boys took their jackets back. But Myrna left her door keys, and didn't miss them until she reached her front door and stuck her hand into the pocket of her jeans.

Her father was still at the theater, so the Topols took her in for the evening. After dinner Kirill adjusted the lamplight until he'd created the correct conditions for shadow play and Myrna put on a little show. Her makeshift shadow puppets quarreled among themselves, hands thrown up, what to do, what to do . . . a spoon-headed creature had suddenly appeared in their midst and befriended their youngest boy. *I promised him he could live with us . . .* The shadow mother forbade this. *Absolutely not! Send this fellow on his way, son.* The boy set up a tent in the garden and courteously asked the spoon-headed creature to enter and consider himself at home. The spoon-headed creature offered to go away, as he didn't want to bother anybody, but the boy insisted. The shadow father was just puncturing the tent with a fork when the Topols' doorbell shrilled. This was followed by urgent knocking and then the sound of very heavy clogs clattering away as fast as they could. Myrna and Mr. Topol ran out onto the street but all they found were ordinary soft-shoed citizens. The lights were on in Myrna's flat; she knocked and waved goodnight to Mr. Topol, but when her front door clicked open, seemingly by itself, she knew that her father wasn't at home. Her father was not a man to hide himself behind a door as he pulled it open.

She called out, "Dad?" anyway, but there was no answer. She only really started shaking when she saw her key ring on the hall table. She considered running to fetch Jindrich or Kirill or both, but she didn't like to turn her back on that open door, and besides, Mrs. Topol had been com- plaining of an especially bad headache all evening and she didn't know how many more times she could politely shrug off the woman's surreptitious attempts to touch her before the situation became awkward. So she called Jin- drich Topol on the telephone even though he was only a flight of stairs away; she talked about nothing and kept talking about nothing as she walked through the flat room by room. Everything was just as usual in every room except her bedroom, where, being well versed in horror story search procedures, Myrna looked under her bed last and found Rowan Wayland lying flat on her back, filled with loathing for keys. A key ring gets left in your care and you reject all responsibility for it yet can't bring yourself to throw it away. Nor can you give the thing away—to whom can someone of good conscience give such an object as a key? Always up to something, stitching paths and gateways together even as it sits quite still; its powers of interference can only be guessed at. The wooden devil suspected keys cause more problems than they solve, so she followed Myrna with one plan in mind, to do her bit to restore order. Myrna's home had seemed like a clever—and strictly temporary—hiding place. But with typical slyness the keys had let Rowan in and then been of no assistance whatsoever when it came to getting out.

ALL THAT SKINSHIP shared by friends, families, and lovers— Myrna had seen plenty of it and had proudly despised them for needing such comforts. Now that she had tried and liked a little of it—shyly, Myrna reached for Rowan again, touched her wooden wrist, and felt something like a pulse flicker through it—she feared it would be hard to go on without any more. It took time for Rowan and Myrna to understand each other's words; they had to take hold of each other and think clearly, then know. Finder's keepers. *Zabaveno nálezcem* . . . and humans only lived a few years, so afterward Rowan could go home again, back to half-sleep and voices that asked nothing of her. She and Myrna took their time presenting the situation to Professor and Mrs. Semyonov. They waited until the family was reunited in London, their chief concerns being that Mrs. Semyonova might call in an exorcist and the professor might try to find out how to make more living puppets by taking Rowan apart. But the Semyonovs weren't like that. There were a few words of Neruda's they were fond of:

> *I don't know anything about light, from where*
> *it comes, nor where it goes*
> *I only want the light to light up . . .*

Rowan took a little bow, to indicate that he'd told all that he wished to tell.

"What are you going to do?" I asked.

He sighed. "I'm afraid Myrna is not turning out well. All she seems to have learned is a way to take pain away without touching anybody."

"And that's bad?"

"It is if your method involves causing the pain in the

first place. But don't worry, I'll deal with her and Tyche both. But the main thing for you is that though you wish to alter your condition that wish will not be granted through me, if at all."

I made no reply, since he'd given me much to consider.

(How much of this do I tell Radha?

As much as will change her feelings.

None of it, then.)

Rowan carried me home in his rucksack—to Radha's house, not Myrna's. Gustav answered the door. Behind him Radha was practicing a choreographed dance with Petrushka and Loco Dempsey, jumping in and out of different pairs of shoes.

"I'm sorry," Rowan said, as he set me down on the doorstep.

"For what?" Gustav asked, laughing, but Rowan just plugged his earphones in and sauntered off.

TYCHE AND MYRNA came back from Scotland with tender new constellations, one tattooed on Tyche's left arm and the other on Myrna's right. They'd chosen a configuration of four brilliant stars collectively called the Chameleon. Rowan looked on impassively as Myrna tucked notes into Tyche's locker for her to read later. Tyche whispered her replies into

Myrna's ear and Myrna smiled in a way that most onlookers took as confirmation of erotic intimacy, though knowing what I did about Myrna's aversion to flesh I doubted it. As for Radha, the fight never quite went out of her—she admired the tattoos, continued to fluster Myrna by cheerfully calling her "wife" to her face, and invited Tyche and Myrna puppet shopping, though she returned from those trips empty-handed. Music was the only thing that exposed her; she found that she was too easily brought to tears by it, and skipped so many tracks on her playlists that I lost my temper and switched the music off altogether, leaving her to work at her desk amid a silence she looked grateful for. At times she held her head in her hands and laughed softly and ruefully. She found notification of a missed call from Gustav on her phone one night and made no attempt to return the call but stayed up late, very very late, in case he tried again. (He didn't.) Ah, really, it was too annoying how bold these ones were when they were in each other's company and how timid they were when apart. It was beneath me to knock all their pretty heads together and shout, "Exactly what are you trying to do with each other?" but it was my hope that Rowan would. Rowan was more interested in knitting a snowflake shawl, so Radha continued writing for Gustav's puppets unhindered. She was scripting her contribution to the school's end-of-term show; the working title was *Polixena the Snitch* and all that I was permitted to know about it was that it was mostly set in a karaoke bar for gangsters.

THE SEGMENT following *Polixena the Snitch* belonged to Tyche and Myrna, who were working on an idea of Tyche's they called *The shock of your life or a piece of cheese*. We, the audience, received cards in advance: One version of the card read *Shock,* and beneath that word was an instruction to write a name *(CANNOT BE YOUR OWN)*. The other version of the card read *Piece of Cheese,* and again there was space to write a name that was not your own. These cards provoked shudders of euphoric terror that only increased as the day and then the hour itself drew ever closer. The cards spoke to a suspicion that many whose work is play can never be free of: that you can only flaunt your triviality for so long before punishment is due. A date has been selected, and on that day there will be a great culling . . .

WE FILED into the school theater chattering with nerves. The volume increased when we were handed pens at the entrance and informed that choices made in pencil would not be accepted. When we sat down nobody removed their coats or bags; everybody was ready to evacuate immediately.

Poor Radha and Gustav . . . their performance was merely something to sit through as we got ready for our shocks or our pieces of cheese.

Gustav's puppet troupe was already onstage, seated on chairs with their backs to us. Brunhild the shipbuilder was tallest of them, and I could see the top of her head. There was a strangeness in the way that head was positioned: I accept that this is an almost meaningless thing to say about the posture of a puppet, which is intrinsically all sorts of strange. But still. I began to mention this to Radha, but Tyche and Rowan sat down beside us and I thought better of it. Tyche asked Radha which card she'd got: shock or piece of cheese? Radha smiled very sweetly and said, "Wait and see," and Gustav walked onstage to the sound of TLC's "No Scrubs." As he did the puppets' chairs turned, and after that everything compressed into a split second; we saw that every single one of the puppets' throats had been slashed wide open so that they erupted strings; they'd been hacked at so savagely that even those internal strings were cut. And when Gustav saw them he lost consciousness. He didn't collapse, exactly—it was more as if he'd been dropped from a height. He fell plank straight, and without making a sound, and that fall of his was just as unreal to us as the glazed eyes with which the puppets onstage surveyed their own innards. Their expressions were the kind that couldn't be altered unless physically dismantled, each smile, scowl, or beseeching look disappearing piece by piece. Laughter was the first response, perhaps the only natural response to such excess. It felt intended that we laugh. Puppets and puppeteer slain by an unknown hand; for about thirty seconds the scene was so complete that no one dared intrude upon it. Then Gustav's friends began to call out to him, reminding him that they'd always known he was too serious for comedy, demanding the next scene, telling him that it was time to get up, that they needed to know if he was OK. From where we sat he seemed to be comfortably asleep, and "No Scrubs" played on and on until Radha ran onto the stage, lifted the boy into her arms, turned his head to the side, and we saw that his eyes were open. Then it became official that Gustav wasn't sleeping. Those of us in the front row even saw his eyes; they were like a void made visible. Professor Semyonova himself climbed onto the stage, checked vital signs, and shouted for someone to call an ambulance. The professor called for his daughter too, and she arrived on the stage among a swarm of other students proffering bottles of water and Tiger Balm and scarves and asking: "Is he breathing? Is he breathing?"

TYCHE, ROWAN, and I were the only ones who stayed where we were. That probably made us look guilty of something,

but moving closer to the stage would have broken our
concentration. Myrna said something to Radha that caused
her to release Gustav and turn her attention to the maimed
puppets, gathering the bodies one by one, running her
fingers through Hamlet's hair, knocking on Petrushka's
helmet, closing eyes pair by pair. As she did so Myrna
clasped Gustav to her ("Did you know she liked him that
much?" I heard one boy ask another), all of her body
against all of his body. He moved his head, seemed to
return to himself, and pushed her away, his hand seeking
only Radha's. Myrna stepped back into the crowd with a
look of shock. What caused it; that the dose she'd given was
enough for him? Or the way Radha bent over him looking
into those sad eyes that had grown even sadder from the
day he'd chosen her? My guess: The biggest surprise was
that by looking at each other in this way they were hurting
Myrna. A little pain—just enough to quicken her breathing.
Tyche was half out of her seat trying to decide whether to
go to Myrna or not, and Rowan tried to give me a high
five, which I ignored. "As expected," he said, and looked
about him with an air of fulfillment that made it plain he
was referring to more than just my snub.

drownings

This happened and it didn't happen:

A man threw a key into a fire. Yes, there are people who do such things. This one was trying to cure a fever. He probably wouldn't have done it if he'd had his head on straight, but it's not easy to think clearly when rent is due and there isn't enough money to pay it, and one who relies on you falls ill for want of nourishment but you have to leave him to walk around looking for work to do. Then even when you find some there still isn't enough money for both food and shelter, and the worry never stops for a moment. Somehow it would be easier to go home to the one who relies on you if they greeted you with anger, or even disappointment. But returning to someone who has made their own feeble but noticeable attempts to make the place a little nicer while you were gone, someone who only says "Oh, never mind" and speaks of tomorrow as they turn their trusting gaze upon you . . . it was really too much, as if tomorrow was up to him, or any of us . . .

THERE'S THAT difficulty with delirium too: You see it raging in another person's eyes and then it flickers out. That's the most dangerous moment; it's impossible to see something that's so swiftly and suddenly swallowed you whole. Arkady's debts were so numerous that when he found himself being beaten up by strangers he no longer bothered to ask who they were or why they were hitting him—he just assumed it was something to do with his repayments. Instead of putting up much of a fight he concentrated on limiting damage to his internal organs. A friend of a friend of his knew a woman who bought people's organs in advance of their death. This woman bought your organs and then made your death relatively nice for you, an accident when you least expected it, a surprise release from life. Once that was taken care of she paid the agreed sum in full, cash in the hands of a person of your choice. Arkady felt his heart and lungs throughout the day—they felt hardy enough, so he had a Plan Z. Why go straight to Z, though?

THROWING THE KEY into the fire was the first step of this man's fever-born plan. The second step involved the kidnapping of a girl he had seen around. He felt no ill will toward this girl, and this was in itself unusual, since his desperation had begun to direct him to linger on the street wishing misfortune upon everyone he saw. That lady's maid hurrying out of the jeweler's shop—he wished she would lose some item of great value to her mistress, so that he might find it and sell it. Yes, let the lady's maid face every punishment for her carelessness, he wouldn't spare a single thought for her. As he passed the grand café on his city's main boulevard he wished a dapper waiter carrying a breakfast tray would slip and fall so that he could retrieve the trampled bread rolls. And how would it be if this time the waiter had slipped and fallen one time too many and was dismissed? *Even better—then I can replace him.*

THE GIRL he planned to kidnap happened to be a tyrant's daughter. Hardly anybody disliked her; she was tall and vague . . . exceedingly vague. Her tendency toward the impersonal led to conversations that ended with both parties walking away thinking: "Well, that didn't go very well." If you mentioned that you weren't having the best day she might tell you about certain trees that drank from clouds when they couldn't find enough moisture in the ground beneath them. She was known as Eirini the Second or Eirini the Fair, since she had a flair for the judicious distribution of cake, praise, blame, and other sources of strife. In terms of facial features she didn't really look like anybody else in her family. In fact she resembled a man her mother had secretly loved for years, a man her mother had never so much as spoken to until the day the tyrant decided to have his wife Eirini the First stoned for adultery. He did give her a chance, one chance. He asked her to explain why his eyesight kept telling him that his daughter was in fact the child of another man, but the woman only answered that there was no explanation.

THE MAN EIRINI the First loved heard about the resemblance between himself and the child and came down to the palace to try to stop the execution. He swore to the tyrant that he and Eirini the First were as good as strangers, but the tyrant waved him away and signaled his executioners to prepare themselves, at which point the man Eirini the Fair resembled ran into the center of the amphitheatre where Eirini the First stood alone with her arms forming a meager shield for her face and chest. The man Eirini the Fair resembled stood before her with his back to the executioners and the tyrant and told her to look at him, just to keep looking only at him, and that it would be all right. It seemed he intended to protect her from the stones until he couldn't anymore. This was intolerable to the tyrant; he could not allow these two to exit together. There was also a sense of having just witnessed the first words they'd ever said to each other. The tyrant feared a man who had no qualms about involving himself in a matter such as this, so instead of going ahead with the execution he had his wife returned to the palace.

AS FOR THE MAN Eirini resembled, he asked to see the child just once—he'd never been more curious about anybody in his life, he said—but his request was denied and the tyrant had him drowned, as had been the case with all other enemies of the tyrant's state. All any citizen had to say was, "The last king was better," and somehow or other Eirini's father got to hear of it and then you were drowned in the gray marshlands deep in the heart of the country, far from even the most remote farmhouse. The air was noxious where the drowned were. The water took their bones and muscle tissue but bubbles of skin rose from the depths, none of them frail, some ready for flight, brazen leather balloons. Houses throughout the country stood empty because the tyrant had eliminated their inhabitants; the swamp of bone and weights and plasma also had house keys mixed into it, since many had been drowned fully clothed along with the contents of their pockets. Eirini the Fair was aware of the keys. She visited the marshlands as often as she dared, crossing narrow stone bridges with a lantern in her hand. She went there to thank the man she resembled for what he had done, but he couldn't be separated from the rest of the drowned; Eirini the Fair swung her lantern around her in a circle and when her tears met the water they told their own meaning as they flowed from eye socket to eye socket.

Among those the tyrant hadn't had drowned yet there was a great eagerness to be rid of him, and Arkady knew that if he went through with his plan to kidnap the tyrant's daughter he would not be without support. The tyrant had started off as an ordinary king, no better or worse than any other, until it had occurred to him to test the extent of his power. And once he found out how much power he really had, he took steps to maintain it. A ration system was in place, not because resources were scarce or because it was necessary to conserve them, but because the tyrant wished to covertly observe the black market and see what exchanges people were willing and able to make. Not just goods, but time . . . How much time could his subjects bear to spend queuing for butter? What about medicine? This was the sort of thing that made life for his subjects harder than life was for citizens of neighboring countries.

EIRINI THE FAIR was sure that her father was detested. He was a man who only laughed when he was about to give some command that was going to cause widespread panic. She didn't doubt that if anybody saw a way to annoy her father by harming her, they might well do it. But she was well guarded, and it escaped her notice that she was being intensely observed by the kind of person who would melt a key.

THE TYRANT had orphaned him, had had Arkady's mother and father drowned in the middle of the night, so that the boy woke up in an empty house wondering why nobody was there to give him breakfast. Young Arkady prepared his own breakfast that day and continued to do so until there was no more food, and then he went out onto the street and stayed there, leaving the front door open in case anybody else had a use for his family home.

Two companions crossed his path—the first was Giacomo, the one who came to depend upon him. Arkady had
happened to overhear a grocer trying to make Giacomo
pay three times the going rate for a bar of soap. "I know
this soap looks just like all the rest, but it'll actually get you
thrice as clean . . ." Giacomo was cheerfully scraping coins
together when Arkady intervened, inquiring whether the
grocer was enjoying his existence as a piece of garbage,
whether it was a way of life the grocer felt he could recom-
mend. Giacomo was not a person who knew what a lie was
or why anybody would tell one; his mind worked at a different speed than usual. Not slower, exactly, but it did take
him a long time to learn some things, especially practicali-
ties regarding people. Light felt like levitation to Giacomo,
and darkness was like damnation. How had he lived so
long without being torn apart by one or the other? He was
so troublesome, taking things that then had to be paid for,
paying for things that shouldn't have cost anything; he
taught Arkady patience, looking at him with wonder and
saying: "Arkady is good." It was Giacomo who was good.
His ability to give the benefit of the doubt never faltered.
The swindlers didn't mean it, the jeerers didn't mean it,
and those who would stamp on a child's hand to make
her let go of a banknote she had been given, those people
didn't mean it either.

Their other companion was a vizsla puppy, now a deep gold–colored dog, who began to follow Arkady and Giacomo one day and would not be shooed away, no matter how fierce an expression Arkady assumed. Since Giacomo's alphabet and numerical coordination were unique to him, it was rare for him to be gainfully employed, so the dog merely represented an additional mouth for Arkady to feed. But the vizsla's persistence and tail-wagging served him well, as did his way of behaving as if he had once been a gentleman and might yet regain that state. The vizsla waited for Giacomo and Arkady to help themselves to portions of whatever meals they were able to get before he took his own share, though sometimes Giacomo pressed the dog to begin, in which case he took the smallest portion and not a bite more. Giacomo named him Leporello. On occasions of his own choosing Leporello turned backflips and earned coins from passersby. And yet he couldn't be persuaded to perform on demand; no, he would give looks that asked Arkady to perceive the distinction between artist and mere entertainer.

THE THREE of them settled in a building at the edge of the city. The view from the building's windows was an unexpectedly nice one, covering miles and miles of marshland so that the mass of drowned flesh looked like water, just muddy water, if not wholly pure then becoming so as it teemed toward the ocean.

ONE DAY WHILE ARKADY was out working one of his three jobs Giacomo came home from a long walk, stopped on the wrong floor of their building, and accidentally opened the door to a flat that wasn't the one he shared with Arkady and Leporello. The tenant wasn't at home, so Giacomo could have seen or taken anything he wished. But what he sought was a view from a new window, and that was all he took. Ten minutes looking out to sea. And he soon discovered that the same key opened every door in the building; their landlord counted on it not occurring to any of the tenants to try opening doors other than their own. When Giacomo told Arkady of his discovery, Arkady was all for having their locks changed. They could be murdered in their beds! They could be robbed at any time! It was bad enough that they lived under the rule of a tyrant who was slowly but surely squeezing the life out of everybody, but now their neighbors could get at them too . . .

Giacomo just laughed and pulled Arkady into one of the flats that stood empty between tenants on a floor higher than theirs; Leporello came too, and barked at the moonlight as it washed over their faces. Their fellow tenants continued to identify their doorways with care, and were too busy and too tired to go anywhere but home.

HAVING SECURED Giacomo's assurance that he'd be very, very careful with these trespasses of his, and Leporello's assurance that he'd help Giacomo keep his word, Arkady's worries were lessened for a time. One of his jobs was assisting the tyrant's physician, who did not choose to be known by her true name—or perhaps was yet to discover it—and went by the nickname Lokum. Like the confection she left traces of herself about anybody she came into contact with—sweetness, fragrance. "Ah, so you have been with her . . ."

Lokum kept the tyrant in perfect health, and perfectly lovesick too. Like the tyrant's wife, Lokum had no lovers: Anybody who seemed likely to win her favor was immediately drowned. Arkady swept and mopped Lokum's chambers, and he fetched and carried covered baskets for her, and he also acted as her test subject—this was his favorite job because all he was required to do was sit on a stool and eat different-colored pieces of lokum that the physician had treated with various concoctions. He was also required to describe in detail what he felt happening in his body a few minutes after the consumption of each cube, and some of the morsels broke his cells wide open and made it all but impossible to find words and say them, though for the most part accurate description was no great task for him, and it paid more than his other two decidedly more mundane jobs. "Open your mouth," she'd say, and then she placed a scented cube on his tongue. He'd warned himself not to behave like everybody else who came within ten paces of her, but once as the lokum melted away he found himself murmuring to her: *I remember a dawn when my heart / got tied in a lock of your hair.* Her usual response was flat dismissal—she all but pointed to the door and said, "Please handle your feelings over there," but this time she took one end of the scarf she wore and wrapped it around his neck, drawing him closer and closer until her face was just a blur. "Listen, listen," she said. "People have been drowned for saying much less."

Arkady could make no retort to that. She was only telling the truth. He thought that was the end of the matter, but as he was leaving she told him not to come back. She said jealousy lent people uncanny powers of detection, and that it was better not to be so close within the tyrant's reach if he wanted to go on living. He protested—without the wages she paid him, he, Giacomo, and Leporello could hardly keep afloat—but she shook her head and motioned to him to be quiet, mouthed, *For your own good*, scattered a trayful of lokum on the floor, shouted, "That's enough clumsiness from you" loudly enough for the guards just outside the door to hear, and sent him on his way, flinging the tray after him to complete the dismissal scene.

He didn't like that, of course, Lokum's taking it upon herself to decide what was for his own good. He could drown if he wanted to. In the weeks that followed that unfillable gap in his funds drowned him anyway—unpaid bills and nobody willing to employ him without speaking to Lokum, who refused to show him any favor. Giacomo and Leporello spoke less and stared out of the windows more. Arkady knew that they weren't getting enough to eat but Giacomo wasn't the sort to complain and Leporello dared not. Giacomo's fever didn't take hold until Arkady missed three rent payments in a row and the trio were evicted from the building with the views that Giacomo was so fond of. Arkady was able to find them a room, a small one with a small grate for cooking. It was a basement room, and Giacomo seemed crushed by the floors above them. He wouldn't go out. He asked where the door was and searched the walls with his hands. Leporello led him to the door of the room but he said, "That's not it," and stayed in the corner with his hands reverently wrapped around a relic, the key to their previous flat: "The key to where we really live, Arkady . . ." How Arkady hated to hear him talk like that.

GIACOMO AND LEPORELLO had stolen the key between them, Leporello putting on a full acrobatic display and then standing on his back legs to proffer a genteel paw to the landlord while Giacomo made a getaway with the key. In his head Giacomo pieced together all those views of the same expanse. Sometimes he tried to describe the whole of what he saw to Arkady, but his fever made a nonsense of it all. Arkady took the key from Giacomo to put an end to his ramblings, and he threw the key into the fire to put an end to the longing that raged through his body and vexed his brain. "This is where we really live, Giacomo, here in a basement with a door you say you cannot find."

THEN ARKADY turned his back on Leporello's growling and Giacomo's sobs as he tried to snatch the key back from the grate. He fell asleep with the intention of kidnapping Eirini the Fair in the morning. The palace watchwords hadn't changed; he had checked. He would be glib and swift and resolute and have the girl at his mercy before she or anyone grasped the situation. He would demand that the tyrant take his damn foot off the nation's neck and let everybody breathe. Money too, he'd ask for a lot of that. Enough for medicine and wholesome meat broth and a proper bed and all the sea breeze his friends could wish for.

HE DREAMED of the key writhing in the fire, and he dreamed of faces coughing out smoke amidst the flames, each face opening up into another like the petals of a many-layered sunflower, and he was woken by police officers. They shone light into his eyes and pummeled him and ordered him to confess now while they were still being nice. Confess to what? The officers laughed at his confusion. Confess to what, he was asking, when the building he'd been evicted from had burned to the ground overnight and he'd been the one who'd set the fire. Almost half the inhabitants had been out working their night jobs, but everybody else had been at home, and there were nine who hadn't escaped in time. So there were nine deaths on his head. Arkady maintained that he'd set no fire, that he hadn't killed anybody, but he knew that he'd been full to the brim with ill will and still was, and he thought of the burning key and he wasn't sure . . . he believed he would have remembered going out to the edge of the city, and yet he wasn't sure . . . he asked who had seen him set the fire, but nobody would tell him. Giacomo and Leporello were so quiet that Arkady feared the worst, but when he got a chance to look at them he saw that one of the policemen had somehow got a muzzle and leash on Leporello and was making gestures that indicated all would be well as long as Giacomo stayed where he was. After a few more denials from Arkady his friends were removed from the room: Giacomo asked why and was told that his friend had killed people and wouldn't admit it, so he was going to have to be talked to until he admitted it. At this Giacomo turned to Arkady and asked: "But how could Arkady do this, when he is so good?" Arkady forgot that his words could be taken as a confession, and asked his friend to understand that he hadn't meant to do it. *I didn't mean it. I didn't know*—Giacomo nodded at those words and said: "Yes, I understand." Satisfied with Arkady's self-incrimination, the officer holding Leporello allowed the dog to stand on his hind legs and pat Arkady's cheek and then his own face; he repeated this a few times as a way of reassuring Arkady that he would be by Giacomo's side until the truth came out. Leporello seemed confident that the truth would come out very soon, and Arkady remembered the vizsla puppy he'd tried to drive away and was glad he'd failed at that.

THOUGH ARKADY BROKE down and confessed after being shown photographs of the five men and four women who'd died in the fire, his confession was never entirely satisfactory. He got the timing and exact location of the fire he'd set wrong, and his statement had to be supplemented with information from his former landlord, who identified him as the culprit before a jury, pointing at Arkady as he described the clothing the police had found him wearing the morning they arrested him. The inconsistencies in Arkady's account troubled the authorities enough to imprison him in a cell reserved for "the craziest bastards," the ones who had no inkling of what deeds they might be capable of doing until they suddenly did them.

ARKADY'S MEALS were brought to him, and his cell had an adjoining washroom that he kept clean himself. He no longer had to do long strings of mental arithmetic, shaving figures off the allowance for food as he went along—after a few days his mind cleared, he stopped imagining that Giacomo and Leporello were staring mournfully from the neighboring cell, and he could have been happy if he hadn't been facing imprisonment for deaths he dearly wished he could be sure he hadn't caused. His cell was impregnable, wound round with a complex system of triggers and alarms. Unless the main lock was opened with the key that had been made for it, he couldn't come out of that cell alive.

THE TYRANT held the key to Arkady's cell, and liked to visit him in there and taunt him with weather reports. He hadn't been interested in the crimes of the other crazy bastards who'd once inhabited this cell, so they'd been drowned. But as somebody who had by his own admission dispatched people and then gone straight to sleep afterward, Arkady was the only other person within reach that the tyrant felt he had a meaningful connection with. Arkady barely acknowledged his questions, but unwittingly gained the affections of the guards by asking a variant of the question "Shouldn't you be staying here in this cell with me, you piece of shit?" each time the tyrant said his farewells for the day. As per tyrannical command the guards withheld Arkady's meals as punishment for his impudence, but they didn't starve him as long they could have. One night Arkady even heard one of the guards express doubt about his guilt. The guard began to talk about buildings with doors that could all be opened with the same key. He'd heard something about those keys, he said, but the other guard didn't let him finish. "When are you going to stop telling old wives' tales, that's what I want to know . . . anyway no landlord would run his place that way."

LOKUM AGREED to marry the tyrant on the condition that there would be no more drownings, and he sent Eirini the First and Eirini the Fair across the border and into a neighboring country so that he could begin his new life free of their awkward presence. After a long absence, the tyrant appeared before Arkady to tell him this news, and to inform him that he'd lost the key to Arkady's cell. The key couldn't be recut either, since he'd had the only man with the requisite expertise drowned a few years back. Lokum had a point about the drownings being counterproductive, the tyrant realized. "Sorry about that," he said. "Maybe it'll turn up again one of these days. But if you think about it you were going to be here for life anyhow."

"No problem," Arkady said. And since it was looking as if this was the last time the tyrant was going to visit him, he added casually: "Give my regards to Lokum."

The tyrant looked over at the prison guards, to check whether they had seen and heard what he'd just seen and heard. "Did he just lick his lips?" he asked, in shock. The guards claimed they couldn't confirm this, as they'd been scanning the surrounding area for possible threats.

"HMMM . . . SPRING the lock so that the cell kills him," the tyrant ordered as he left. The guards unanimously decided to sleep on this order; it wasn't unheard of for the tyrant to rethink his decisions. The following day the tyrant still hadn't sent word, so the guards decided to sleep on it another night, and another, until they were able to admit to themselves and to each other that they just weren't going to follow orders this time. Their first step toward rebellion, finding out that disobedience didn't immediately bring about the end of the world . . . the prison guards cautiously went into dialogue with their counterparts at the palace and at border crossings, and a quiet, steady exodus began.

THE NEIGHBORING countries welcomed the escapees, and with them the opportunity to remove the tyrant's power at the same time as playing a prank on him by helping to empty out his territory. If the tyrant noticed that the streets were quieter than usual, he simply said to himself: "Huh, I suppose I really did have a lot of these people drowned, didn't I . . ." It probably wouldn't have helped him one way or the other to notice that as the living people left, the marshland stretched out farther and farther, slowly pulling houses and cinemas, greengrocers, restaurants, and concert halls down into the water. If you looked down into the swamps (which he never did) it was possible to see people untangling their limbs and hair, courteously handing each other body parts and keys, resuming residence in their homes, working out what crops they might raise and which forms of energy they could harness.

MEANWHILE THE TYRANT was congratulating himself for having dealt with Arkady. He had disliked the way Lokum had begged for Arkady's life, and cared even less for her expression upon being told her pleas came too late. He didn't think they'd had a love affair (that lanky pyromaniac could only dream of being worthy of Lokum's attention), but Lokum's behavior was too similar to that of the man Eirini the First loved. What was wrong with these people?

THE TYRANT set Lokum alight on their wedding day. Thanks to Arkady, fire had risen to the top of his list of elimination methods. He forced her to walk to the end of the longest bridge spanning the marshlands, and he drenched her in petrol and struck a flame. He'd given no real thought to decreasing his own flammability, so the event was referred to as an attempted murder-suicide. "Attempted" because when he tried to run away, the burning woman ran after him, shouting that she'd just that moment discovered something very interesting; he couldn't kill her, he could never kill her . . . she took him in her arms and fed him to the fire he'd started. There was still quite a lot of him left when he jumped into the swamp, but the drowned held grudges and heaved him out onto land again, where he lay roasting to death while his bride strolled back toward the city, peeling blackened patches of wedding dress off her as she went. She put on some other clothes and took food to the prison where Arkady sat alone contemplating the large heap of questionable publications the guards had left him on their departure. Before Arkady could thank Lokum for the food (and, he hoped, her company) she said, "Wait a minute," and ran off again, returning an hour later with his two friends. Leporello shook Arkady's hand and Giacomo licked his face; this was a joke they'd vowed they'd make the next time they saw Arkady, and they thought it rather a good one. Arkady called out his thanks to Lokum, but she had no intention of staying this time either: "We've got to get you out of there," she said, and left again.

"It's autumn, isn't it?" Arkady asked Giacomo. He'd seen that Giacomo's shoes and Leporello's feet were soaking wet too, but he wanted to finish eating before he asked about that.

"Yes! How did you know?"

"I don't know. Could you bring me some leaves? Just a handful . . ."

Giacomo brought armfuls of multicolored leaves, and Leporello rushed through them like a blizzard so that the richest reds and browns flew in through the prison bars.

"Giacomo?"

"Yes, Arkady?"

"Is it right for me to escape this place? Those people where we used to live—"

"There was a fire and they couldn't get out. They would have got out if they could, but they couldn't, and that's what killed them. If you can escape then you should."

"But am I to blame?"

Giacomo didn't say yes or no, but attempted to balance a leaf on the tip of Leporello's nose.

WHAT ABOUT EIRINI the Fair? For months she'd been living quite happily in a big city where most of the people she met were just as vague as she was, if not more so. She ran a small and cozy drinking establishment and passed her days exchanging little-known facts with customers in between attending to the finer details of business management. Her mother had drowned soon after their arrival in the new city: This might have been an accident, but Eirini thought not. The river Danube ran through her new city of residence, and her mother had often said that if she could drown in any river in the world she wished for it to be the Danube, a liquid road that would take her body to the Carpathians and onward until it met the Iskar as it crossed the Balkan mountains, washing her and washing her until she lost all scent of the life she'd lived. Then let the Iskar take her to lie on beds of tiny white flowers in old, old glades, high up on the slopes. Or if she stayed with the Danube, let it draw her along miles and miles of canals to collect pine needles in the Black Forest. As many as her lap could hold . . .

Thinking of her mother's words, Eirini the Fair had journeyed farther up the river and given the ashes into its care. Arrivals from her father's territory frequented her bar and freely cursed the tyrant's name as they told tales that intrigued her. If what these people were saying was true, then the tyrant's drownings had come to an end. It was said that her father's territory was mostly underwater now, that there was no king, no flag, and no soldiers, that there were only cities of the drowned, who looked as if they were having a good time down there. Eirini the Fair heard that one of the only pieces of land yet to be submerged was notable for having a large prison on it. The man who told Eirini this paused for a moment before asking if he could buy her a drink, and she left an even longer pause before accepting. He was handsome but the scent of his cologne was one she very strongly associated with loan sharks. Even so, can't loan sharks also be caring boyfriends, or at the very least great in bed?

"Hi, excuse me, sorry for interrupting," a glamorous newcomer said, as she took a seat at the bar beside the probable loan shark. "Can we talk in private?"

ALL LOKUM wanted to know was what Eirini the Fair had taken with her when she'd left the palace. Eirini had neither the time nor the inclination to provide a list of articles to her father's plaything. But Lokum rephrased her question to ask if Eirini had taken anything of her father's while leaving the palace, and then Eirini remembered the key. Just a metal shape on his dressing table, bigger than most keys she'd seen, but still small enough to pocket while she

bade her father farewell and hoped she'd managed to in-
convenience him one last time.

JUST BEFORE she and Lokum reached the prison gates,
Eirini the Fair looked over the side of their boat and saw
that her mother had found her way to the drowned city
that now surrounded the building. She wasn't alone; there
was a man with her, the one Eirini the Fair had never
met but wanted to. They both waved, and Eirini the First
held up a finger and then wistfully rocked an invisible
baby, motions easily interpretable as an appeal for grand-
children. "Lovely," Eirini the Fair murmured, drawing her
head back into the boat and pretending she hadn't seen
that last bit.

presence

Jill Akkerman's husband had been wanting to have a talk with her for weeks, and she was 200 percent sure that it was going to be an unpleasant one. The signs were subtle, but she was a psychologist. So was he; she'd been warned that this would probably be her toughest marriage. In the month before their summer holiday he was so busy that she hardly saw him at home, and when he was in she used the unofficial zoning of their household to postpone the talk. No harsh words were to be said in bed, or in the kitchen. Neither of them had made these rules, but since this had somehow become part of their code of conduct, Jill and Jacob continued to do their bit toward keeping their meals and their dreams untainted. Conversation in the bedroom and kitchen tended toward the light-hearted, so she stuck to those rooms as often as possible when she wasn't at work. Jacob had had the house reno-vated to her wishes; there weren't many changes, just the addition of a few extra doorways. She preferred rooms with a minimum of two doorways, so you had options. You didn't have to go out the same way you came in. In the bedroom she moved from the bed to the floor and back again with her books and gadgets. Sex was out of the ques-tion. He didn't even raise the question, just watched her with a glint of amusement in his eyes. In the kitchen she cleaned diligently and sharpened knives until they broke. Jacob bought more and presented them to her with witty asides she heard only dimly beneath the louder fear that he might add: "Can I see you in the living room for a minute?"

HE DID CATCH her in the living room once but she ran so fast around the edge of the room and out of the nearest door that she toppled and broke a painted jug they'd chosen together on their honeymoon.

Jill wouldn't have minded receiving some advice but ul-timately opted not to mention this situation to anybody outside of the marriage. Not to her own therapist and certainly not to Lena or Sam. Jacob was about to leave her. She didn't want him to, but this was her third marriage and his second; she knew how these things went. She'd met Jacob's new colleague over dinner and the colleague, Viviane, was well dressed, husky-voiced, and generally delightful company, knowledgeable on a number of topics and curious about a variety of others. Jill had found herself joining Jacob in addressing her as "Vi," and when Vi left the table for a few moments to answer a phone call Jill whispered: "You realize she's got a crush on you?"

Jacob laughed and leaned toward her with his lips all smoochy, but she pushed his face away with a breadstick. "Did you hear what I just said?"

He leaned in again. Not close enough for a kiss this time, but close enough for her reflection to almost completely fill his irises. Portrait of cross forty-two-year-old with, hey, really nice boobs actually. "Yes, you said you think Vi has a crush."

"I'm two hundred percent sure about that."

"Two hundred percent? Oh. Even if you're right it'll pass, J."

J. Vi. And he still called his first wife Dee.

"Why don't you just make the most of it, run off with her, and be half of a beautiful black intellectual couple just like you always wanted?"

Husbands one and two, Max and Sam, were white—Sam was a few years younger than Jill, but both he and Max tended to look old stood beside her. Well, not elderly. Just older than her. Whereas side by side she and Jacob looked about the same age. What age was that? If you didn't know them you couldn't even give a rough estimate. Jacob picked up a breadstick of his own, crunched half of it, stabbed her in the arm with the other half, and asked: "Do you really think you can do this here?"

He rarely appeased her. She wasn't sure what to make of that given his attitude toward almost all his other friends, loved ones, clients, the efforts he made to ensure everybody else's comfort. When he was with Jill he made her wonder whether he'd been sent to destroy her. Take the time she'd invited him to sample the first viable batch of tea leaves from the greenhouse she part-owned. Chun Mei, with its taste of sweet springtime grass. He'd sauntered downstairs inexplicably wearing a denim shirt over jeans, taken the teacup from her, and filled his cheeks with tea. "And how is this superior to a nice cup of Tetley?"

The combination of barbaric taste buds and denim on denim had set Jill's teeth so sorely on edge that her jaw locked for a couple of minutes. Enough time for him to stare her down and walk out unadmonished. He knew what he was doing, he knew! For her part she'd given up trying not to be quite so in love with him at some point in their late teens when she'd clocked that, without deliberately cultivating any particular scent, Jacob Wallace managed to smell exactly like a just-blown-out candle. But if the feelings on his side weren't there anymore then it was better for him to just go. His contributions to their joint bank account tripled hers but she wouldn't have a problem doing without handwoven rugs at home and boutique hotels abroad. Doing without Jacob himself was going to make her a little bit crazy for a long time, so no she wasn't going to make it easy for him to say his piece and then leave.

WITH A WEEK to go before their summer holiday Jacob all but ambushed Jill at a Tube station. She was adding another month's worth of public transport to her Oyster card when an arm slipped around her neck and her husband murmured: "Jill, Jill . . . you can't fight this any longer. I need to ask you something . . ."

She could've feigned alarm for just a couple more moments and elbowed him in the groin, but instead she turned her head and hissed: "Whose idea was it to get married in the first place, eh? Why don't you ask around and get back to me?"

She wasn't going to let him off just like that but he'd

better not be hoping she'd cling to him either! If she didn't feel like being on her own she could get another husband if she wanted.

(Jill had run into Max outside their friend Mary's bakery the other day, and he'd held her at arm's length, given her a long, admiring look, and said: "God, you're deteriorating fast. Lucky me, getting out while the going was good, eh?"—his eyes directly contradicting his remarks. Not that she'd ever go back to Max, with whom wedded bliss had been nowhere to be found. It had made her nervous that almost all her new in-laws were Swiss bankers, but also there were the terrific nightlong rows she and Max got into. If she protested Max's shameless revisionism by making reference to something he himself had said just the day before, he'd become "concerned" about her negativity or would hit her with some barbed comment somebody else had apparently made to him about her demeanor—it wasn't clear whether he made them up or merely saved them. She never stopped liking Max, but did grow weary at the thought of him.)

Jill went over to the blue stand where issues of the *Evening Standard* were stacked, but Jacob handed her his copy.

"I know whose idea it was to get married," he said. "I don't need to ask around—I was there. And so were you, just another stunner among the many, many stunners of London town, drunk on a sofa with one of your best mates—"

"Excuse me . . . the best mate may have been legless, but seeing as I'm a hero of the kingdom of alcohol, I was mildly tipsy. Also don't forget to mention that this best mate was a moderately attractive man who'd never once made so much as a hint of a move on me in all the twenty-eight years we'd known each other . . ."

"Maybe he thought it was too obvious. I mean, Jack and Jill? Anyway the two of you were thirty-nine years old, prime of life, and both solvent to boot, so the man plucked up the courage to say . . . Hang on, what did I say again?"

Do you think that maybe we're able to love someone best when that person doesn't know how we feel? That's what Jacob had said, and she'd looked at him and asked if he was about to say something weird to her. She'd rather he didn't. Having weird things said to her was a large part of her day job and why couldn't she have time off? Jacob's answer was that he was about to say something weird, but only a tiny bit, and maybe what he wanted to say wouldn't come out sounding as wrong as they thought it would. Maybe it would sound normal.

Let's get married and have sublime blasian babies before it's too late, Jacob had blurted after she'd nodded at him to continue. Jill stretched an arm out and refilled both their shot glasses. It was already too late for babies. She'd had a sort of deadly serious running joke with both her previous husbands that having children would have to wait "until the war's over." But none of the ongoing wars looked likely to ever end, and she could no longer see carrying a child in her future. Not physically, and not mentally either. Maybe that had always been the case.

"I'm not going to marry you, mate."

"Oh. That's . . . well, I mean, why not? Because I said blasian? Because we haven't known each other for long enough?"

In her head she'd replied: *Because I can't just keep getting married all the time, and also because I'm pissed off with you for making me sit through two of my own weddings and one of yours before it occurred to you that maybe we should have tried it together first.*

Aloud she'd said that they were too old, adding that they didn't need to get married. She said they could just see each other, if he wanted. She advised sleeping the question off. Maybe he'd wake up and realize that he only wanted to get married when he drank a lot of soju.

"But that wasn't good enough for the rejected suitor," Jacob continued, settling down into the Tube seat beside hers. "He'd been wanting to marry this woman for ages, long before the adult realization that marriage isn't all that necessary . . . so he proposed again the following evening. The babies don't have to happen, he said, and then he sang the cheesiest Korean song he could find . . ."

Was Jacob about to sing "What's Wrong with My Age" right there on the Tube with all these boys and girls and men and women looking? They were already looking, since he hadn't bothered to keep his voice down.

Still, she stuck up for "What's Wrong with My Age." "It's not a cheesy song! It's your singing that makes it cheesy. I love that song."

"Me too. But I'm afraid it is inherently cheddar, J."

Jacob turned to Jill, opened his arms and sang, in Korean, of staring into the mirror and bidding time to stand aside. The lyrics sprang to her own lips as she listened, and by the time he was challenging her to deny that his age was the perfect age for love, she was smiling the words right back at him.

As he sang, she realized something. He hadn't been thinking about leaving her. Whatever he'd been working up to asking her, it was about something else entirely. She placed a finger over his lips: "And when they wed their parents and all their friends stood up in the church pews and sang 'At last' . . ." but Jacob made a halfhearted attempt to bite her, then said: "Hey! Hey Jill. Are you thinking about leaving me?"

She didn't answer that. One of the things she'd learned about him early on was that he had an inbuilt and near-infallible lie detector, and all of a sudden she wasn't sure whether what she'd really been doing for the past few weeks was skillfully molding her own desire to be single again into an image of his. It could be that all Jill's leaving and being left had now made it impossible for her to stay with anyone.

FOR MOST of their lives she and Jacob had both been afraid of the same thing: not being deemed worthy to share a home with a family. They were both foster kids. Nobody ever said you were unworthy, not to your face, but there was talk of adults and children not being "the right fit" for each other. The adults were the ones who decided that, so when "fit" was brought up they were really talking about the child. This left Jacob, and Jill, and Lena (Jill's onetime foster sister during an idyllic but brief lull) ever-ready to have to leave a home, or to be left. Jacob became extremely capable, a facilitator, someone you wanted around because he smoothed your path—whether through his skill as a polyglot or his general aura of "can do." Lena was pretty much lawless, used to wear a pair of sunglasses on the back of her head and a badge that said HELL, which she tapped whenever anyone asked her where she was "originally from," and she was so clearly somebody that you could trust with your life that reform always seemed possible for her. Jill advanced an entirely false impression of herself as biddable and in need of protection. *Ah, I'm just a little chickadee who won't survive the winter unless I nestle under your life-sustaining wing.* Far from original, but it worked.

THEY WENT OUT to dinner at their favorite restaurant—the benefits were twofold: delicious chargrilled broccoli plus the discussion of Jacob's question without having to bring it into the house with them. Jacob proposed sacrificing their summer holiday to a project of his, an idea he was developing as part of his work as a bereavement counselor. So that was it, the question he'd been building up to for weeks. Do you mind giving up your holiday to test-run my project? She was embarrassed that he felt he'd had to work up to asking her this; it was a question that would've been easily raised and just as easily settled with an unselfish part-ner. Regarding him her support was in fact unconditional and to date she'd thought she adequately expressed this; now she fought demoralization as she heard him out. His project focused on a particular type of experience that a large number of his clients reported having undergone. "To oversimplify the descriptions I've been given, this experience presents as . . . an implosion of memory. And as the subjects drift through the subsequent debris, they calmly develop a conviction that they do not do so alone. These presences aren't reported as ghostly, but living ones . . . minutes, sometimes hours when the mourner feels as if they've either returned to a day when the deceased was still alive or the deceased has just arrived in the present time with them . . . and what's interesting about these lapses people experience is that most of them happen under fairly similar physical conditions."

"So you've put together some sort of program that induces this feeling of . . . presence?"

"Well, that's what I'm aiming for. Of course it'd only be for mourners who need that feeling from time to time and can't make it happen by themselves. We're calling it 'Presence.' And now we've got some funding . . ."

"You clever thing."

"Really it was Vi who got the funding together. She's a bit of a whiz at that. Lots of international contacts."

"I'm sure that's only the tip of Vi's iceberg." She made a quick attempt to estimate the extent to which new information concerning the relationship between Vi and Jacob might shake her. Sam had had his affairs, and Jill had come to an understanding of them as a form of boundary setting, actions taken against a fear that any one person could or did know "everything" about you. Jill was never more aggravating than when she got busy understanding things, and yet these rationalizations of hers might not be such a big problem this time around, as she was finding that the thought of various deep, sweet secrets between Jacob and Vi had something of a mechanical effect on her. Air seeped out of her and very little came back in—she breathed as though subject to strangulation and sat on her hands to suppress tentacle-like tendencies such as thrashing about, and clinging. The more Jacob told her about the testing of his program, the more she wondered if her first misgivings hadn't been right after all. He was genuinely willing to be a guinea pig for his own prototype, she could see that, but maybe this was also Leaving Jill, Phase 1: Practice.

"OK, I'LL HELP. But since I don't know anyone else who'd ask me to spend two weeks pretending he's no longer in the world, tell me this first: Are you really not thinking about leaving me?" she asked.

That glint of amusement again. "Get this through your head, Jill Akkerman: I'm not leaving you. And you—are you leaving me?"

"I'm not leaving you, Jacob Wallace."

She watched him put her expression, posture, and phrasing through his lie detector. She passed. His gaze lost intensity.

"Remember that psychologist who said we had an unhealthy dependence on each other?" asked the boy who'd learned Korean along with Jill and the couple who'd eventually adopted her. Her parents had wanted to have a new family language, and Jacob had learned too, so that he could be a part of that family. He'd been an honorary Akkerman for over half his life now.

"Yeah . . . we owe our careers to him, I think. He made us want to see what his job would be like if someone did it properly."

"He might have been right, though," Jacob said.

"Oh?"

"I just mean . . . if it was healthy, it might be easier to give up."

She poured him more wine and they raised their glasses to unhealthy dependencies. Then he told her the specifics of their test for Presence. They needed two bases. Jacob would stay at their Holland Park house with the projection of Jill's presence and Jill would need to stay at her flat in Catford, a parting gift from Max that she would've rejected if that hadn't meant starting another fight with him. Jill's current tenants were away in Prague until the autumn and when she called them to ask if they were all right with her being in the flat for a couple of weeks they said it was fine. "Just don't break anything . . ." Radha said. Workmen came to the flat to make some adjustments to wiring and to secrete the contents of what looked like gas canisters into the walls. Jacob gave her a full list of the substances she'd be breathing in. While they were all substances found unaltered in wildlife, mixing them was bound to be a different matter.

"This is essentially going to be like an acid trip that lasts for two weeks, isn't it?"

Jacob only said: "Not really. You'll see."

After the necessary alterations had been made to both houses Jill and Jacob recorded three conversations—the purpose of which was to place the mourner in the midst of a familiar exchange, the kind we're always having with friends and family, repeating ourselves and repeating ourselves, going over what we know about each other to prove that we still know these things and will not, cannot, forget them. Vi set up a camera at Jacob's office and filmed Jacob's face as he and Jill repeated the conversation they'd had on the Tube about whose idea it had been to get married. They talked about their earliest impressions of each other too, and by the time it came to filming their third conversation they couldn't think of anything else they wanted to say, so they kept it brief. Sex returned to the Akkerman-Wallace bedroom—to every room in their house in fact, their sweat mingling in the summer heat.

A day later Vi provided them with a transcript of what they'd said in each of the conversations they'd filmed in Jacob's office, and Jill was irritated by this (was this Vi's way of telling them to make certain that their claims matched up with what they really felt?) until she recalled that they were going to be filming all three conversations again in her own office, with the camera focusing on Jill's face this time. They had to make an effort to get the conversations in sync. If she or Jacob couldn't "get hold" of each other in their separate bases they were to put headphones on and reengage in the conversation, responding to each other's words, saying their own parts as they remembered them.

JACOB PHONED her when he and Vi arrived at the prison where she worked. The timing was inconvenient because Jill had just made accidental eye contact with the governor of the prison and had done what she usually did when that happened—she'd walked around the nearest corner to hide. She was well aware that the governor thought she was useless. Not Jill as an individual, necessarily, but her role within the framework of the prison. "Letting young offenders have half an hour a week tapping out fuchsia landscapes on a chromatic typewriter doesn't really do much toward turning them into better citizens, does it?" Not a fair summation of her work, but getting on with her job was Jill's only answer, amiable until some bureaucratic roadblock popped up. And once it had been dealt with she was a nice person once more, even nicer than before. She and Jacob repeated their three conversations for the camera and then she went back to work.

Jill knew what all the boys had done, or as much as they would admit to, anyway. They all received treatment; they could talk to her as long as they tried to say what was true for them. Everything they said was recorded, and her office door stayed open whenever a boy was in there with her. There was a guard at the door too, just in case, but problems between her and the boys were infrequent. Many of them called her "Miss," quite tenderly—*Tell me if anyone's rude to you, Miss. Just tell me his name, yeah?*—as if she was their favorite teacher at school. She had hope for them, even though the things they told her made her shake like a jellyfish when she got a moment in her office alone.

Ben and Solomon were the two boys whose progress she dwelled on the most, and they came to see her that afternoon, one after the other. Ben was deeply introverted, coping relatively well with his incarceration and mostly harmless—if only she could get him to express some, or any, emotion to her so that she could confirm or revise these impressions of his coping and his harmlessness. He had language and could understand everything that was said to him, but his introversion was so deep that he often looked as if he no longer knew whether he'd spoken aloud or not; he was irked when she pressed him to answer her questions: *I already answered, Miss . . .*

A phone had recently been discovered in Ben's cell; there were no incoming or outgoing calls or messages recorded on it. Nobody could explain how Ben had come by the phone but it was easy to tell how long he'd had it because the photo album was full of selfies he'd taken. He posed in exactly the same way in each one, fingers held up in a peace sign. Only the backgrounds were different. He favored empty rooms and, occasionally, the backdrop of two or more of his fellow inmates doing their best to bash each other's heads in.

SOLOMON WAS MUCH more communicative with her, but that didn't mean she understood him any better. His record was something of a puzzle in that he'd only turned to a life of crime relatively recently. For the first fifteen years of his life his record was spotless, then one day he'd approached a gang whose members had been torturing him on and off, joined, and became their leader. His explanation of the change he'd made: "It was time."

Jill was aware that Solomon's younger brother had been struggling with illness for years, and that the brother's brain tumor had gone into remission when Solomon was thirteen. The beginning of Solomon's career of criminal violence coincided—if you could really call that a coincidence—with doctors detecting a recurrence of cancerous cells in his brother's brain. This made Jill afraid for Solomon, and afraid of him too. He admitted to wanting to help his brother, but would say nothing more about it. He was like a boy in a fairy tale; there was a set of steps he was to follow with no concession whatsoever as to how others viewed his actions. Then at the end of it all there'd be a reward. Solomon had just heard from his family—his brother's cancer was back in remission. But the young man showed no relief; the news only deepened the look of concentration in his eyes. This is what Jill saw when she tried to see life Solomon's way: Your brother had been selected at random and hurt, so by selecting others at random and hurting them, you won relief for your brother. If that's how it was then Solomon would eventually be compelled to select one more person at random and kill them so that his brother could live. Much of what she said to him was mere diversion, her attempt to knock down the tower of logic he was building. Sometimes she thought it was working. Sometimes he cried when she made him realize a little of what he was doing. He wasn't a sniffler so the tapes didn't catch his remorse. And when she asked herself whether she'd support a recommendation for his early release a year from now, she very much doubted being able to do that. For a while he would hate his false friend Doctor Akkerman, obsess, fixate, and possibly decide that the life he'd take for his brother's sake should be hers. She was only 100 percent sure of these things, and had no clear idea of how far the boy's attempt would progress before he was restrained or what injuries would be sustained. Perhaps none, perhaps none . . .

Still, it was Jill's duty to mention this likelihood, and she'd do so in her reports closer to the time.

"Have a good holiday, Doctor Akkerman," Solomon said at the end of their session. The only boy to acknowledge they wouldn't be seeing each other for the next two weeks.

JILL TOOK HER suitcase over to the Catford flat and slept there the night before Presence was due to begin. Jacob wasn't dead to her yet, so they played at a long-distance love affair over the phone. Jill had Radha and Myrna's permission to take down any images that might interfere with Jacob's presence, so as she talked to her husband she walked around the flat dropping pictures of the intimidatingly photogenic couple and their puppet and human friends (hard to tell which was which) into a jewelry box. She heard no echoes of Max's ranting or her own frenzied screeching, and when she went into the bedroom where she'd slept so that she wasn't tempted to injure Max in the night she found it full of small stages. Some cardboard, some wood and textile, and there were silky screens for casting shadows through too. "Looks like only playfights are allowed in here now," Jill said to Jacob, and then, as she opened the fridge and took note of its being crammed with bottles full of something called "Kofola": "I was thinking— won't it be easier for you to get hold of my presence over there than it will be for me to get hold of yours over here? You've never been here."

"I'm curious about that too," Jacob said. "People who end up using Presence may need to be able to travel with it, use it in a new house, and so on . . ."

Two minutes until midnight. She looked around at the pale blue walls, then out of the window and into the communal garden; there was a night breeze, and the flowers were wide-awake.

"Is there a button I press to . . . activate or something?"

"Vi's going to start it remotely."

"For both of us?"

"Yes . . . goodnight, J."

"Goodnight."

She drew the curtains, switched off the lights, and was knocked down onto the bed by a wave of darkness so utter her eyes couldn't adjust to it. It felt as if she'd fainted . . . that was what she liked about fainting, the restful darkness that bathed your eyelids. After what felt like an hour (or two?) she held her phone up to her face to check the time, still couldn't see anything, and decided she might as well just sleep.

SHE WOKE UP feeling chilly; her feet were sticking out from under the covers. A head had been resting on the pillow beside hers—all the indentation marks were there. She picked up her notepad and wrote that down. Even though she'd made the marks herself they contributed to a sense of not having slept alone. It was twelve-thirty, the latest she'd woken up in a while, and the room temperature was unusual for an early afternoon in July. She checked the thermometer and wrote the temperature down. Low, but it felt even lower. She put two jumpers on, made tea, plugged headphones in, and called up the first recorded conversation on her computer screen. There was Jacob, smiling at her, speaking. At a much lower pitch she heard her voice answering his: "Your singing makes it cheesy. I love that song . . ." There were strings of words that she remembered in the correct order, and she tried to say them before her recorded voice did, but the cold threw her off balance and she was left just listening and watching instead of participating. She added that observation to the others in her notepad.

A VISIT TO HER greenhouse in Sevenoaks yielded a discovery: She hadn't woken up at twelve-thirty. Twelve-thirty was still two hours away. When she checked her phone on the train the time changed, and she asked five other overground passengers, six . . . *Yes, yes, it really is ten-thirty.* Sam and Lena were at the greenhouse, tending to the tea plants beneath swiveling lamps. They were wearing matching floral-print wellies and Sam preempted her derision: "Yeah I know, we deserve each other."

Jill hesitated before she told them about Presence. What if they said *Jacob? Who's Jacob?* or reminded her in voices full of pity that Jacob had been "gone" for months now? She couldn't be confident in what she said to them when she'd just stepped out of an icebox into a sunny July day and the time outside wasn't the same as the time in her flat. Well, they were her friends. If at all possible your friends have a right to be notified when you've downright lost it. But it seemed she was still sane. Lena and Sam had a lot of questions, Lena kept checking her pupils, and they both wanted to come over to the flat and verify her experience. Lena was most intrigued by the wall clocks

("They all read twelve-thirty? Did you hear them ticking?

"Come to think of it, no—no ticking.")

and Sam wondered about the cold.

"Talk to Jacob . . . maybe he'll test the next phase on you two . . ." They said they'd like that. She didn't think she'd told them anything that made Presence seem like good fun, so it was most likely that they were just being supportive. Sam gave her a pouchful of Assam leaves: "Let me know what you think . . ." On the way home she stopped at a supermarket and bought winter groceries. Lemsip, hot chocolate, ingredients for soup and for hot toddies. She put it all through self-checkout so she wouldn't have to make any small talk about summer colds. Then, wondering how Jacob was doing, she checked their joint account and saw that he'd made a card payment at a Waitrose about an hour ago, for more or less the same amount as she'd just spent. She wouldn't mention this in her notes; it was cheating. She shouldn't be able to guess whether or not he was cold too.

SHE'D FORGOTTEN to lock the front door. Just like waking up at twelve-thirty, it'd been years since she'd last done that. People told horror stories about Catford but she would've been more worried about going in if it was the Holland Park front door she'd forgotten to lock. The stakes were higher over there. She dumped her shopping bags in the kitchen and went back to the front door, locking it behind her with exaggerated care. Jacob came out of the room filled with puppet stages and looked around him, nodding. "Not bad," he said. According to the clock just above his head it was still twelve-thirty. He took a step toward her and she took a step back.

"What are you doing here?"

"Why are you shivering?" he asked back.

"Er, because it's bloody cold in here?"

He held out his hand for her to touch; he was warm, and she closed both her hands around his palm. He winced, removed his hand from hers, and brought her two more jumpers to put on. He didn't need to be told where to find the jumpers. She went back into the kitchen, found her notepad, and made a note of that. Then she put the kettle on, and Jacob asked if he should do the same with the central heating.

"Yes please." She measured tea into a teapot, put the shopping away in the cupboards. The tea brewed and then she and Jacob sat down in the living room, he took a couple of sips and said: "Remind me how this is superior to a nice cup of Tetley?"

She couldn't really taste the tea herself. She was sweating, and Jacob wasn't. He was comfortable, right at home. She took a jumper off, to see if she'd feel the cold less that way. Putting on jumpers and turning on the heating only seemed to increase the cold. When she looked at Jacob from the side she could see that he wasn't her husband. He had no shadow and he didn't smell like her husband—he didn't smell of anything—he was warm and he could drink tea and be snarky about the tea, and perhaps she would've been more willing to keep him around if he'd been shadowless but smelled right. But the way things were she was too conscious of this person not really being Jacob.

"Sorry, but I think you'd better go," she said, checking her watch for some reason. *It's twelve-thirty, time for you to go.*

He set his cup down on the coffee table. "OK. But if you tell me to leave I won't come back."

She patted his knee. "That's fine. Thanks for understanding."

He stood up, and so did she. "I'm leaving, but everything that's between us will stay."

She couldn't help laughing at that. "You're so soppy, Jacob."

He laughed too, then put an abrupt brake on the laughter. "I didn't mean it in a soppy way."

"Er . . . OK . . . Bye . . ."

"Good to see you," he said, and left the room. She stayed still for hundreds of heartbeats and thousands of shivers but didn't hear the front door open or close. At twelve-thirty she got up and made sure that he was gone, then she recorded the entire encounter in her notebook and broke a rule of the test by phoning Jacob. *If you tell me to leave I won't come back,* now that she thought about it she didn't like the sound of that. Jacob took a long time to answer the phone; she'd almost given up when his voice came down the line: "J?"

"Jacob! Are you OK?"

"Yeah . . . you?"

"Fine, just . . . Have you seen me at home yet?"

"No. Not yet," he said. Something else had happened. He'd gone out for a bit and come back to find the front door open (she bit her lip so that she didn't interrupt him) and an intruder in the hall. Some old black guy talking at him in Portuguese, begging forgiveness for something.

"Did you call the police?"

Jacob was silent.

"You didn't call the police, Jacob?"

He thought the intruder might have been his dad. "You know, my bio dad. I got him to slow down and he seemed to be talking about how I'd weighed on his conscience."

"Interesting. Is he still there with you?"

"Nah . . . once I realized who he was or might be or whatever, I told him to get the fuck out. And guess what he said—"

"He said, 'OK, but if you tell me to leave I won't come back'?"

"And I said, 'Well, you'd best not!'"

"And then he said, 'I'm leaving, but everything that's between us will stay'?"

"No, he didn't say that. And hang on, how did you . . ."

Jacob's voice fizzed and wavered, stopped altogether, and was replaced by a smoother, happier version. Audio of the second conversation they'd filmed.

"To be honest, Jill, I didn't think you were going to get adopted. You played too many mind games with the people who tried to take you on . . . when you were together in public you'd act all cowed and hurry to do everything they said, acting as if they beat you at home. And you didn't eat at home either, did you?"

"No! I'd stuff my face in school so it looked like I wasn't getting fed. Looking back I was a scary kid," Jill said, in perfect time with the recording of her own voice.

"But the Akkermans just kept telling you they really liked you, and even when you pulled stunts like that Sabine would say, 'Nope, sorry and God help us, but we still really like you,' and she and Karel wouldn't eat until you ate . . ."

"So then I'd worry that I'd brought them to the brink of collapse and ended up spoon-feeding them rice, two spoons for each of them and then one for me . . . important to keep your strength up when you've got parents to feed . . ."

There was no room to ask what had happened; Jacob had been there on the other end of the line but now he was gone and it was a week ago again. The blue wall in front of her was more pacifying than sky, its color more even. Icicles hung from her nostrils; they were long, thin, and pearly gray . . . *Like enchanted spindles,* Jill thought, but it was only mucus, so she reached for tissues. She and Jacob were talking about the Wallaces now. Jill had always been sure that

Jacob would get adopted. It was just a question of his coming across grown-ups who didn't try to pull the wool over
his eyes: Even the whitest of lies made him act out, and
then he was discovered not to be "the right fit." But along
came Greg and Petra Wallace, and it was heartwarmingly
weird that a pair of super-white Conservative politicians
had fallen for Jacob as hard as they had. It took a long time
for their foster son to stop anticipating some hidden motive
on their part. Jacob had been wary of being dragged out in
public with the parental bodies, wary of a fatherly hand
settling on his shoulder while reporters took down remarks
like, "Take this hardworking young man . . . a far better
role model for our disadvantaged youth than some benefits
scrounger . . ." Nothing of the kind ever came to pass, and
the Wallaces had shown such steadfast and enthusiastic
support of all things Jacob that he (and Jill) had had to
give in.

BEFORE GREG AND PETRA none of the people who'd invited
Jacob to "make himself at home" had really meant it . . .
wanting to mean it didn't count. The Wallaces gave Jacob
a front door key and one day Jill had temporarily
confiscated it, just to see how disconsolate Jacob would be
at the prospect of a delay in getting home. She'd found that

Jacob Nunes, a boy who was usually up for one more three-legged race, one more game of knock down ginger, one more *WWF SmackDown!*, was now very disconsolate indeed at having to endure one more anything before hometime. And the Wallaces were so jolly it seemed bad manners not to like them back. Jacob's Labor Party membership probably saddened his parents more than they could say, but you can't have everything . . .

AT TWELVE-THIRTY Jill went into the bathroom, found some shampoo, and washed the sweat out of her fringe. She used the hot tap and saw the water steaming but it splashed her skin blue instead of pink. Never mind; she couldn't feel any of it anyway. She was a bit peckish, though. *Gherkins.* She'd seen a jar of them in the cupboard when she was putting the shopping away. She fetched them, walking carefully so as not to slip on the water she was dripping. "Yaaaay, gherkins!" But she couldn't get the jar open. She heard a voice in the next room (Jacob's again, after she'd told him to leave?) and went to have a look. It was only the TV. She surfed channels, since it was on. "Remember when almost everybody on TV was older than us, Jacob?"

She wrote these things down in her notepad, hurrying because it was almost twelve-thirty, bedtime, darkness, instant and complete, another head on the pillow beside her, maybe she grew one more in the night and that's why the night sleep was so deep, it was a matching pair of sleeps.

A NEIGHBOR BANGED on the door and woke her to complain about wailing coming from her flat. The neighbor was a middle-aged brown man in an unusually close-fitting dressing gown, and she didn't even need to warn him not to try to come in—he stood well away from the front door. He felt the cold. His beard was attractive; it was clear he took good care of it.

"Were you playing some kind of world music or do you need an ambulance, or . . . ?"

"Or," she told him. "Or." And she apologized, and promised the noise would stop, though she wasn't sure it actually would. It must have, because she didn't hear from him again.

AT TWELVE-THIRTY she got up again, to go to the toilet. The TV was on again (or still?) so she switched it off. She walked past the kitchen and then went back and looked at the kitchen counter. There was the jar of gherkins, where she'd left it. But now the lid was off. Good! She ate a gherkin and checked the room temperature, which had dropped even further. She'd forgotten to find out whether Presence was potentially life-threatening. It looked nice outside; she'd go out soon. Maybe at twelve-thirty. Rain fell through sunlight. This was what Sabine Akkerman called fox rain. In her mind's eye Jill's mother shook iridescent raindrops off her umbrella and said: "Wolves are hosting wedding feasts and witches are brushing their hair today."

Presence certainly met its objective but perhaps the objective itself was flawed and warranted adjustment. Jill wrote that down in her notebook.

THE NEXT TIME she went into the kitchen there was a boy sitting at the table eating toast. Twelve years old, maybe twelve and a half. He looked like Jacob and he looked like Jill, and he had mad scientist hair that looked to be his own invention. She had to quickly pop back to the fifteenth century to find a word for how beautiful he was. The boy was makeless. From head to toe he couldn't be equaled, the son she and Jacob hadn't had time to have, their postwar baby. Having a kid of your own, yes, now she saw what all the fuss was about. "Thanks for opening the gherkin jar, my strong man," she said, taking his other piece of toast. He could make more. He flexed his puny biceps and said: "You're welcome."

He was so new that all his clothes still had price tags attached; they looked the price tags over one by one: "Oh my god, *how* much? Thieves and bandits! This isn't even going to fit you five minutes from now." Her son rubbed her hands until they were warmer. She liked that, didn't matter if he was just sucking up in the moments before he asked her for something. He wanted a skateboard, and launched into a list of reasons why she should let him have one, but she just said: "Yes. Stay there." There was a fifty-pound note in her purse, and she went to get it. When she came back he was still there but a bit older now, about fifteen and a half, and he didn't want a skateboard anymore, he wanted some video game console or other. She gave him all the cash she had on her and told him he'd have to get the rest from his dad.

Hugs, kisses; ah good, they'd raised him to be tactile. "You're the best, Mum."

"Yeah, yeah . . ."

He dried her sudden tears. "Don't cry while I'm out, Mum."

"You're really coming back?"

"Yeah, but if you send me away I won't."

"I'm bloody well not sending you away."

"Great. Bye for now then." He threw his plate into the sink—more at the sink, no, really he threw the plate as if it were a Frisbee. But it did land in the sink. Sheer luck.

"Hang on . . . what's your name?"

"Alex, innit."

"Have you got friends? Who are your friends?"

He rolled his eyes, showed her a few photos on his phone, scrolled past certain other photos at lightning speed. "Mum, it's almost twelve-thirty so . . . see you later, yeah?"

She didn't bother listening for the front door this time. She wanted to say something to her husband about their son. She switched on her laptop and drafted an e-mail to Jacob with the subject line *Have you seen what we made???* and plugged her headphones in instead of sending it. She played the third conversation they'd filmed. One question and one answer.

What's the hottest time of day?

The answer, known only to them and hundreds of thousands of disciples of a certain K-pop band, was 2PM.

On-screen, Jacob waited for her question.

"Hey Jacob, what's the hottest time of day?"

His reply: "The hottest time of day is 2PM."

That niggled at her. Jill frowned. Actually two things

bothered her—his having said, "The hottest time of day is 2PM" when the usual answer was simply "2PM," and then there was the appearance of Vi's hand in the shot. It was only there for a moment before it was withdrawn from the space in front of the lens with a barely audible "oops," but Jill could see now that the waving hand was probably the reason why Jacob laughed a little as he talked his way back toward the answer (could be that he'd momentarily forgotten the question): "The hottest time of day is 2PM."

Alex returned before she could replay the third conversation again. He was in his early twenties now, and was sporting chin stubble and red chinos. He didn't grumble as much as she expected when she made her request that they just watch some telly together. He quite happily complied, putting his arm around the back of the sofa and keeping her warm that way. She didn't have a clue what they were watching, but took the time to absorb every detail of his face so that later, when he was gone again and it was twelve-thirty at night, the man who looked like her and Jacob was superimposed on the darkness.

IN THE MORNING Alex came back in his late thirties with photos of his wife Amina and her granddaughter. Jill went down to the corner shop to try and prepare herself for her son's arrival in her own decade of life. She hadn't looked into the mirror before going out of the front door—Darren at the corner shop was shocked and asked her if she was OK. She told him she was fine, and asked about the date and time. It was four p.m. in the outside world, and a week and five days had passed since she'd begun testing Presence. Fox rain was falling (still?) and Jill said: "Time flies, time flies." Darren asked her if she was OK again, and this time she asked him how he was. Darren was fine too, or so he said. *Can't complain* . . . She bought some lip balm and went home.

SHE'D MISSED Alex's forties: "I'm in my fifties, now, Mum . . ." He didn't look it . . . maybe he was lying, maybe your baby's just always your baby. But she didn't feel able to stay at home with her son who was now older than her. There was a lot she could've learned from him, she knew, but that would've meant staying in that flat where the temperature was so far below zero that the numbers were now meaningless. She didn't feel able to send Alex away either. She washed. Not just her fringe, she washed all over. And she took a different outfit out of her suitcase and put it on. She didn't say good-bye to Alex, but left him sleeping on a mattress they'd set up in the second bedroom, between the puppet stages, still makeless, though by twelve-thirty his presence would have faded away altogether. Jill locked the front door behind her and made two journeys: first stop work, to ask after her boys, the ones she still had hope for. The front desk warden made a few phone calls in a low voice with her back turned, then told her they were fine, nothing out of the ordinary had happened, and wasn't it tomorrow that she was due back?

"Good, yes, that's right . . . see you tomorrow."

JILL'S SECOND JOURNEY ended at home in Holland Park. On the train she thought about the likelihood that Vi would be there with Jacob. She'd been there in the camera shot with Jill and Jacob, however momentarily. His answer had still come to her, and when she got home the front door was unlocked and she found the house as dark and as cold as the flat she'd left earlier; it was twelve-thirty and she found Jacob slumped over the kitchen table with his headphones on. She took them off and asked him again: "What's the hottest time of day?"

The answer, without verbal deadweight this time: "2PM . . ."

His arms around her, and hers around him, knots and

tangles they could only undo with eyes closed. "You're so warm."

"About Presence," she said. "Scrap it. Don't do this to anyone else."

"Agreed."

JACOB MENTIONED ALEX once, as they were comparing notes. "I wish we had a picture, at least," he said, and Jill knew what and whom he was referring to. She didn't agree, but neither did she contradict his wish. It was his own, after all.

a brief history of the homely wench society

From: Willa Reid <stonecoldwilla@hotmail.com>

To: Dayang Sharif <okinamaro1993@gmail.com>

Date: November 12th 2012, 18:25

Subject: JOIN US

Dear Dayang,

Among Cambridge University's many clubs, unions, academic forums, interest groups, activist cells and societies, there's a sisterhood that emerged in direct opposition to a brotherhood. What this sisterhood lacks in numbers it more than makes up for in lionheartedness[1]:

---

[1]*This is Grainne's self-perception. If you can overlook her narcissism you may come to care for her one day.—M.A.*
You sayin' you care for me, Marie?—G.M.

The Homely Wench Society. The Homely Wenches can't be discussed without first noting that it was the Bettencourt Society that necessitated the existence of precisely this type of organized and occasionally belligerent female presence at the university.

The Bettencourt Society has existed since 1875. The Bettencourters are also known as "the Franciscans" because a man gets elected to this society on the basis of his having sufficient charisma to tame both bird and beast. Just like Francis of Assisi. Each year at the end of Lent term the society hosts a dinner at its headquarters, a pocket-sized palace off Magdalene Street that was left to the university by Hugh Bettencourt with the stipulation that it be used solely for Bettencourt Society activities. If you've heard of the Bettencourters you may already known the following facts: No woman enters this building unless a member of the Bettencourt Society has invited her, and no Bettencourt Society member invites a woman into the building unless it's for this annual dinner of theirs. And getting invited to the dinner is dependent on your being considered exceptionally attractive.

The Homely Wench Society has only existed since 1949. The women who were its first members had heard about the Bettencourt Society and weren't that impressed with what they heard about the foundational principles of these so-called Franciscans. As for their annual dinner . . . hmm, strangely insecure of intelligent people to spend time patting each other on the backs for having social skills and getting pretty girls to have dinner with them. But people may spend their time as they please. No, the first Homely Wench Society members didn't have a problem with the Bettencourt Society until Giles Rutherford (Bettencourt Society President, 1949, Ph.D. Candidate in the Classics Faculty) was writing a poem and got stuck. What he needed, he said, was to lay eyes on a girl whose very name conjured up the idea of ugliness the same way invoking Helen of Troy did for beauty. Luckily for Giles Rutherford's poem, the first wave of female Cantabs working toward full degree certification were on hand to be ogled at. Rutherford sent his Bettencourt Society brethren out into the university with this task: "Find me the homeliest wench in the university, my brothers. Search high and low, do not rest until you've sketched her face and form and brought it to me. Comb Girton in particular; something tells me you'll find her there."[2] The Bettencourters looked into every corner of Newnham and Girton and found many legends in the making. They compiled a list of Cambridge's homeliest wenches, a list which later fell into the hands of one of the women who had been invited to the Bettencourt's annual dinner. This lady stole the list and sought out other women who'd accepted invitations to this dinner. Having gathered a number of them together she showed the list of homely wenches around and asked: "Is this kind of list all right with us?"

---

[2]*At least that's what Grainne Molloy imagines Rutherford said. This is not verifiable!—T.A.*

Bah, history students.—G.M.

"No it jolly well isn't," the others replied. "This is Cambridge, for goodness sake—if a person can't come here to think without these kinds of annoyances then where in this world can a person go???"[3]

They hesitated to involve the women whose names they'd seen on the list. Some of the Bettencourt dinner invitees were friends with the homely wenches, and didn't want to cause any upset. Who wants to see their name on such a list? But in the end they decided it was the only way to gather forces that would hold. Honoring delicacy over full disclosure only comes back to haunt you in the end. Moira Johnstone, the first of the homely wenches to be informed of her place on the list, had to suspend a project she'd been working on in her spare time—the building of a bomb. She'd been looking for an answer to a question she had regarding the effects of a particular type of explosion, but the temptation to test her model on a bunch of fatheads was too strong. The others had similar responses, but soon settled on a simple but emphatic riposte. As they worked through this riposte, the Bettencourt dinner invitees and the homeliest wenches discovered that, by and large, they liked each other and were interested in each other's work; they thereby declared themselves a society and gained the support of new members who hadn't been featured on either list. Nonetheless the members of this new society dubbed themselves Homely Wenches one and all.

---

[3]*Again with the unverifiable exchanges, Grainne . . .—T.A.*
Leave me alone, Theo . . .—G.M.

The 1949 Bettencourt Society Dinner began pleasantly; lots of champagne and gallantry, flirtation and the fluent discussion of ideas. They were served at table by waiters hired for the evening, and whenever a Bettencourter disagreed with one of the guests he made sure he mitigated his disagreement with a compliment on his opponent's dress, thereby reminding her what the true spirit of the evening was. Fun! At least it was for the boys, until a great crashing sound came from the next room as the waiters were preparing to bring in the first course. Rutherford called out to the head waiter for the evening; the head waiter replied that "something a bit odd" had happened, but that service would be up and running again within a matter of moments. Waiting five minutes for a course was no great hardship—more compliments, more champagne—but when the head waiter was asked to explain the delay he asked jocularly: "Do you believe in ghosts?"

The lights in the kitchen had been switched off and then switched on again as the food was being plated, and then the waiters had heard footsteps in the next room, and then the portrait of Sir Hugh Bettencourt in that very same room had fallen off the wall. The Bettencourt boys laughed at this, but their guests turned pale and went off their food a bit. Who could say what might have happened to it when the lights had gone out? The Bettencourt boys laughed even more. Even the cleverest woman can be silly. When the same sequence of events occurred between the first and second courses—footsteps and falling objects, this time all along the floor above the dining room— the Bettencourters stopped laughing and looked for weapons that would assist them in apprehending intruders, spectral or otherwise. Their guests were one step ahead of them and already had a firm hold on every object that could conceivably be used to stab or whack someone, including cutlery. "Do you want us to go and have a look?" asked Lizzie Holmes, first-ever Secretary of the Homely Wench Society.

"No no, you stay there, we'll take care of this," Bettencourt President Rutherford said, adding a meaningful "Won't we?" to his patently reluctant brethren.

"Yes, yes of course . . ." The Bettencourters had to go forth unarmed, since the frightened women refused to release even one set of ice tongs. Up the stairs they trooped, with no light to guide them ("We'll just wait in the kitchen," the waiters said) and they searched each room on the first floor and found no one there. When they filed back into the dining room, however, it was full of uninvited women, each of whom had taken seats emptied by the Bettencourters and were tucking into the platefuls of food the Bettencourters had temporarily abandoned. "Sit down, sit down, join us," cried Moira Johnstone, number one Homeliest Wench. The Bettencourters looked to Rutherford to see how they should proceed; he decided the only sporting response was a good-natured one, so he and his brethren had another table brought into the room, had the waiters set places at it and sat there and ate alongside all the Wenches. Their plan had been just as you must've guessed by now: Earlier that evening the last of the "most attractive" women to enter Bettencourt headquarters had lingered at the door and let the first of the "homeliest wenches" into the building.

As far as we know, the Bettencourt Society never compiled another list of homely wenches. The Homely Wenches Society flourished for a time, and then membership dwindled as ensuing generations of female Cantabs saw little need to label themselves or to oppose the Bettencourters (whose numbers remain steady). The activities of the Homely Wench Society mainly come under the banner of "Laughs, Snacks and Cotching," but in response to advice from Homely Wenches who've since graduated, the society produces a termly journal. Mostly for the purpose of posterity; we have no real readership other than ourselves.

So if you want to join, our questions to you are:

Who are the homely wenches of today?

What makes you think you're one of us?

Your answer is a key that will unlock worlds (yours, ours), so please make it as full and as *bigarurre* as it can be.

Hope to hear from you soon,

Willa Reid (third-year History of Art, Caius)

Ed Niang (second-year NatSci, Clare)

Theo Ackner (second-year History, Emma)

Hilde Karlsen (third-year HSPS, Girton)

Grainne Molloy, (second-year Law, Peterhouse)

Flordeliza Castillo (first-year CompSci, Trinity)

and

Marie Adoula (third-year MML, King's)

———

IT TOOK DAYANG SHARIF (second-year Eng. Lit, Queen's) days to think up an answer that was full and *bigarurre*. As soon as she read the e-mail she wanted in—actually as soon as she'd met Willa and Hilde on the train she'd wanted in— but as with all groups the membership hurdle wasn't so much to do with convincing the Wenches that she was one of them as it was to do with convincing herself. She looked the word *bigarurre* up and found that it meant both "a medley of sundry colors running together" and "a discourse running oddly and fantastically, from one matter to another." "Medley of sundry colors running together" made her think of her Director of Studies, Professor Chaudhry, saying: "I saw you with your Suffolk posse, Dayang. A colorful gang!" She'd looked at him to check what he meant by "colorful" and deciphered from his grin that other definitions included "delightful" and "bloody well made my day."

DAY COMPOSED an answer that centered on the evening she'd met Hilde and Willa. She'd got on at Kings Cross with Pepper, Luca, and Thalia, all four of them covered in sweat and glitter—they'd had their Friday night out in London town and now they were ready to get back to Day's room and crash. Hilde and Willa sat opposite them sharing a red velvet cupcake. Day remembered trying not to fret about two whole girls afraid to eat a whole cupcake each. She didn't know them or their fears. She noticed Willa's long chestnut hair and Hilde's eyes, which were like big blue almonds. She'd never seen them before but nodded at them, and they nodded back and continued their conversation, which seemed to be a comparison between medieval and modern logistics of kidnapping. Pepper and Luca were attempting to address Thalia's complaints about art school, and Day was about to throw in her own tuppence worth when five boys who looked about the same age as them came swaying through the carriage singing rugby songs. Actually Day didn't know anything about rugby so they might not have been rugby songs per se, but the men definitely had rugby player builds. They stared as they passed Day and her friends; Day felt a twanging in her stomach when they walked back a few paces and their song died away. She could see them thinking about starting something, or saying something. If these boys said something Luca would fight, and so would Pepper, and then what were Day and Thalia supposed to do—broker peace? Hardly. Day could punch . . . her parents had only been called into school for emergency meetings about her twice, and both times had been about the punching. Not necessarily the fact of her having punched someone, no, it was the style of it. Day punched hard, and when she did so she gave little to no warning. She punched veins. Aside from being disturbing to witness, the vein punching was extremely distressing for Day's target; the link between heart, lungs, and brain fizzed and then seemed to snap, then the target's limbs twitched haphazardly as they tried to recover some notion of gravity. Every now and again Day's sister requested punching instruction from her, but this wasn't something Day could teach. She just knew how to do it, that was all. She thought it might be connected to anxiety and the need to be absolutely certain that it was shared. And she really didn't feel like punching anybody that night. She'd had a good time and just wanted to keep having one . . .

A COUPLE of the rugby boys were black. They both caught Pepper's eye, and all three looked apologetic for staring. But that didn't mean there wasn't going to be a fight. So Day, T, Pepper, and Luca tensed up. Day saw something interesting: Chestnut Hair and Blue Almond Eyes were no longer eating cake and had tensed up too. Not the way you tense up when you're about to run away, but the way you tense up when you're not about to have any nonsense. And actually, looking around, Day saw that Chestnut Hair and Blue Almond Eyes weren't the only ones. Others scattered across the carriage had become alert too, looking up from the screens of their phones, some even rolling their sleeves up. "Jog on, lads," a barrel-chested man advised, and the boys seemed to reflect on numbers, then left and took their thoughts of starting something with them. When they'd gone Chestnut Hair leaned across the table and said, "I'm Willa." Blue Almond Eyes introduced herself as Hilde and said, apropos of nothing: "When we were little we had chicken pox together."

"Ah," Luca said, sagely. "So you two are close."

Willa rubbed her nose. "Oh, but we didn't do it on purpose . . ."

Willa was seriously posh. She tried to sound estuary but couldn't go all the way. At the station Hilde turned to them and asked: "Are you students here?"

T, Pepper, and Luca talked over each other: As if! Yeah right . . . and all three pointed at Day: "There she is, Miss Establishment . . ."

"Please just live your hate-filled lives happily, guys," Day said.

Willa took Day's e-mail address and said she'd be in touch. "We should all cotch sometime."

Cotch? Pepper thought that sounded sexual. Luca said: "Maybe something to do with horse riding? That one blatantly rides horses." Thalia just giggled.

———

THE MEETING on the train sort of answered the question of what made Day think she could be a Homely Wench, but it didn't answer the question of who a Homely Wench is. Second year was a year of conscientious study for Day; she couldn't have another exam result fiasco like last year (too much time spent visiting Pepper at Oxford Brookes), so she could only return to her questions of wenchness after she'd done as much work toward her degree as was possible, all the reading and note-taking and following up on references that she could do in a day. Queen's was in Day's blood, since it was her father's college too. In his day he'd flown thousands of miles specifically to enroll, whereas she'd come in from Suffolk. Her college library was at its best late at night. At night the stained-glass figures in the windows seemed to slumber, and the lamps on each desk gently rolled orange light along the floors until it formed one great globe that bounced along every twist and turn of the staircase to the upper levels. When she surveyed the entire scene it seemed to be one that the stained-glass figures were dreaming. And she was there too, living what was dreamed. She stretched, sighed. *Well, I'm a fanciful wench, but am I a homely one?* Her sister Aisha was gunning for Murray Edwards, their mother's college.

DAY HADN'T SIGHED quietly enough: A few desks away Hercules Demetriou (first-year Law) looked over at her and smiled. She looked away. She didn't think he was evil or anything, but he was a problem. The issue was all hers for fancying him even though he'd already been elected to the Bettencourt Society. The boy was tall and well built and had wavy hair, excellent teeth, and unshakable equilibrium. Up close you saw smatterings of acne but that was no comfort. His skin tone lent him enough ethnic ambiguity for small children whose parents had a taste for vintage Disney to run up to him and ask: "Are you Aladdin?" He'd flash them a dazzling smile and answer: "Nah, I'm Hercules."

Hercules of Stockwell. So full of himself. This was not an attraction that Day could ever confess to anybody. Hercules talked to her, though. He'd say, "See you in the bar, yeah?" as he and his friends walked past her and her friends. Then Mike or Dara or Jiro would turn to her and say things like, "So *will* you see him in the bar? Or his bed, for that matter?" Horrible. When Hercules Demetriou spoke to Day her heart beat loudly and her loins acted as if they didn't know what the rest of her knew about him. What was he after? Day didn't actually think she was unattractive: Her appearance was mostly passable, and sometimes even exceeded that. Two things that were not in her favor were her spectacles, which often led people (including herself) to incorrectly anticipate a sexy librarian effect. You know . . . the glasses come off, the hair tumbles down, and there she is. Nope. She had unreasonably large feet too. She'd never walk on moonbeams. *Why* would the perfectly proportioned Hercules Demetriou keep trying to befriend her? It made no sense. Unless the slimy Betten-courters were compiling another List after all.

THE YOUNG HERO was still looking over. Day took her glasses off, cleaned them, put them back on, and then typed a couple of paragraphs.

WHO IS A HOMELY wench? Is a girl who exhaustively screens every man her mother contemplates seeing a homely wench? Leaving these things to Aisha meant just letting it all go to hell. How about a girl who sometimes finds it easier to talk to her dad's boyfriend than she does to her dad—what manner of wench is she? Day's dad still fasted at Ramadan even though he didn't go to mosque anymore, and from time to time he flared up at signs of Day and

Aisha's "secular disrespect," which he was almost sure they were learning from their mum. (They weren't. If anything they were learning it from Dad's boyfriend, Anton.) But apart from being less hung up on manners, Anton was less sensitive than Dad. Day had once mentioned being envious of her friend Zoe for having two mums—she'd been talking about the miracle of having two mums who were both so cool, but her dad had taken her words to mean that she didn't want all the family she had, and he'd looked so crestfallen that she'd spent ages explaining her original comment and making it sound even more dismissive of him and Anton until he'd had to laugh.

A GIRL at the desk next to Hercules'—Lakmini, Day thought her name was—wrote him a note; must have been a hot note because he fanned himself with it. But Miss Dayang Sharif couldn't have cared less what the note said, no way.

WHO ARE THE Homely Wenches of today?

SHE WROTE about her first boyfriend, Michael, her first and only boyfriend to date. She'd been in love with him and they broke up but the love didn't. In fact the love got—not truer, just better. Their friend Maisie's parents were away on the same weekend as the Eurovision Song Contest Grand Final so Maisie opened up her house to "all my Eurovision bitches," which turned out to be not that many. Just Maisie, Day, and Aisha, until Michael showed up, with two friends, Luca and Thalia. A taxi pulled up outside of Maisie's house and Michael, Luca, and Thalia got out, the three of them dressed in silk sheaths—real, heavy silk. Maisie rushed to the front door: "What? Who are they? Are the Supremes really about to come in right now? I must have saved a nation in a past life . . ."

IT TOOK DAY A COUPLE of hours to get around to talking to Thalia and Luca. She only had eyes for Michael. For the first time she was seeing that he had everything she coveted from pre-Technicolor Hollywood. Hip-swinging walk, lips that tell cruel lies and sweet truths with a single smile, eyelashes that touch outer space. If Bette Davis and Rita Hayworth had had a Caribbean love child, that child would be Michael just as he was that night. They hugged for a long time, and later they talked on the balcony outside. "Thank God for the Internet," he said. "I wouldn't have found Luca and T without it. All sorts of nutters out there, but mine found me . . ."

He settled on the name Pepper. Day remembered the rest of that night in stop-motion—galloping, shimmying, the speakers turned up so loud that the singing shook the air and the beat of the music was like being knocked on the head. The backbeat was a hammock you fell into. Ring a ring o'roses, pan flutes, trumpets, and yodeling—Day was holding hands with Luca, who held hands with Aisha, who held hands with Maisie, who held hands with Pepper, who held hands with her, dancing around in a circle with bags and coats stacked in the center, cheering for the countries whose stage performances made the most effort or projected the most bizarre aura. Luca and Thalia became Day's too. "For life, yeah? Not just for Eurovision . . ."

Thalia didn't even like Eurovision. She said she'd come along to meet Day. "This one's always going on about you," she said, gesturing toward Pepper.

DAY'S STEPDAD, Anton, who'd had trouble remembering Michael's name, hailed Pepper with joy, even as he teased Day about the times she'd said Michael was the one. Day just shrugged. Pepper wasn't always on the surface, but whether she was with Pepper as Pepper or Pepper as Michael, Day had found the one she'd always be young with, eating Cornettos on roller coasters, forever honing their ability to combine screams with ice cream.

SO . . . WHO is a Homely Wench?

DAY WROTE about Luca, muscular and much-pierced Luca, and how that first Eurovision they spent together his hair was the same shade of pastel mint as the dress he wore. He and Thalia were a bit older, in their early twenties. By day he sold high-fashion pieces: "Everyone wants to fly away from here but not everyone can make their own wings . . . so they buy them from me . . ." By night he was an unstoppable bon vivant, deciding what kind of buzz was right for that night and mixing the pharmaceutical cocktail that had the least tortuous hangover attached. He'd had nights so rough he could hardly believe he was still alive: "But this can't be the afterlife. Ugh, it can't be." Luca laughs long and loud and his body shakes as he does so. He's better at forgetting than forgiving; he says this is the only thing about himself that scares him. Speaking of him Day's father says, "So . . . vulnerable," at the same time as her stepdad says, "Brazen!" Neither is quite right. When Luca was younger he got kicked out of his parents' house for a while; they'd hoped it'd make him less brazen, but it didn't—he stayed with friends and got brasher, and when he came home it was like he took his family back into his heart rather than the other way around. Day knew Pepper and Luca were together. She'd also heard that Luca liked to pursue straight men. Thalia referred to this tendency as "Luca's danger sport." Pepper said Luca'd be fine. "He's got us."

OH, AND THALIA—DAY had to talk about T. Thalia's aesthetic was the most civilian (Pepper had learned the most from her YouTube makeup tutorials) and Thalia was her full-time name. She was composed, reserved, she lived with an older man none of her friends had met; the only reason her friends even knew about the older man was because of a week when T had been ecstatic because she'd sold five triptychs and received a really considered, insightful note about them from the buyer. But then she found out the buyer was her boyfriend, so she was furious for a couple of days, and then the fury mingled with elation again. Luca argued that the boyfriend was merely investing in an artist who'd be famous one day, and whenever Thalia heard this she said, "Care," to indicate that she didn't. Thalia painted scenes onto mirrors, dramatic televisual two-shots from stories that had only ever been screened in Thalia's mind. Her mirror paintings left gaps where the facial features of the characters would normally be, so that your face could more easily become theirs. T's brushstrokes are thin, translucent, and mercurial in their placement; they swirl into one other. Her colors are white and silver. Around the images Thalia paints a few words from the script: an alphabet frame. Day's favorite was a voiceover:

The poison taster is feeling a bit ill. He's well paid but he hates his master so much that today, the day he finally tasted poison, he's eaten a lot and is managing to keep a normal expression on his face until his master has eaten at least as much as he has. Eat heartily, boss, don't stop now . . .

Who's a homely wench? Luca is, and Day is, and so are Pepper and Thalia and Hilde and Willa and anyone who is not just content to accept an invitation but wants more people to join the party, more and more and more. Day can just hear Pepper and Luca climbing up onto a tabletop at such a party and screaming out (they'd have to scream through megaphones, as she's envisioning a gathering that'd fill Rome's Coliseum many times over): *Hello everyone, it's great to see you all, you homely beasts and wenches.*

Send.

THE HOMELY WENCHES have no fixed headquarters, and all the members agree that this keeps them humble, relying as they do on the soft furnishings and snack-based offerings of whichever member is host to Wench meetings for the month. February was Day's month for hosting meetings, and this particular meeting had been called to discuss articles for the Lent term edition of *The Wench*. There were to be two interviews: one with a bank robber who'd turned down a place at Cambridge and now half regretted it. Marie was covering that story; she had a feeling for bittersweet regret and mercenary women. The other interview was with Myrna Semyonova, author of a novel, *Sob Story*, which she'd written to make her girlfriend laugh, consisting as it does of a long, whisky-soaked celebration of all the mistakes two male poets (one young, one middle-aged) had made and were making in their lives. The narrator of the novel was the bar the two poets drank at, and since Semyonova had published the book under the pen name Reb Jones she was hailed as the new Bukowski. Willa was covering that, and her reaction to *Sob Story*'s being taken so seriously was the same as that of Semyonova's girlfriend: It made the joke twice as funny. Ed was working on a piece about hierarchies of knowledge for female love interests in the early issues of her favorite comic books; how very odd it must be to operate within a story where you're capable, courageous, droll, at the top of your field professionally and yet somehow still not permitted the brains to perceive that the man you see or work with every day is exactly the same person as the superhero who saves your life at night. "Seems like someone behind the scenes clinging to the idea that the woman whose attention you can't get just can't see 'the real you,' no?"

DAY LOOKED FROM face to face. Marie might get on with Thalia; they both favored grave formality and never letting a single hair fall out of place, though Marie's Zaire French accent and her tendency to wear jackets over her shoulders without putting her arms in the sleeves gave her attitude more impact than Thalia's. The society was too small to have a leader, but if they'd had one, Marie would've been it. Sometimes, when Marie and Willa spoke together in French, glancing around as they did so, Day felt that they were disparaging her mode of dress, but Ed had reassured her that that was just how people who could only speak English naturally responded to fluent French speakers. Ed, named after Edwina Currie, was much easier to get to know. You could chat to her about anything. If she didn't understand a reference you made she just said so. Rare, very rare for anyone Day had met at Cambridge to admit to gaps in their understanding . . . but Ed would ask to hear more. This puckish, boyish young woman was black like Marie and a Londoner like Willa, but, as she put it herself, "a different kind of black, and a different kind of London"—it was hard to picture a time, place, or opportunity other than university and the Homely Wench Society for the likes of Ed, Willa, and Marie to find out that they really got on. For one thing all three had a tendency to assume that everybody else was joking all the time and responded accordingly—Willa with breezy levity, Marie with frank disappointment, Ed with various micro-expressions, semi-smiles, really, that made you want to laugh too, even if you really did mean what you'd just said.

THEO AND HILDE, on the other hand, didn't think anybody was joking about anything unless they were explicitly told so. Theodora Ackner, Nebraska's finest, was still disconcerted by Europe's ghosts. Hilde, Ed, and Grainne could no longer hear them, but the ghosts seemed to wake up again around Theo, since she actively listened for them.

Lisbon, Paris, and Vienna were tough places for her, beauties clotted with blood. Hilde refused to accompany Theo to Oslo. "About a quarter of my family lives there, Theodora. Let me know these things in my own way."

AND THEN THERE was Grainne Molloy, who had lobbied to be recorded in the annals of the Homely Wench Society as "the irrepressible" Grainne Molloy, unsuccessfully, since, as Hilde pointed out: "Sometimes you are repressible, though." While Grainne did truly lose her temper several times a day, that frenetic energy of hers occasionally served to obscure another trait: the cool and calculated collection of incriminating anecdotes.

THE NEWEST HOMELY WENCH was half in love with every single one of her fellow Wenches, but she wasn't sure what she, Dayang, brought to the mix. She'd been a member for just over three months and hadn't had an idea for an article or a group activity yet. She snapped the group photos so she wouldn't have to see physical proof of her being odd man out. Maybe she could do something toward recruitment; a few of her friends from college and faculty had seemed interested when she mentioned the Wenches.

———————

FLORDELIZA, the youngest Wench, their first-year, arrived late. As expected. "Afternoon, ladies!" She grabbed a handful of biscuits and flopped down onto Day's bed. She'd been growing out a side Mohawk since the summer, so her front hair was still much longer than it was at the back. Her clothes were crumpled and she'd clearly slept without removing her eyeliner; Day had barely noted this before Flor announced that she had a tale of shame to tell. But also a tale of possibility.

"Go," Theo commanded from the window seat; she'd arranged Day's curtains about her so that they resembled a voluminous toga.

"OK, first of all, you're not allowed to judge me . . ."

"We're all friends here," Marie said, sternly.

Flordeliza revealed that a member of the Bettencourt Society was into Yorkshire Filipinas. "Or maybe just into this?" She pointed at herself.

"Oh God," Grainne shouted. "Oh God, Flordeliza, what did you do?"

DAY WAITED to hear about Flor and Hercules. She felt a bit sick but that was just obstructed emotion, a sensation the

Dayang Sharifs of this world know all too well. Spring was definitely in the air, even as early as February. Everyone except Day was in some sort of romantic relationship— Marie with a townie who rode a motorbike, Willa with a curator at the Fitzwilliam, Theo with a guide who led tours of Dickensian London, Ed and Grainne with each other, and now Flordeliza with her Bettencourt boy. Day's only hope was that Hercules Demetriou would come out of this story sounding so greasy that Day's physical response to his proximity would be mercifully dulled forever.

(The other day she'd passed him and a few other boys she suspected were Bettencourters on King's Parade, apparently conducting a survey that involved soliciting the opinions of women. "More like ranking them," she muttered, and Hercules had smiled at her and said: "Sorry, what was that?"

"Nothing. Hello."

"Hi. Listen, do you want to—"

"Sorry, I can't. Bye!")

Flor wasn't talking about Hercules, but about a third-year at her college named Barney Chaskel, a boy she hadn't pegged for a Bettencourter because, "Well, he's sort of low-key and makes fun of his own obsession with conspiracy theories and . . . he's sweet."

"Sweet?!" came at her from every corner of the room. Day asked it loudest, more with curiosity than incredulity. Hilde said: "Flor, aren't you going too far?"

"Look . . . on the way over I actually thought about presenting all this as if I'd seduced him on purpose to get info, but the truth is I didn't know Chaskel was a Bettencourter until this morning! I said I had to run to a Wench meeting, and he was like . . . surely not the Homely Wenches? And I was like, yeah, the very same, and then he went, 'How funny, I'm a Bettencourter . . .'"

"'How funny' . . . ? This 'Barney Chaskel' thinks our decades of enmity are just a bit of fun . . . ?" Theo wondered aloud.

"Flor," Marie said, in sepulchral tones. "So far this is the tale of our enemies evolving into ever more superficially pleasing forms. You mentioned that this was also a tale of possibility?"

"Flordeliza, if there's a twist introduce it now or there might be beats in store for you . . ." Ed added.

But Flor did have something good for them after all. She'd followed Barney Chaskel to Bettencourt Society headquarters and had seen him punch in the code that let him into the building. That was why she was late: She'd seen the sequence, but not its exact components. So she'd cased the joint, observed that the Bettencourters left through another door, and given herself three chances to repeat the code Barney had punched in.

"Babe," Willa said. "BABE. Third time lucky?"

Flor laughed and said: "Second."

Grainne and Willa hooted and jumped on her, but Hilde, Ed, and Theo were unmoved.

"There's no need for us to enter Bettencourt premises," Hilde declared.

Theo agreed: "The Wenches made the ultimate gesture years ago."

"No, come on, come on, we've got this so it'd basically be folly and sin not to use it!" Grainne said.

But Ed backed up Hilde and Theo: "Yeah, it'd be nice to fuck with the Bettencourters' heads a bit more, but I'd rather we move on, concentrate on building ourselves up. We need more pieces for *The Wench* . . . weren't we just about to hear an idea from you, Day?"

"I think we should go in," Day said. Everybody went quiet, but her words were mainly for Marie, who hadn't expressed an opinion either way. "I think we should go in and do a book swap."

"A book swap?" Marie echoed.

"Yup. I'm betting the Bettencourters don't have many,

or maybe even any, books by female authors on their bookshelves. And speaking collectively we don't have that many male authors on our own shelves—"

"Yes, but that's personal preference and our desire to honor what's ours, Day," Hilde said.

"I know," said Day. "And I do. But I want to read everything. When it comes to books and who can put things in them and get things out of them, it's all ours. And all theirs too. So we go in, see what books they have, take a few and replace them with a few of ours."

"No muss, no fuss," Theo said, grudgingly.

"I'd have voted to trash the place but I don't care what we do as long as we do something," Willa said. "I suppose that would've wrecked Flor's budding romance, though."

Flor covered her face but didn't deny being keen on Barney Chaskel.

Marie spoke up: "I do want us to do something. I have been waiting for a chance to do something to the Bettencourt Society, ever since a Bettencourter used me as a human shield on my very first Thursday at this university . . ." She stared out of Day's window and into the very moment of the incident. Her face was transfigured with wrath.

"Another guy was chasing him," Grainne whispered to Ed and Flor. "He said he never thought the other guy would hit a girl . . ."

"So I am in favor of Dayang's proposal," Marie concluded. "All others in favor of Dayang's proposal, raise your hands." Day raised her hand, as did Flor, Grainne, Willa, and Theo. Theo said she was only coming along to make sure they did it right.

DAY FOUND Hercules Demetriou sitting at her usual desk in the library. Rather than talk to him she went to his usual desk, which was unoccupied, and set up her laptop there. He looked over at her three times; she looked over at him once. Just once, and he came over. Argh, was it that pitifully obvious?

He drew a chair up to her desk and leaned on the corner of it. Everything about him was dark, delicious, fluid— that gaze especially. If she moved her arm just a little it'd touch his. There was an envelope in his hand.

"Listen, I heard you like John Waters," he said.

"I do," she said. "So?"

His sister ran a cinema in Stockwell . . . he described it as "pocket-sized." Big Sis had given Hercules two tickets for a screening of *Female Trouble*, and . . .

"No."

"Are you sure?"

"Are you finding it hard to believe that a girl wouldn't want to go and see a film with someone as amazing as you?"

He drew back, but didn't retreat. Instead he subjected her to a deeper look. The first to break the gaze would lose, so she didn't blink. "I was just finding it hard to believe that a John Waters fan wouldn't want a ticket to *Female Trouble*," he said, then dropped his gaze, laughing a little. "Here. Take two." He put the envelope down in front of her and went back to his desk.

Then he came back: "Dayang, can I ask you something?"

Oh my God. "If you must."

"Why did you come here?"

"Here?"

"Here, to this university."

She thought of Professor Chaudhry, one of the professors who'd interviewed her, and how he'd said he liked the connections he could see her making in her mind, and the way that she tried to tend them so that they thrived. Nobody had ever said anything like that to her before. Usually it was "Aren't you overthinking things, Day?" But a gardener growing thoughts—she liked that.

Hercules tired of waiting for Day to answer him: "Didn't you want to see who else was here?" he asked. "I know that's part of the reason why I came. It's the reason why I go to most parties."

Parties? She couldn't stop herself from smiling. "OK . . . same."

"So," he said. "I'm here. You're here. You find me off-putting at the moment, but why don't you try treating me like a person? You might like me."

"Bettencourter," she said.

His eyebrows shot up and he said: "Ah." Not an enlightened "ah." If anything he was more puzzled.

"It's Lent term. Aren't you supposed to be looking for someone to bring to that dinner of yours?"

The penny dropped. "You're a Homely Wench, aren't you?"

"And proud."

He gathered up his things and left the library, shaking his head and muttering something she didn't catch. Day took the cinema tickets out of the envelope and texted the date on them to Pepper:

Female Trouble in London yes or yes??

YESSSSSS

————————

THE BETTENCOURTERS were well-read in various directions; that's what their bookshelves said about them, anyway. Plenty of stimulating-looking books, less than 10 percent of which were authored by women. The substitutions were made by torchlight, as nobody thought it was a good idea to switch on the house lights at four a.m. and risk some passing Bettencourter coming round to see if any of his brethren was up for another drink. (The keys to the rooms of the house were on a hook beside the light switch in the entrance hall, so the girls peeped into the Bettencourt Society drinks cabinet too. It was more of a walk-in closet than a drinks cabinet, a closet vertically stocked with hard liquor from floor to ceiling. There were even little ladders for more convenient perusal. Day had never seen anything like it.)

Flor, Day, Willa, Marie, and Theo unloaded their rucksacks and filled them again with books from the Bettencourt shelves. Not having read any of the books she was taking, Day made her exchanges based on thoughts the titles or authors' names set in motion. She exchanged two Edith Wharton novels for two Henry James novels, Lucia Berlin's short stories for John Cheever's, Elaine Dundy's *The Dud Avocado* for Dany Laferrière's *I Am a Japanese Writer*, Dubravka Ugrešić's

Lend Me Your Character for Gogol's *How the Two Ivans Quarreled and Other Stories*, Maggie Nelson's *Jane: A Murder* for Capote's *In Cold Blood*, Lisa Tuttle's *The Pillow Friend* for *The Collected Ghost Stories of M. R. James*. She stopped keeping track: If she kept track she'd be there all night. But she left with what looked like a quality haul, and so did the others. The Wenches had their noses in books that were new to them for weeks. They waited for some challenge to be issued from Bettencourt headquarters, but none came forth. The boys didn't seem to have noticed that their library had been compromised. Maybe a drink swap would have been more effective.

FLOR AND BARNEY of the Bettencourters really seemed to be becoming ever more of an item; it was gross, but the Wenches acted as if they didn't mind so as not to encourage a Romeo and Juliet complex. Besides, Theo summed up what all the Wenches were feeling about the Bettencourt book haul when she looked up from the pages of Kim Young-ha's *Your Republic Is Calling You* and said resentfully: "They have good taste, though."

HERCULES DEMETRIOU didn't show his face at the *Female Trouble* screening. That didn't matter; there was popcorn and Pepper and so much divine and diabolical mayhem onscreen, plus Cookie Mueller telling it exactly like it is: *Just 'cause we're pretty everybody's jealous!*

"Were you expecting to see someone?" Pepper asked her, as they walked out of the cinema. "You kept looking round."

She lied that she'd been watching the audience. It was a plausible lie because she was the kind of person who watched audiences.

HERCULES WAS WAITING on the staircase that led up to her room, his legs stretched all along the step, his feet jammed into two slots in the banister. He was reading one of the books Flor had left at Bettencourt headquarters: *for colored girls who have considered suicide / when the rainbow is enuf.* When he saw her he scrambled to his feet and hit his head on the stone ceiling. She felt his pain, so she patted his shoulder as he went by; he took her hand and followed her up the stairs until she came to a halt.

"What?"

"Is this yours?" he asked, holding up the book.

"No."

"But you've read it?"

"Yup."

"It's great, isn't it? It sort of rocks you . . . reading it is sort of like reading from a cradle hung up in the trees, and the trees rock you with such sorrow, and as the volume turns up you realize that the trees are rocking you whilst deciding whether to let you live or die, and they're sorry because they've decided to smash you to pieces . . ."

"But then you're put back together again, in a wholly different order . . ."

"And it hurts so much you don't know if the new order will work."

"It'll heal. It has to hurt before it heals, don't you think?"

He was smiling at her again. He hadn't let go of her hand yet. It was nice until he invited her to the Bettencourt dinner. She hesitated for a surprising length of time (surprising to her, anyway) before she said: "Herc, I can't."

He wasn't daunted; she'd shortened his name, that had to mean something! "You're a Homely Wench. I'm not saying I understand all that that entails, but I don't think the Bettencourters and the Wenches are that far apart in the way they see things anymore. Laughs, snacks, and cotching, yeah? And we have a journal too: a journal read only by us. Can't we read each other's? I know you want me to pretend you don't look like anything much, but you're a beauty. Sorry. You are. Just come to the dinner, come and meet the Bettencourters and actually talk to them, come and meet the people they think are beauties too. We're not like last century's Bettencourt Society. I guarantee you'll be surprised."

They both laughed at this closing speech of his. She didn't want to blush but blushed anyway, and he saw that. He thought she was a beauty! What a wonderful delusion. And she liked the idea of the Societies reading each other's journals. She could just about imagine putting on a slinky dress and going along to this little dinner, making the acquaintance of his brothers in charisma and the boys and girls they'd brought along. But she could also picture the looks that some of the diners would give other diners, the words that'd be murmured when the subject of evaluation left the room. *Really . . . her?* Or *Nice, nice.* Both possibilities made her feel weary. With boys there was a fundamental assumption that they had a right to be there—not always, but more often than not. With girls, *Why her?* came up so quickly.

"I can see you believe you lot are new and improved, but to have this dinner where each of you brings one person to show off to the others . . ."

"Isn't that what all socializing's like when you're in a relationship?" Hercules asked, resting his chin on her palm. This boy.

"Yes, well, I don't know about that—"

"Never had a boyfriend? Girlfriend?"

She took her hand back, stood on tiptoe, and whispered into his ear: "Ask someone else."

"You'll be jealous," Hercules whispered back.

Day waved him away and climbed the last few steps to her door. "I won't. Goodnight, Herc."

He cupped his hands around his mouth and walked backward down the stairs, calling out: "You like me. She likes me. She doesn't know why and she can't believe it, but Dayang Sharif likes me!"

THE HOMELY Wench Society's final meeting of Lent term was held in Flordeliza Castillo's room at Trinity. Plans for a trip to Neuschwanstein Castle had been finalized and there was no real business left to discuss, so Dvořák's *The Noon Witch* was playing, Grainne was sitting on the windowsill puffing away at an electronic cigarette with a face mask on ("A ghost! A well-moisturized ghost!"), Flor was lying with her head in Day's lap having *Orlando Furioso* read to her, Ed and Marie were mixing drinks, and Theo carried Grainne's to the window and then back to Flor's desk as Grainne's smoke went down the wrong way and she staggered over to Ed, sputtering: "Bettencourters incoming . . . Bettencourter invasion!"

Flor must have been in on it. Must have. Her room wasn't easy to find. As a matter of fact, who's to say that the events of that historic afternoon weren't the culmination of a scheme Flor and Barney had hatched between them way back in September?

THE SMALL but lionhearted Homely Wench Society gathered at Flordeliza Castillo's window and looked down upon the mass of menfolk below, many of them bearing beverages and assorted foodstuffs. At their head, in place of their president, was Hercules of Stockwell, waving a white flag with much vigor and good cheer.

dornička and the st. martin's day goose

Matko, matičko! řekněte,
nač s sebou ten nůž béřete?
"Mother, dear mother, tell me, do—
why have you brought that knife with you?"

—FROM "THE GOLDEN SPINNING WHEEL,"
KAREL JAROMÍR ERBEN

Well, Dornička met a wolf on Mount Radhošt'.

Actually let's try to speak of things as they are: It was not a wolf she met, but something that had recently consumed a wolf and was playing about with the remnants. The muzzle, tail, and paws appeared in the wrong order. Dornička couldn't see very far ahead of her in the autumn dusk, so she smelled it first, an odor that made her think *gangrene*, though she'd never smelled that. The closest thing she could realistically liken this smell to was sour, overripe fruit. And then she saw a fur that buzzed with flies, pinched her nostrils together and thought: *Ah, why? I don't like this.* She'd gone up the mountain to look at a statue of a hypothetical pagan god; she'd taken a really long look at him and for her he remained hypothetical. But it had been a good walk up a sunlit path encircled by bands of brown and gray; it had been like walking an age in a tree's life, that ring of color in the trunk's cross section. As she walked she'd been thinking about city life, and how glad she was that she didn't live one. According to Dornička, cities are fueled by the listless agony of workers providing services to other workers who barely acknowledge those services. You can't tell Dornička otherwise; she's been to a few cities and she's seen it with her own eyes, so she knows. City people only talk to people they're already acquainted with, so as to avoid strangers speaking to them with annoying over-familiarity or in words that aren't immediately comprehensible. And everybody in the city is just so terribly bored. Show a city dweller wonders and they'll yawn, or take a photo and send it to somebody else with a message that says "Wow." The last time Dornička had been to Prague she'd made some glaring error as she bought a metro ticket—she still didn't know what exactly her error had been . . . an old-fashioned turn of phrase, perhaps—and her goddaughter Alžběta had clicked her tongue and called her a country mouse. Instead of feeling embarrassed Dornička had felt proud and said: "Come and visit your country mouse at home sometime." So Alžběta was coming. Her arrival was a week away, and she was bringing her own daughter, Klaudie. Dornička's anticipation of this visit was such that she'd been having trouble sleeping. Klaudie and Alžběta had visited before, had filled her house with hairpins and tone-deaf duets inspired by whatever was on the radio, and she longed to have them by her again. Dornička liked her work and her friends and the town she lived in. She liked that she made enough of a difference to the education of her former pupils for them to write to her and sometimes even visit her with news from time to time. But she really couldn't get used to being a widow (she would've liked to know if there was anybody who got used to that state of affairs) and didn't often feel as if she had anything much to look forward to. If it hadn't been for Alžběta and Klaudie's forthcoming visit she might have succumbed to the "wolf" at once. But since she had to live for at least another week she pinched her nostrils together and thought: *Ah, why?* Like it or not the "wolf" was standing there in her path so that she couldn't get by. As for "why," it must have been due to her red cape. Our Dornička had decided that once you reach your late fifties you can wear whatever you want and nobody can say anything to you about it. Looks like Mount Radhošt' is different, eh, Dornička?

THE "WOLF" approached, paying no attention to Dornička's repeated requests that it do no such thing. It pushed back the hood of her cape.

"Oh!" said the "wolf," and shuffled back so that it was standing on the side of the path, out of her way.

Somewhat offended, Dornička stared over her shoulder and into the "wolf's" glassy eyes.

"Am I that bad?" she asked.

"Not at all, not at all, no need to take that tone," the "wolf" demurred. "I just thought you were young, that's all."

"Nope, just short," Dornička said, pulling her hood back up.

"Yes, I see that now, so please be on your way."

"But surely you can't be him," Dornička declared, with a cutting glance.

"Him?"

"The Big Bad Wolf, of course."

The "wolf" tugged its whiskers with an air of self-consciousness. "The truth is, that fellow is modeled on me . . ."

"Wasn't he killed by the woodchopper?"

"Yes, yes, but go back to the beginning and there he is again, ready for action. This is the beginning again, and I thought you were her. In a way it's good that you're not her. The wolf gets to eat a lot before she comes along . . ."

"*She* being . . . ?"

"Never mind, never mind—I'll just wait for the next one," the "wolf" muttered. And Dornička wondered what on earth could be inside that rotting skin.

"Good . . . you do that," Dornička replied, and then, a few steps down the path, thinking of "the next one," she sighed and returned to the "wolf." "But what is it you need, exactly? You can't be hungry; you just ate an entire wolf."

The "wolf" shrugged its shoulders and said: "You wouldn't understand."

The forlornness of its voice prompted Dornička to coax: "Come now, you can tell me."

"Life," said the "wolf." "I need more life . . . do you think it's easy for the seasons to change here amidst all this stone?"

"I see," said Dornička. "It must take a lot."

"I almost have enough, but I just need a crumb more. Something juicy and young."

Ah, whatever you are, you really stink. The "wolf's" haphazard configuration made her own feel loose; she tapped her thighs and forearms. They hadn't changed. She'd scowled whenever her Tadeáš had slapped her bum and chuckled, "Built to last," but for now that was a blessing. A group of hikers strolled by; as they realized they were witnessing the encounter of age-old adversaries they booed the "wolf" and urged Dornička on toward her fated triumph, and would have taken photos if it weren't for the fact that Dornička refused to drop the hood and reveal her side profile. The "wolf" was happy to pose . . .

"What an irregular costume . . . interesting!" The hikers moved on, but one of their party, a rosy-cheeked girl who looked to be sixteen or so, knelt on the ground to retie her shoelaces. Dornička watched the "wolf" stir.

"What can I do to help you change the season here?" she asked, snapping her fingers in front of the "wolf's" snout.

A tongue darted out across a flaccid muzzle. "Send me something juicy and young."

"Then I will," Dornička promised. "But you can't go after anyone. Just be patient and I'll send you something nice. OK?"

"OK . . ." said the "wolf." "But just to be sure . . ."

It raised its paw and dealt her a staggering blow to the

hip; by rights this should have shattered the bone but it didn't. It just hurt an awful lot. "That should do it . . ."

The "wolf" padded up the mountainside and folded its carcass into a rocky crevice, awaiting the arrival of the morsel Dornička had agreed to send.

Dornička limped home, and from there to the emergency room of the local hospital, where she was assured that no part of her body had been sprained or broken. But a bruise grew over her left hipbone; it grew three-dimensional, pushing its way out of her frame like a king-sized wart. The bruise wasn't colored like a bruise either—it was a florid pink, like a knob of cured ham. At times she felt it contract and expand as if it were suckling at her hip joint. The sight and feel of that made her nauseous, but a doctor scanned and prodded both Dornička and her lump and said that Dornička was in fine fettle and the lump would fall off on its own. When Dornička was fully clothed it looked as if she was pregnant or experiencing extreme and left hip–specific weight gain. People remarked upon it, so the day before Alžběta and Klaudie arrived, Dornička took a carving knife, put her left foot on the edge of the bathtub, and cut the ham-like knob off. As she'd suspected the severance was painless and actually relieved the tension she'd been feeling, as if she was a patient in an era in which bloodletting was still believed to be a procedure that brought balance to the body's humors. She treated the wound, wrapped gauze bandages around it, washed and dried the heavy, oval-shaped lump of flesh. Was it fat, muscle, a mix of both? She pushed her finger into the center of the oval. Soft, but elasticity was minimal. Like lukewarm porridge. Lukewarm . . . *Ah, this thing had better not be alive.* Of course it wasn't, of course it wasn't. She thought about weighing it and decided not to. She also thought about taking the severed lump to the "wolf" but that would be a wasted journey, since this flesh didn't meet the "wolf's" requirements. She buried it in the garden beneath an ash tree. Then she put her considerable talent for making nice things to eat to Alžběta and Klaudie's service, simmering and baking and braising through the night.

KLAUDIE had nineteen years behind her and who knew how many ahead; her eyes sparkled and did not see. Sometimes she used a cane, sometimes not, depending on her own confidence and the pace of the crowd around her. In Ostrava she didn't use her cane at all. That autumn she went around Dornička's pantry lifting lids and opening cupboard doors: "What is that delicious smell? I want a slice right now!" Alžběta and Dornička served up portions of everything that was available, tasting as they went along, but Klaudie sniffed each plate and dismissed its contents. Then she went and stood under Dornička's ash tree and drew such deep and voluptuous breaths that Dornička began to have the kind of misgivings one doesn't put into words.

"Come, Klaudie," she called. "I need your help with something."

The project Dornička invented wasn't especially time-consuming, but it was better than nothing. Klaudie took up a power drill and Dornička a handsaw and ruler and they made a small, simple but sturdy wooden chest, and when they had finished Alžběta fetched out her own bag of tools and fitted the wooden chest with a lock—"Free of charge, free of charge, and I hope it holds your treasures for you for years to come, dear Dornička," she said, giving her godmother a big kiss before turning in for the night. Even though the locked chest was empty Dornička slept with her fingers wrapped around the key that fit its lock; that hand made a fist over her stomach.

DORNIČKA was one of twelve caterers who made meals for the town's coal miners. Alžběta and Klaudie helped her deliver her carloads of appetizing nutrition; they were well-beloved at the mine and there was much laughter and chatter as they stacked lunchboxes on the break room counter for later. Several fathers had Klaudie in mind for a daughter-in-law and sang their sons' praises, but most of the others warned her against chaining herself to a local: "Travel the world if you can, Klaudie—go over and under and in between, and if there happens to be a man or three on the way, that's well and good, but afterward just leave him where you found him!"

Klaudie listened to both sides; these were people who felt the movement of the earth far better than she, and when she visited Dornička she thought of them often as they moved miles beneath her feet. Tremors that merely rumbled through her soles broke the miners' bodies. They knew risk, and when they encouraged her in one direction or another they had already looked ahead and taken many of her possible losses into account. There was one among them who kept his mouth shut around her, as he was a coarse young man who didn't want to say the wrong thing. When Klaudie spoke to him he answered "Eh," and "Mmm," with unmistakable nervousness, and she liked him the best. Dornička favored candlelight over electric light, and as Klaudie went about Dornička's living room lighting candles in the evening the wavering passage of light across her eyelids felt just like the silence of that boy at the coal mine. Dornička invited the boy to dinner but the invitation agitated him and he refused it. Alžběta, whose snobbery was actually outrageous, said that the boy knew some things just aren't meant to be.

". . . . OR these things just happen in their own time," Dornička told her, partly to annoy her and partly because it was true.

ALL SOULS' DAY came and the three women went to the churchyard where so many who shared their family names were buried. They tidied the autumn leaves into garland-like arrangements around the graves, had friendly little chats with each family member, focusing on each one's known areas of interest, and all in all it was a comfortable afternoon. There was a little sadness, but no feelings of desolation on either side, as far as the women could tell, anyway. In a private moment with Tadeáš, Dornička told him about the "wolf" that had punched her and the lump that had grown and been buried, and she told him about Klaudie going on and on about a delicious smell and then suddenly shutting up about the smell, and she told him she'd found telltale signs of interrupted digging beneath her ash tree.

Tadeáš's disapproval came through to her quite clearly: *You shouldn't have promised that creature anything.*

But she couldn't regret her promise when it had been a choice between that or the "wolf" waiting for the next one.

But how are you going to keep this promise, my Dornička?

Don't know, don't know . . .

Tadeáš relented, and it came to her that the very least she could do was dig the lump up herself and put the new wooden chest to use. That night Alžběta took Klaudie to visit old school friends of hers and Dornička did her digging and held the lump up to her face, looking for nibble marks or other indicators of consumption. A dead earthworm had filled the hole she'd poked into the lump, but apart from that the meat was still fresh and whole. In fact it was pinker than before. Klaudie had described the smell as that of yeast and honey, like some sort of bun, so Dornička did her best to think of it as a bun, locked it up in the chest and put the locked chest on the top shelf of the wardrobe beside the hat box that contained her wedding hat. In the days that followed she would often find Klaudie in her bedroom "borrowing" spritzes of perfume and the like. A couple of times she even caught Klaudie trying on her red cape; each time brought Dornička closer to a heart attack than she'd ever been before. But the key never left her person, so all she needed was a chance to build a little bonfire and put the lump out of reach for good.

THAT YEAR it was Klaudie who chose the St. Martin's Day goose. The three women went to market and Klaudie asked Pankrác the goose farmer which of his flock was the greediest—"We want one that'll eat from morning 'til night . . ." All Pankrác's customers wanted the same characteristics in their St. Martin's Day goose, but Pankrác had his reasons for wishing to be in Dornička's good graces, so when her goddaughter's daughter asked which goose was the greediest he was honest and handed over the goose in question. The goose allowed Klaudie to hand-feed her some scraps of lettuce and a few pieces of apple, but seemed baffled by this turn of events. She honked a few times, and Alžběta interpreted: "Me? Me . . . ? Surely there must be some mistake . . ."

"Thanks, Pankrác . . . I'll save you the neck . . ." Dornička spread newspaper all along the backseat of her car and placed the caged goose on top of the newspaper. The goose honked all the way home; they'd got a noisy one, but Dornička didn't mind. When Klaudie said she felt sorry for the goose and wished they'd just gone to a supermarket and picked a packaged one, Dornička rolled her eyes. "This city child of yours," she said to Alžběta, and to

Klaudie: "You won't be saying that once you've tasted its liver."

The goose quieted down a bit once she'd been installed in Dornička's back garden. She would only eat from Klaudie's hand, so it became Klaudie's job to feed her. It's well-known that geese don't like people, so the companionship that arose between Klaudie and the goose was something of an oddity. Klaudie spoke to the goose as she pecked at her feed, and stroked the goose's feathers so that they were sleek. Dornička harbored a mistrust of the goose, since she pecked hard at the ground in a particular patch of the garden—the patch where Dornička's infernal lump had been buried. No wonder Klaudie and the goose got along; maybe they had long chats about all the things they could smell. The goose was extraordinarily greedy too, Dornička's greediest yet: "Eating us out of house and home," Dornička grumbled when Klaudie knocked on the kitchen door to ask if there were any more scraps.

Alžběta was more concerned about Klaudie's fondness for the goose. "She might not let us kill it," she said. "And you know I like my goose meat, Dornička!"

"It's all right, it's all right," Dornička said. "Trust me, that goose's days are numbered."

She caught Klaudie in her bedroom again and almost fought with her.

"For the last time, Klaudie, what are you doing in here?"

Klaudie fluttered her eyelashes and murmured something about scraps. *Any scraps for the goose, Dornička . . . ?*

That gave Dornička an idea.

Again, let's not dress anything up in finery, let's speak of things as they are: While Klaudie and Alžběta were sleeping, Dornička fed her lump to the goose. The flesh was gobbled up without hesitation and then the goose began to run around the garden in circles, around and around. This was dizzying to watch, so Dornička didn't watch. She dropped the key inside the empty chest and poured herself a celebratory shot of *slivovice.* Good riddance to bad rubbish.

THE NEXT DAY Klaudie was bold enough to bring the empty chest to Dornička and ask what had been in it.

"Kids don't need to know. Please feed the goose again, Klaudie."

But Klaudie didn't want to. She said the goose had changed. "She doesn't honk at all anymore, and she seems aware," she said.

"Aware?"

Dornička went to see for herself; she took a bucket of waterfowl feed out to the back garden.

The goose appeared to have almost doubled in size overnight.

Her eyes were bigger too.

She looked at Dornička as if she was about to call her by name.

Dornička threw the bucket on the ground and walked back into the house very quickly.

"See what I mean?" Klaudie said.

IT WAS THE EVE of St. Martin's Day, November 10th. The first snow of the winter was close by. Dornička abandoned reason for a few moments, just the amount of time required to switch on her laptop and order another red cape. Child-sized this time. Express delivery. When it arrived she left it in the back garden with the waterfowl feed and said prayerfully: "What will be will be."

SHE LEFT THE BACK door open that night, and when the St. Martin's Day goose came up the stairs and into her bedroom, she wasn't taken by surprise, not even when she saw that the goose was wearing the red cape and had Dornička's car keys in her beak.

"Thank you, goose," she said. "I appreciate you."

She drove the goose to the foot of Mount Radhošt' and watched her waddle away up the mountain path, a bead of scarlet ascending into ash.

Thank you, goose. I appreciate you.

Alžběta the goose-meat lover didn't even complain that much in the morning. She just glared at Klaudie and told her to forget about choosing the Christmas carp.

freddy barrandov checks . . . in?

As I was saying, I'm an inadequate son. I didn't really notice this until I reached the age my father had been when he was imprisoned for repairing the broken faces of clock towers without authorization. He'd incurred the wrath of those who require certain things not to work at all. That's what the broken clock towers had been designated as: remembrances of a civil war that stopped time at various locations scattered across my father's country. Fixing the mechanisms seemed political, though it was impossible to agree on the exact meaning of the gesture. When my dad saw his first splintered clockface he just thought it was a proud and beautiful work that, if restored, would take the mortal sting out of being told how late you are, or

how long you've been waiting, or how much longer you'll
have to wait.

MY MOTHER affirms life in her own way: She did some of
her most thorough affirmation on behalf of a government-
sponsored literary award that posed as a prize sponsored
by a company that made typewriters. One year the writer
chosen to win the award declined without giving a reason
and asked that her name not be mentioned in connection
with the award at all. Unfazed, my mother congratulated
the next best writer on his win, but was almost laughed
off the phone line: "It's sweet of you to try this, but everybody knows my book isn't that good," he said. He
named another writer and suggested the prize go to her,
but the recommended writer didn't fancy it either. There
had to be a winner, so my mother went through all the
shortlisted writers but it was "Thanks but no thanks" and
"Oh but I couldn't possibly" all round, so she went back to
the originally selected winner and made some threats
that caused the woman to reconsider and humbly accept
her prize.

Even though all went on as before, Mum's developed a
sort of prejudice against writers; there are behaviors she
now calls "writerly," but I think she actually means un-

cooperative. Anyway, my mother agreed with my father about the clockfaces they saw; she wanted to organize the ruin away. So the newlyweds had worked at this project together, though he never allowed anybody to even suggest that she'd been involved, taking all the blame (and speculation, and, in some quarters, esteem) onto his own shoulders. In court my father pleaded that he'd thought he was demonstrating good citizenship by providing a public service free of charge, but was asked why he'd provided this public service anonymously and at dead of night . . . why work under those conditions if you believe that what you're doing is above reproach? And then all he could say was, *Right, I see. When you put it like that it looks bad.*

Another thing the law didn't like: He'd broken into the clock towers, and left them open to people seeking shelter, attracting all sorts of new elements into moneyed neighborhoods and driving established elements out into shabbier neighborhoods so that it was no longer clear what kind of person you were going to find in any part of the city.

MY FATHER got a three-year prison sentence and came out of it mostly in one piece due to his being a useful person; a sort of live-in handyman. He gained experience in tackling a variety of interesting technical mishaps that rarely occur in small households, and now works alongside my mother at a niche hotel in Cheshire . . . Hotel Glissando, it's called, and it's niche in a way that'll take a while to describe. Dad's Chief Maintenance Officer there. He more or less states his own salary, as the management team (headed by my mother) hasn't yet found anyone else willing and able to handle all the things that suddenly need fixing at Hotel Glissando.

As Frederick Barrandov Junior, there was an expectation that I'd follow in Frederick Barrandov Senior's footsteps, that at some point I'd leave my job as a nursery school teacher and join Hotel Glissando's maintenance team.

A MONTH or so after I'd turned thirty-three I learned that Mum had assured the hotel's reclusive millionaire owner that I'd join the team before the year was out.

She broke this news to me over lunch.

"Where do you see yourself in ten years' time?" she asked.

My answer: "Not sure, but maybe on a beach reading a really good mystery. Not a murder mystery, but the kind where the narrator has to find out what year it is and why he was even born . . ."

Would I have answered differently if I'd known that

Mum intended this to be a proper talk about my future? Probably not.

Mum was livid.

"Sitting on a beach reading a good mystery novel? Sitting on a beach reading a good mystery novel?? If that's the height of your ambition you and I are finished, Freddy."

"Come come, Mother . . . How can we ever be finished? I'm your son."

"I'm going to give you one more chance," she said. "What are your plans for the next few years? What motivates you?"

I spoke of the past instead of the future; a past, it turned out, I had neither lived for myself nor been told about. I remembered a sign that read REBEL TOWN, but not in English. I remembered people striding around with cutlasses, and a nursemaid who was a tiger—her lullabies were purred softly, and the melodies clicked when they caught against her teeth: *Sleep for a little while now, little one, or sleep forever . . .*

"That was my childhood, not yours," my mother snapped. "Yours is a pitiful existence. I had you followed for six months and all you did apart from turn up to play in a sandpit with infants was go to galleries, bars, the cinema, and a couple of friends' houses. What kind of person are you? I spoke to your weed dealer and he said you don't even buy that much. You are without virtue and without serious vice. Do you really think you can go on like this?"

"What shall I do then?"

"You'll start working at Hotel Glissando next week."

"Will I? Can't somebody else do it?"

"No, Freddy. It's got to be you."

THIS WAS SEXISM; my younger sister Odette is much handier than me. I pointed this out, but my mother seemed not to hear and proposed that I shadow Dad at the hotel for a few months in order to acquire the skills I lacked. I told Mum that I wouldn't and couldn't leave Pumpkin Seed Class at this crucial moment in the development of their psyches. Mum told me her career was at stake. A bright-eyed, bushy-tailed, and unscrupulous woman who was just below Mum in the chain of command was gunning for her job, subtly and disastrously leaving my mother out of the loop so that she missed crucial directives and was left unaware of changes to the numerous hourly schedules and procedures that it was her task to oversee and complete. I could see my mother's stress as she spoke: It was there in her hair, which usually looks thoroughly done to a state-regulated standard. But now there were knots in my mother's hair. I'd never seen that before.

———————

HAVING SAID I'd sleep on my decision I went over to my sister's flat and we talked all night. We both like the Glissando well enough. Discretion is its main feature: You go there to hide. The furnishings are a mixture of dark reds and deep purples. Moving through the lobby is like crushing grapes and plums and being bathed in the resultant wine. There are three telephone booths in the lobby. Their numbers are automatically withheld and they're mainly used for lies. Once as I was leaving the hotel after running an errand for my dad I saw a man in a trench coat stagger into one of those phone booths. He had what looked like a steak knife sticking out of his chest and must've trailed some blood into the booth and lost a lot more at quite a rapid rate thereafter, though I didn't see much of this. Blood's a near-perfect match for the color scheme— each drop is smoothly stirred in.

I lingered in order to provide assistance; the man with the knife sticking out of his chest picked up the phone, dialed, and explained to somebody on the other end that he was working late. "Heh—yes, well, save me a slice!" His voice was so well modulated that if I hadn't been able to see him I wouldn't have entertained even the faintest suspicion that there was a knife in him. Then he phoned an ambulance and collapsed. That man impressed me . . . he impressed me. As he waited for the paramedics his eyes darkened and cleared, darkened and cleared, but he gripped the knife and his grip held firm. He looked honored, extraordinarily honored, seeming to care more for that which tore his flesh than he did for the flesh itself, embracing the blade as if it were some combination of marvel and disaster, the kind that usually either confers divinity or is a proof of it. To the boy gawping through the glass it seemed that this man strove to be a worthy vessel, to live on and on at knifepoint, its brilliance enmeshed with his guts. If he was a man without regrets then he was the first I'd seen. And I remember thinking: *Well, all right.* I wouldn't mind ending up like that.

AT THE FRONT desk of the Glissando, guests can request and receive anything, anything at all. Odette was there when a man with very bad nerves had asked for a certificate guaranteeing that the building's foundations were unassailable; this man was convinced that he was pursued by a burrowing entity that lived beneath any house he lived in and raised his floors by a foot every year, the entity's long-term goal being to raise his quarry so high that he could never again descend into the world of his fellow human beings. Our mother made no comment on this man's convictions but provided him with a certificate stating that there never had been and never could be room for any form of other dwelling beneath the Hotel Glissando. The only thing a hotel guest may not ask for is, for some reason, an iguana-skin wallet. The woman who requested one was told to "Get out of here and never come back." And as the doorman threw the ex-guest's luggage out onto the street he said: "An iguana-skin wallet? Where do you think you are?"

As far as we know, that's the only time a Glissando guest's request hasn't been fulfilled. For years Odette and I have felt that our parents' dedication to taking care of Hotel Glissando's guests borders on the unnatural. Odette has told me that in some way the hotel and its guests are like the broken clockfaces, except that Mum and Dad are compensated for their work instead of being punished.

Even so: "They've given the best years of their lives to that place, and that's their own business—but now they want to throw my life in too?" That was how I put it to Odette. Odette said she felt I was overlooking something: For as long as we've known our parents, my mum's professional value has been dependent on my dad's. She's been treated as a facilitator for his talents for so long that she's come to believe that's what she's here for. Mum brought

Barrandov Senior to Hotel Glissando, so by hook or by crook she'll bring Barrandov Junior there too.

"I don't know . . . if I give in to this won't I be setting that image in stone? Is that really good for Mum?"

Odette's eyes twinkled. She said she thought I'd actually ruin the image, since there was no way I could match up to Dad.

"Thanks, sis . . . many thanks . . ."

"I, however, *can* match up to Dad, and maybe even outdo him."

Was Odette's confidence well-founded? I thought so. She'd always wanted to learn all that Dad had wanted to teach us. And when we asked Dad which of us he'd prefer to work with he said: "Odette, obviously." My sister was making a killing as a self-employed plumber, but she gave all that up to be there for my parents. She had no regrets either: said she loved the work and could see why our parents were so committed to the Glissando. I asked her to elaborate and she became so emotional that it made me feel lonely.

I, ON THE other hand, lost my way for a while. Mum took to behaving as if I'd never even existed: "Imagine if I'd only had one child . . . one child who'd throw my life's work away in favor of Hayseed Class or whatever it's called," she told Odette. Dad and I spent Sunday evenings at the pub as usual, but it just wasn't the same. I hadn't realized how important it was for me to have both parents on my side. Mum did a lot for us when we were coming up. Just like all their other work, she and Dad split their share of raising us right down the middle, finding mostly trustworthy grown-ups to be with us when they couldn't, keeping track of all our permission slips, hobbies, obsessions, allergies (both faked and genuine), not to mention the growth spurts, mood swings, the bargaining for their attention, and the attempts to avoid their scrutiny. I remember Mum repeatedly telling us we had good hearts and good brains. When she said that we'd say "thanks" and it might have sounded as if we were thanking her for seeing us that way but actually we were thanking her for giving us whatever goodness was in us. She didn't believe I was giving my all to teaching and she was right. She wants to see good hearts and good brains put to proper use, but I'm not convinced that everybody ought to live like that, or even that everybody can.

AISHA TOLD me—what did she tell me, actually? What does she ever tell me? She's what people call an "up-and-coming" filmmaker; far more accustomed to showing than telling. So what did she show me? Plenty, but not everything. We live in the same building and met in the stairwell: I'd locked myself out and was waiting for my flatmate Pierre to come home. It was going to be a long time before he came home: You see, being a key part of the socialization process for Poppy Class is only Pierre's daytime identity. At weekends he turns into the lead singer for a band, Hear It Not, Duncan, and their gigs go on forever. Of course I couldn't get him on the phone, and it seemed every other friend who lived on our bus route was at the gig too, so I sat outside my front door going through all the business cards I'd ever been given and dialing the mobile numbers on them, getting voicemail each time since nobody likes surprise phone calls anymore.

Aisha walked past me as I was leaving somebody a rambling voicemail message about the time I was walking past a neighbor's front door, stuck my hand through the letterbox on a whim only to have that hand grabbed and firmly held by some unseen person on the other side of the door—that really happened, and I've never been so frightened or run so fast since. Aisha walked past and heard me saying this, and she smiled. She smiled. I'm a simple lad, unfortunately the kind that Aisha can't really smile at unless she wants a boyfriend. I told her I was locked out and did all I could to inspire pity; she asked me if I had a car and asked if we could go and pick up hitchhikers and take them to their destinations. She'd always wanted to do that, she said. "Yeah, me too!" I said. We drove up and down the A534 but couldn't persuade anybody to get into the car with us: Maybe we seemed too keen. We got back at dawn and Pierre had come home; I wonder what would've happened if he hadn't.

AISHA TOOK to knocking on my door as she went past, inviting me to screenings and more, but no matter what meeting time we agree on she arrives half an hour later than that, sometimes forty-five minutes late. I'd probably wait for an hour or longer but she mustn't ever discover that. Perseverance doesn't seem to move her: I only ever get to seduce her up to a very specific point. I've tried to think this through, but I only get as far with the thinking as I do with the seduction. When entwined, our bodies build the kind of blaze in which sensation overtakes sense—it becomes possible to taste sound—that half hiccup, half sigh that tells me she likes what my tongue is doing to her. And so we each take a little more of what we like and lust swells until, until she pulls away. No penetration permitted, no matter how naked we are or how good the stroking and sliding feels, no matter how delectably wet she is when I nudge her legs open with my knee. I look into her eyes and see craving there, but there's also what seems to be abhorrence. Then she breaks contact.

Could it be that nobody likes a man without ambition and everything is withheld from him until he changes his ways? Is A saving herself for some fictional character, Willow Rosenberg or fucking floppy-haired Theodore Lawrence or someone like that? Is there somebody else, somebody nonfictional? Is she doing this to make me tell her in words that I want her? I don't like saying that kind of thing. So for now, if she doesn't want to then I can't. This sounds completely obvious but I've heard stories, from men, from women, that demonstrate that that's not how it is for others. Consent is a downward motion, I think—a leap or a fall—and whether they'll admit it or not, even the most decisive people can find themselves unable to tell whether or not their consent was freely given. That inability to discover whether you jumped or were pushed brings about a deadened gaze and a downfall all its own.

PIERRE SAYS it sounds like Aisha "just doesn't want dick."

"So she prefers pussy?"

"Perhaps, but the only thing that concerns you in particular is that she doesn't want dick. I just mean . . . OK, so there's some guy, and he's absolutely desperate to get inside you. Maybe it's a bit off-putting?"

I can always count on Pierre to offer his honest opinion. Or to try to give me some sort of complex. Or both.

Here's the thing that keeps me from trying anything rash: Aisha's other passions expose her. She loves cinema so well that I can find her there, hints and clues in each of her favorites. I know whose insolent lip curl she imitates when she hears an order she has no intention of following, and I know who she's quoting when she drawls, *Oh, honey, when I lose my temper you can't find it anyplace!* Full carnal knowledge of this woman eludes me, true—yet I know her. Aisha used to want to write poetry, since she liked reading it. But the muse spake not unto her. Then she'd wanted to write prose, but had stopped bothering when she realized she couldn't bring herself to write about genitalia. "A real writer has to be able to write about the body. They have to. It's where we live."

So A's foible could simply be this: She doesn't want lust to be the one to lead me in. It may be that lust is a breathtaking traitor, the warden's daughter seen in the walled city at all hours of the night singing softly and teasing the air with a starlit swan's feather. Lust, the warden's daughter; a little feckless, perhaps, but not one to cause injury until the day her telescope shows her that troops are marching on the walled city. When darkness falls she slips through the sleeping streets, meets the foe at the city gates, and throws those gates wide open: *Take and use everything you want and burn the rest to the ground . . .*

. . . When it's all over no observer is able to settle on a motive for this brat's betrayal, illogical or otherwise. Historians dissect her claims that she was sleepwalking. Such are the deeds of lust, a child of our walled cities. But say whatever you want about her, she will not be denied. Or will she???

I DRIFTED into unemployment without really noticing; I hung around in the lobby of the Glissando so much I didn't have time to go to work. Somebody at the hotel might need some skill of mine and then I could rejoin the rest of my family and continue the Barrandov tradition of providing debatable necessities. But nobody had need of me. I watched my mother dashing to and fro muttering into a walkie-talkie and my dad and Odette striding about with their thumbs tucked into the vacant loops in their tool belts. Had I missed my chance? As I ran through my savings I decided to work on developing ambition at the same time as amusing myself. I stole expensive items and in the moment of acquisition found that I didn't want to keep them and couldn't be bothered to sell them. I returned them before anybody noticed they were gone. The trickiest and most pleasing endeavor (also the endeavor that required going up to London and applying the most detailed make-up and speaking with a Viennese accent that was perfect down to the pronunciation of the very last syllable) was the theft and fuss-free return of a diamond necklace from Tiffany's on Old Bond Street. I almost didn't put the necklace back, but Aisha didn't like it and I couldn't think of anybody else to give the thing to. The diamonds looked muddy. Upon stealing the necklace my first impulse was to give it a good wipe.

THERE'S A SHORT film of Aisha's I watched more than a few times during this period. It's called *Deadly Beige*, is set in Cold War–era St. Petersburg, and relates the dual destruction of the mental health of a middle-aged brother and sister. The siblings share a house and are both long-standing party members, employed as writers of propaganda. One night they receive notification from Moscow that it's time for them to do their bit toward helping keep the party strong. They are to do this by raising subtle suspicion among their fellow party members that they, the brother and sister, are in fact spies and observing the investigation into their activities at the same time as doing their genuine best to thwart this investigation. Discussion of this "exploratory exercise" is prohibited, so the siblings are unable to discern whether their St. Petersburg colleagues are aware of this exercise. Neither do they have the faintest idea who to report back to in Moscow. The letter they received was stamped with an authentic, and thus unrefusable, official seal, but was unsigned. This letter is delivered to them very late at night—the sister takes it from the trembling hand of a man who is then shot by a sniper as he walks away from their front door. The siblings then hear further shots at varying heights and distances that suggest the sniper has also been shot, followed by the sniper's sniper. There can be no doubt that disobedience would be stupid. So would half-hearted obedience: If the brother and sister fail to perform their tasks satisfactorily they will receive "reprimands"—what does that mean, what is this suggestion of plural punishment per failed task? The first task is to tear the letter up and eat it. In order to receive their instructions they take turns visiting a derelict house on the outskirts of the city, where they find that week's instructions written on a bedroom wall. They're instructions for setting up various staged liaisons and the preparation of coded, nonsensical reports. Having read and memorized the instructions, they are to paint over them. The brother and sister are forbidden to enter the house together. So she enters alone, he enters alone, and it wasn't so bad concocting slanders against each other as long as they took care not to look each other in the eye. Another concern: Some of the staged liaisons they set up feel all too genuine.

The siblings are so very unhappy. They can't understand how this could be happening to them when they've never put a foot wrong. A colleague makes a jocular comment at lunch and introduces the possibility that someone in Moscow is pissed off with the wonder siblings, finds them insincere, has settled on this tortuous scheme to force them to dig their own graves. As you watch these siblings squabble over daily chores and exchange bland commentary on the doings of their neighbors there are unfortunate indications that every word of praise these two write actually is profoundly insincere, and has been from the outset. They have denied themselves all social bonds; everybody's just an acquaintance. Now they search their souls, discern silhouettes of wild horses stampeding through the tea leaves at the bottom of their cups . . . What omens are these? "The horses are telling us to drink something stronger than tea." This counsel is invaluable—the siblings dearly wish to be quiet, and it's been their experience that alcohol ties their tongues for them. So they drink that at the kitchen table, facial expressions set to neutral, knees scraping together as each stares at the amply bugged wall behind the other's head.

IT'S A SPECTRAL wisp of a film, film more in the sense of a substance coating your pupils than it is a stream of images that moves before you. It's all felt more than seen; tension darkens each frame; by the end you can see neither into these siblings' lives nor out. Neither, it seems, can they. The film seems to be a judgment upon the written word and the stranglehold it assumes. Woe to those who believe in what is written, and woe to those who don't.

I put this to Aisha and she shook her head.

"It's a puppet show," she said. Yes, it's that too. The film's siblings are played by two feminine-looking puppets and voiced by a singer and a puppeteer, both friends of A's stepfather. The sister towers over the brother; she's wooden. The brother's made of metal, and his face is one of the most arresting I've seen, composed entirely of jagged scales—scales for eyelids, a button-shaped scale for a nose. When he opens his mouth to speak, it's as if the sea is speaking.

I'd decided to show the film to my own sister Odette, and as I waited in the lobby of Hotel Glissando I used the free Wi-Fi to watch it again in miniature, on my phone. A man tapped me on the shoulder and I looked up: He was a black man about my father's age and half a head shorter than me. Those sideburns: I'd seen them (and him) before, but couldn't think where. The man was talking. I pulled my earphones out.

". . . looking well, Freddy. How have you been?"

"Yeah, really well, thanks. And yourself?" I hadn't a clue who he was, but as long as one of us knew what was going on I didn't mind chatting.

He nudged me with his elbow, winked. "You're surprised to see me, eh? Thought I was dead, didn't you?"

When he said that it all came back to me; this man really was supposed to be dead. He was my godfather, and I'd last seen him at my christening. I might have gone to his funeral but I'm not sure: I've been to so many they all blur together.

"Gosh, yes! So you're alive after all? Excellent. How did you manage that? I mean, you went—"

"Sailing, yes," he supplied, beaming.

"Right, sailing, you were circumnavigating the globe in your boat, and then there was that Cuban hurricane and bits of the boat washing up on various shores—"

"I ditched the boat pretty early on, Freddy," my godfather said, serenely. "Sailing isn't for me. I only came up with the idea to get away from the wife and kid, really, so once I got to Florida I just let the boat drift on without me."

"So you let your family think you're dead, er—Jean-Claude?"

"That's right. I've been living here at the Glissando for years." His hand moved in his pocket; I could guess what he was doing, having seen others perform the same ritual— he was running his finger around and around the outside of his room key card, doing what he should've done before he checked in and became subject to the rules. Before assuming ownership of a key you should look at it closely. Not only because you may need to identify it later but because to look at a key is to get an impression of the lock it was made for, and, by extension, the entire establishment surrounding the lock. Once you check into Hotel Glissando there's no checking out again in your lifetime: I imagine this is a taste of what it is to be dead. In many tales people who've died don't realize it until they try to travel to a place that's new to them and find themselves prevented from arriving. These ghosts can only return to places where they've already been; that's all that's left for them. Depending on the person that can still be quite a broad existence. But whether its possessor is widely traveled or not, the key card for each room at Hotel Glissando is circular; if you took the key into your hand and really thought about it before signing the residency contract, this shape would inform you that wherever else you go, you must and will always return to your room.

"It's nice and quiet here and every morning there are eggs done just the way I like them," Jean-Claude said. "Jana divorced me in absentia and remarried anyway; she's fine. And just look how well my boy's doing!" My godfather opened a celebrity magazine and showed me a four-page spread of his son's splendid home. *Chedorlaomer Nachor's House of Locks! Sumptuous! Mysterious!*

"Chedorlaomer Nachor's your son?" I waved my phone at Jean-Claude. "Did you know he's in this film I'm watching?" The film had ended while we'd been talking; I played it again. Jean-Claude's gaze flicked suspiciously between me and the screen of my phone. "All I see are puppets."

"Yes, he's the voice of the brother—" I waited until the silvery face was the only one on-screen and then turned up the volume. Jean-Claude listened for a moment and then nodded.

"What's this film then?"

"Oh, it's my . . . girlfriend's. Well, she wrote and directed it . . ."

Jean-Claude gripped my arm. "You know my Chedorlaomer?"

"Well, not personally, but . . . why, do you want to be . . . you know, reunited?" I hadn't missed my chance after all. Here was a service I could provide to Jean-Claude and his famous son. This would effect my own reunion with my mother, who would acknowledge my existence once more. But Jean-Claude had no wish for a reunion; his accountant advised very strongly against such sentiments. Instead he wanted me to rescue his son from the clutches of a dangerous character.

"Dangerous character?"

"Her name," Jean-Claude said darkly, "is Tyche Shaw."

"Really?"

"You've heard of her?"

I tapped my phone screen again. "She's the voice of the sister!"

Jean-Claude flipped through another magazine until he found photos of Chedorlaomer stepping out hand in hand with a tall, buxom black woman. Her hair was gathered up to bare a neck that tempted me to B-movie vampirism. I wouldn't have guessed she was a puppeteer, and neither would this magazine's caption writer: *Nachor's mystery lady . . . Do you know her? Write in!*

"Freddy," Jean-Claude said. "I've been watching you for a few days now."

"Watching me? From where?"

He pointed to a potted palm tree behind the farthest phone booth. "There's a chair behind it. Yes, I've been watching you, and you look well, you do look well, but you also look as if you're lacking direction . . ."

I didn't dispute that.

"Would you like a bit of gainful employment, Freddy?"

"Well . . . yes."

"Good! I'll pay you this—" Jean-Claude wrote a number on the front cover of the topmost magazine. "If you break those two up as soon as you can."

The figure was high; I had to ask why he was so invested in the breakup.

"I made some inquiries, and I found out some things about Tyche Shaw," Jean-Claude said, his eyes turning to saucers for a moment. "Don't ask me what they are, but let's just say she's not the sort of person my son should be seeing. Save him. If not for the money then at least out of human decency."

"I'll gladly do what I can. But have you tried asking the concierge or my mother about this?"

"Yes of course, but they say it's only in their remit to handle requests that can be fulfilled on the premises."

"I see . . . Well, don't worry, Jean-Claude. I'll deal with this."

"Music to my ears, Freddy. That's the Barrandov Way!"

I was going to have a lot of money soon, but the prospect didn't excite me. Perhaps I'd get more excited as I went along. Aisha introduced me to Chedorlaomer without too much prompting: If anything she seemed amused that she'd discovered the fanboy in me.

Any friend of A's is a friend of mine . . .

Chedorlaomer Nachor had been famous for years. He'd grown accustomed to living well and to feting his playmates; if you said you liked anything of his he gave it to you, even if that meant taking the item off his own body and putting it on yours. He was deliriously happy too— that was part of it. He freely admitted that Tyche was his first love, admitted this to anyone who'd listen. Wherever he was, the delectable, ambrosial Tyche Shaw wasn't far away. They couldn't keep their hands off each other. A blended scent rose from their skins—sulfurous, sticky, sweet. Wasn't he rather old to be falling in love for the first time? And who *was* she? Since Jean-Claude wouldn't tell me what he'd learned about her, I did some research of my own. She was a puppeteer, and very far from a well-known one, though she did associate with the likes of Radha Chaudhry and Gustav Grimaldi. Aisha added in an off-hand manner that Tyche also did odd jobs and invocations. Odd jobs? Was Aisha hinting at prostitution?

Chedorlaomer seemed like a nice person and so did Tyche; if either one was ill-natured they hid it very well. But it didn't matter; I was there to end their romance. They were in love, and laughed at everything, and assaulted me with the odor of all the sex I was being denied. I know I said denied, as if I had a right to it. But those two filled my brain with the filthiest helium—I watched their wandering hands and I watched Aisha's *Deadly Beige* and when I blinked diverse, divine contortions appeared to me, all wrapped up in satin sheets. The bodies I saw and felt combining were mine, Aisha's, Chedorlaomer, Tyche's . . . even the puppets got a look in. I propositioned Chedorlaomer, but the typical halfheartedness of my attempt aside, Jean-Claude's son was immune to my charms. He talked about Aisha and explained that anybody who hurt her wasn't going to find it easy to live with all the injuries he and Aisha's stepdad would inflict upon them. He made these remarks in such dulcet tones that it took me a few minutes to realize he was warning me.

After that I had to let Aisha in on my project, before Mr. Protective told her. Once I'd told her everything she looked at me with the most peculiar expression.

"So you have a tendency not to want anything more than you already have?" she asked.

"Yes."

"And you think that's a problem?"

"Clearly it is: It's a difference that's slowly estranging me from my family!"

"What if I told you that I know both Ched and Tyche well enough to be fairly sure there's no need for you to break them up?"

"I've still got to do it. My word's my bond. I told Jean-Claude—"

"As for Jean-Claude," Aisha said, stirring her tea with sinister emphasis.

"Oh, don't."

"All right, forget Jean-Claude for now. Listen Freddy, you're my guy, and together we can accomplish anything. Here's how you break them up . . ."

"Your *guy* . . . accomplish anything . . . anything, *your* guy," I said, thinking I was talking to myself. But she heard me, and asked if I was OK.

"Me? Yeah? I mean . . . yeah. Always. I— Sorry, I interrupted you, didn't I? Go on."

Aisha knew a man who gave "relationship-ruining head." She suggested getting together with this man and Tyche one evening, giving them both a lot of wine and letting nature run its course. So we did that; I pretended to find it funny when I discovered that this giver of relationship-ruining head was my flatmate Pierre.

TYCHE ARRIVED with Chedorlaomer, and left with him too. Such a companionable couple, enjoying each other and us, his energy so upbeat, she full of quips and observations, both kept revealing their visionary natures, all these hopes and plans, all a bit exhausting really. Meanwhile Pierre drank and drank without getting drunk. He also made meaningful eyes at Aisha. I drank water the whole night; gulped it actually, just trying to cool down. Avoiding inebriation helped me think fast and not write that entire evening off—there on the kitchen counter were the glasses Tyche and Chedorlaomer had drunk out of and then left on the kitchen counter. I swiped them for the next stage of the project.

The results of the DNA test were disappointing. Blood-wise Tyche and Ched were as unrelated as could be, so I'd have to make some effort . . . I looked the results over carefully, consulted friends with some knowledge in the field, and went to work falsifying particulars. The end result only had to look legitimate to two dumbfounded laymen. I stress that this was not about Jean-Claude's Tyche-phobia, or about money, or even about proving to my mother that as a true Barrandov I was equal to any task. I asked them to meet me in the bar at the Glissando.

"What's this about?" Chedorlaomer asked, and Tyche appeared to very briefly meditate on the two envelopes on the counter before me before asking what was in them.

MY MIND TICKED over as I stammered the words I'd prepared; some words about never really knowing our fathers, how we only think we know them, how our fathers' undisclosed dalliances may well cause the world around us to teem with flesh of our flesh and blood of our blood, correspondences we may only recognize subconsciously.

"Exactly what is he saying right now?" Tyche was talking to Ched and looking at me. The voice of reason piped up in my ear, beige through and through: *Freddy's lost his marbles.* Lost them? What was this about loss? Ah well—I'd found something I really, really wanted. It was my dearest wish that Tyche and Chedorlaomer would believe my lie. If they believed me and shunned each other, then I had won. If they believed me and stayed together, then . . . well, that was another version also worth watching, even if it meant I'd lost. I still think I might not have gone as far as I did if they hadn't arrived coated in that scent that drove me to frenzy.

*if a book is locked there's probably
a good reason for that don't you think*

Every time someone comes out of the lift in the building where you work you wish lift doors were made of glass. That way you'd be able to see who's arriving a little before they actually arrive and there'd be just enough time to prepare the correct facial expression. Your new colleague steps out of the lift dressed just a tad more casually than is really appropriate for the workplace and because you weren't ready you say "Hi!" with altogether too much force. She has: a heart-shaped face with subtly rouged cheeks, short, straight, neatly cut hair, and eyes that are long rather than wide. She's black, but not local, this new colleague who wears her boots and jeans and scarf with a bohemian aplomb that causes the others to ask her where she shops. "Oh, you know, thrift stores," she says with a chuckle. George at the desk next to yours says, "Charity shops?" and the newcomer says, "Yeah, thrift stores . . ."

Her accent is New York plus some other part of America, somewhere Midwest. And her name's Eva. She's not quite standoffish, not quite . . . but she doesn't ask any questions that aren't related to her work. Her own answers are brief and don't invite further conversation. In the women's toilets you find a row of your colleagues examining themselves critically in the mirror and then, one by one, they each apply a touch of rouge. Their makeup usually goes on at the end of the workday, but now your co-workers are demonstrating that Eva's not the only one who can glow. When it's your turn at the mirror you fiddle with your shirt. Sleeves rolled up so you're nonchalantly showing skin, or is that too marked a change?

EVA TAKES no notice of any of this preening. She works through her lunch break, tapping away at the keyboard with her right hand, holding her sandwich with her left. You eat lunch at your desk too, just as you have ever since you started working here, and having watched her turn down her fourth invitation to lunch you say to her: "Just tell people you're a loner. That's what I did, anyway."

Eva doesn't look away from her computer screen and for a moment it seems as if she's going to ignore you but eventually she says: "Oh . . . I'm not a loner."

Fair enough. You return to your own work, the interpretation of data. You make a few phone calls to chase up some missing paperwork. Your company exists to assist other companies with streamlining their workforce for optimum productivity; the part people like you and Eva play in this is attaching cold, hard monetary value to the efforts of individual employees and passing those figures on to someone higher up the chain so that person can decide who should be made redundant. Your senior's evaluations are more nuanced. They often get to go into offices to observe the employees under consideration, and in their final recommendations they're permitted to allow for some mysterious quality termed potential. You aim to be promoted to a more senior position soon, because ranking people based purely on yearly income fluctuations is starting to get to you. You'd like a bit more context to the numbers. What happened in employee QM76932's life between February and May four years ago, why do the figures fall so drastically? The figures improve again and remain steady to date, but is QM76932 really a reliable employee? Whatever calamity befell them, it could recur on a five-year cycle, making them less of a safe bet than somebody else with moderate but more consistent results. But it's like Susie says, the reason why so many bosses prefer to outsource these evaluations is because context and familiarity cultivate indecision. When Susie gets promoted she's not going to bother talking about potential. "We hold more power than the consultants who go into the office," she says. That sounds accurate to you: The portrait you hammer out at your desk is the one that either affirms or refutes profitability. But your seniors get to stretch their legs more and get asked for their opinion, and that's why you and Susie work so diligently toward promotion.

But lately . . . lately you've been tempted to influence the recommendations that get made. Lately you've chosen someone whose figures tell you they'll almost certainly get sacked and you've decided to try to save them, manipulating figures with your heart in your mouth, terrified that the figures will be checked. And they are, but only cursorily; you have a reputation for thoroughness and besides, it would be hard for your boss to think of a reason why you'd do such a thing for a random string of letters and numbers that could signify anybody, anybody at all, probably somebody you'd clash with if you met them. You never find out what happens to the people you assess, so you're all the more puzzled by what you're doing. Why can't you choose some other goal, a goal that at least includes the possibility of knowing whether you reached it or not? Face it; you're a bit of a weirdo. But whenever you feel you've gone too far with your tampering you think of your grandmother and you press on. Grandma is your dark inspiration. Your mother's mother made it out of a fallen communist state with an unseemly heap of valuables and a strangely blank slate of a memory when it comes to recalling those hair-raising years. But she has such a sharp memory for so many other things—price changes, for instance. Your grand-mother is vehement on the topic of survival and skeptical of all claims that it's possible to choose anything else when the chips are down. The official story is that it was Grand-ma's dentistry skills that kept her in funds. But her person-ality makes it seem more likely that she was a backstabber of monumental proportions. You take great pains to keep your suspicions from her, and she seems to get a kick out of that.

But how terrible you and your family are going to feel if, having thought of her as actively colluding with one of his-tory's most murderous regimes, some proof emerges that Grandma was an ordinary dentist just like she said. A den-tist subject to the kind of windfall that has been known to materialize for honest, well-regarded folk, in this case a scared but determined woman who held on to that wind-fall with both hands, scared and determined and just a dentist, truly. But she won't talk about any of it, that's the thing. *Cannot* you could all understand, or at least have sincere reverence for. But *will* not?

Your grandmother's Catholicism seems rooted in her approval of two saints whose reticence shines through the ages: St. John of Nepomuk, who was famously executed for his insistence on keeping the secrets of the confessional, and St. John Ogilvie, who went to his death after refusing to name those of his acquaintance who shared his faith. In lieu of a crucifix your grandmother wears a locket around her neck, and in that locket is a miniature reproduction of a painting featuring St. John of Nepomuk, some tall-helmeted soldiers, a few horrified bystanders, four angels, and a horse. In the painting the soldiers are pushing St. J of N off the Charles Bridge, but St. J of N isn't all that bothered, is looking up as if already hearing future confessions and interceding for his tormentors in advance. *Boys will be boys, Father,* St. J of N's expression seems to say. The lone horse seems to agree. It's the sixteenth century, and the angels are there to carry St. John of Nepomuk down to sleep on the riverbed, where his halo of five stars awaits him. This is a scene your grandmother doesn't often reveal, but sometimes you see her fold a hand around the closed locket and it looks like she's toying with the idea of tearing it off the chain.

Suspect me if that's what you want to do.

What's the point of me saying any more than I've said . . . is it eloquence that makes you people believe things?

You are all morons.

These are the declarations your grandmother makes, and then you and your siblings all say: "No, no, Grandma, what are you talking about, what do you mean, where did you get this idea?" without daring to so much as glance at each other.

YOU WERE IN NURSERY school when your grandmother unexpectedly singled you out from your siblings and declared you her protégée. At first all that seemed to mean was that she paid for your education. That was good news for your parents, and for your siblings too, since there was more to go around. And your gratitude is real but so is your eternal obligation. Having paid for most of what's gone into your head during your formative years there's a sense in which Grandma now owns you. She phones you when entertainment is required and you have to put on formal wear, take your fiddle over to her house, and play peasant dances for her and her chess club friends. When you displease her she takes it out on your mother, and the assumption within the family is that if at any point it becomes impossible for Grandma to live on her own you'll be her live-in companion. (Was your education really that great?) So when you think of her you think that you might as well do what you can while you can still do it.

EVA'S POPULARITY grows even as her speech becomes ever more monosyllabic. Susie, normally so focused on her work, spends a lot of time trying to get Eva to talk. Kathleen takes up shopping during her lunch break; she tries to keep her purchases concealed but occasionally you glimpse what she's stashing away in her locker—expensive-looking replicas of Eva's charity-shop chic. The interested single-tons give Eva unprompted information about their private lives to see what she does with it but she just chuckles and doesn't reciprocate. You want to ask her if she's sure she isn't a loner but you haven't spoken to her since she re-jected your advice. Then Eva's office fortunes change. On a Monday morning Susie runs in breathless from having taken the stairs and says: "Eva, there's someone here to see you! She's coming up in the lift and she's . . . crying?"

Another instance in which glass lift doors would be ben-eficial. Not to Eva, who already seems to know who the vis-itor is and looks around for somewhere to hide, but glass doors would have come in handy for everybody else in the office, since nobody knows what to do or say or think when the lift doors open to reveal a woman in tears and a boy of about five or so, not yet in tears but rapidly approaching them—there's that lip wobble, oh no. The woman looks quite a lot like Eva might look in a decade's time, maybe a decade and a half. As soon as this woman sees Eva she starts saying things like, *Please, please, I'm not even angry, I'm just saying please leave my husband alone, we're a family, can't you see?*

Eva backs away, knocking her handbag off her desk as she does so. Various items spill out but she doesn't have time to gather them up—the woman and child advance until they have her pinned up against the stationery cupboard door. The woman falls to her knees and the boy stands beside her, his face scrunched up; he's crying so hard he can't see. "You could so easily find someone else but I can't, not now . . . do you think this won't happen to you too one day? Please just stop seeing him, let him go . . ."

Eva waves her hands and speaks, but whatever excuse or explanation she's trying to make can't be heard above the begging. You say that someone should call security and people say they agree but nobody does anything. You're seeing a lot of folded arms and pursed lips. Kathleen mutters something about "letting the woman have her say." You call security yourself and the woman and child are led away. You pick Eva's things up from the floor and throw them into her bag. One item is notable: a leatherbound diary with a brass lock on it. A quiet woman with a locked book. Eva's beginning to intrigue you. She returns to her desk and continues working. Everybody else returns to their desks to send each other e-mails about Eva . . . at least that's what you presume is happening. You're not copied into any of those e-mails but everybody except you and Eva seems to be receiving a higher volume of messages than normal. You look at Eva from time to time and the whites of her eyes have turned pink but she doesn't look back at you or stop working. Fax, fax, photocopy. She answers a few phone calls and her tone is on the pleasant side of professional.

AN ANTI-EVA movement emerges. Its members are no longer fooled by her glamour; Eva's a personification of all that's put on earth solely to break bonds, scrap commitments, prevent the course of true love from running smooth. You wouldn't call yourself Pro-Eva, but bringing a small and distressed child to the office to confront your husband's mistress does strike you as more than a little manipulative. Maybe you're the only person who thinks so: That side of things certainly isn't discussed. Kathleen quickly distances herself from her attempts to imitate Eva. Those who still feel drawn to Eva become indignant when faced with her continued disinterest in making friends. Who does she think she is? Can't she see how nice they are?

"Yes, she should be grateful that people are still asking her out," you say, and most of the people you say this to nod, pleased that you get where they're coming from, though Susie, Paul, and a couple of the others eye you suspiciously. Susie takes to standing behind you while you're working sometimes, and given your clandestine meddling this watchful presence puts you on edge. It's best not to mess with Susie.

ONE LUNCHTIME Eva brings her sandwich over to your desk and you eat together; this is sudden but after that you can no longer mock others by talking shit about Eva; she might overhear you and misunderstand. You ask Eva about her diary and she says she started writing it the year she turned thirteen. She'd just read *The Diary of Anne Frank* and was shaken by a voice like that falling silent, and then further shaken by the thought of all the voices who fell silent before we could ever have heard from them.

"And, you know—fuck everyone and everything that takes all these articulations of moodiness and tenderness and cleverness away. Not that I thought that's how I was," Eva says. "I was trying to figure out how to be a better friend, though, just like she was. I just thought I should keep a record of that time. Like she did. And I wrote it from thirteen to fifteen, like she did."

You ask Eva if she felt like something was going to happen to her too.

"Happen to me?"

You give her an example. "I grew up in a city where people fell out of windows a lot," you say. "So I used to practice falling out of them myself. But after a few broken bones I decided it's better just to not stand too close to windows."

Eva gives you a piercing look. "No, I didn't think anything was going to happen to me. It's all pretty ordinary teen stuff in there. Your city, though . . . is 'falling out of windows' a euphemism? And when you say 'fell,' or even 'window,' are you talking about something else?"

"No! What made you think that?"

"Your whole manner is really indirect. Sorry if that's rude."

"It's not rude," you say. You've already been told all about your indirectness, mostly by despairing ex-girlfriends.

"Can I ask one more question about the diary?"

Eva gives a cautious nod.

"Why do you still carry it around with you if you stopped writing in it years ago?"

"So I always know where it is," she says.

SUSIE gets restless.

"Ask Miss Hoity-Toity if she's still seeing her married boyfriend," she says to you.

You tell her you won't be doing that.

"The atmosphere in this office is so *stagnant*," Susie says, and decides to try and make Miss Hoity-Toity resign. You don't see or hear anyone openly agreeing to help Susie achieve this objective, but then they wouldn't do that in your presence, given that you now eat lunch with Eva every day. So when Eva momentarily turns her back on some food she's just bought and looks round to find the salad knocked over so that her desk is coated with dressing, when Eva's locker key is stolen and she subsequently finds her locker full of condoms, when Eva's sent a legitimate-looking file attachment that crashes her computer for a few hours and nobody else can spare the use of theirs for even a minute, you just look straight at Susie even though you know she isn't acting alone. Susie's power trip has come so far along that she goes around the office snickering with her eyes half closed. Is it the job that's doing this to you all or do these games get played no matter what the circumstances? A new girl has to be friendly and morally upright; she should open up, just pick someone and open up to them, make her choices relatable. "I didn't know he was married" would've been well received, no matter how wooden the delivery of those words. Just give us *something* to start with, Miss Hoity-Toity.

Someone goes through Eva's bag and takes her diary; when Eva discovers this she stands up at her desk and asks for her diary back. She offers money for it: "Whatever you want," she says. "I know you guys don't like me, and I don't like you either, but come on. That's two years of a life. Two years of a life."

Everyone seems completely mystified by her words. Kathleen advises Eva to "maybe check the toilets" and Eva runs off to do just that, comes back empty-handed and grimacing. She keeps working, and the next time she goes to the printer there's another printout waiting for her on top of her document: RESIGN & GET THE DIARY BACK.

EVA DEMONSTRATES her seriousness regarding the diary by submitting her letter of resignation the very same day. She says good-bye to you but you don't answer. In time she could have beat Susie and Co., could have forced them to accept that she was just there to work, but she let them win. Over what? Some book? Pathetic.

The next day George "finds" Eva's diary next to the coffee machine, and when you see his ungloved hands you notice what you failed to notice the day before—he and everybody except you and Eva wore gloves indoors all day. To avoid leaving fingerprints on the diary, you suppose. Nice; this can only mean that your coworkers have more issues than you do.

You volunteer to be the one to give Eva her diary back. The only problem is you don't have her address, or her phone number—you never saw her outside of work. HR can't release Eva's contact details; the woman isn't in the phone book and has no online presence. You turn to the diary because you don't see any other option. You try to pick the lock yourself and fail, and your elder sister whispers: "Try Grandma . . ."

"Oh, diary locks are easy," your grandmother says reproachfully (what's the point of a protégée who can't pick an easy-peasy diary lock?). She has the book open in no time. She doesn't ask to read it; she doubts there's anything worthwhile in there. She tells you that the diary looks cheap; that what you thought was leather is actually imitation leather. Cheap or not, the diary has appeal for you. Squares of floral-print linen dot the front and back covers, and the pages are featherlight. The diarist wrote in violet ink.

Why I don't like to talk anymore, you read, and then avert your eyes and turn to the page that touches the back cover. There's an address there, and there's a good chance this address is current, since it's written on a scrap of paper that's been taped over other scraps of paper with other addresses written on them. You copy the address down onto a different piece of paper and then stare, wondering how it can be that letters and numbers you've written with a black pen have come out violet-colored. Also—also, while you were looking for pen and paper the diary has been unfolding. Not growing, exactly, but it's sitting upright on your tabletop and seems to fill or absorb the air around it so that the air turns this way and that, like pages. In fact the book is like a hand and you, your living room, and everything in it are pages being turned this way and that. You go toward the book, slowly and reluctantly—if only you could close this book remotely—but the closer you get to the book the greater the waning of the light in the room, and it becomes more difficult to actually move, in fact it is like walking through a paper tunnel that is folding you in, and there's chatter all about you: *Speak up, Eva* and

Eva, you talk so fast, slow down, and *So you like to talk a lot, huh?*
You hear: *You do know what you're saying, don't you?* and *Excuse
me, missy, isn't there something you ought to be saying right now?*
and *You just say that one more time!* You hear: *Shhh,* and *So . . .
Do any of you guys know what she's talking about?* and *OK, but
what's that got to do with anything?* and *Did you hear what she
just said?*

IT'S MOSTLY men you're hearing, or at least they sound male.
But not all of them. Among the women Eva can be heard
shushing herself. You chant and shout and cuckoo call. You
recite verse, whatever's good, whatever comes to mind.
This is how you pass through the building of Eva's quiet-
ness, and as you make that racket of yours you get close
enough to the book to seize both covers (though you can no
longer see them) and slam the book shut. Then you sit on it
for a while, laughing hysterically, and after that you slide
along the floor with the book beneath you until you find a
roll of masking tape and wind it around the closed diary.
Close shave, kiddo, close shave.

AT THE WEEKEND you go to the address you found in the
diary and a gray-haired, Levantine-looking man answers

the door. Eva's lover? First he tells you Eva's out, then he says: "Hang on, tell me again who you're looking for?"

You repeat Eva's name and he says that Eva doesn't actually live in that house. You ask since when, and he says she never lived there. But when you tell him you've got Eva's diary he lets you in: "I think I saw her on the roof once." His reluctance to commit to any statement of fact feels vaguely political. You go up onto the rooftop with no clear idea of whether Eva will be there or not. She's not. You look out over tiny gardens, big parking lots, and satellite dishes. A glacial wind slices at the tops of your ears. If you were a character in a film this would be a good rooftop on which to battle and defeat some urban representative of the forces of darkness. You place the diary on the roof ledge and turn to go, but then you hear someone shout: "Hey! Hey—is that mine?"

It's Eva. She's on the neighboring rooftop. She must have emerged when you were taking in the view. The neighboring rooftop has a swing set up on it, two seats side by side, and you watch as Eva launches herself out into the horizon with perfectly pointed toes, falls back, pushes forward again. She doesn't seem to remember you even though she only left a few days ago; this says as much about you as it does about her. You tell Eva that even though it looks as if her diary has been vigorously thumbed through you're sure the contents remain secret. "*I* didn't read it, anyway," you say. The swing creaks as Eva sails up into the night sky, so high it almost seems as if she has no intention of coming back. But she does. And when she does, she says: "So you still think that's why I locked it?"

acknowledgments

Thank you, Piotr Cieplak, thank you, Marina Endicott, thank you, Tracy Bohan, thank you, Jin Auh, thank you, Bohdan Karásek, thank you, Sarah McGrath. And Kate Harvey—thank you.

Kenneth Gross's absorbing *Puppet: An Essay on Uncanny Life* has also been influential here.